K.L. HESTER

Wounds of Ash

BOOK ONE OF THE VENDI CHRONICLES

Wounds of Ash: Book One of the Vendi Chronicles

For information contact:
K.L. Hester
klhesterwrites@gmail.com

Cover design by GetCovers
Author Photo by Holly's Hobby's Photography
ISBN: 9781088141632

First Edition: June 2023

10 9 8 7 6 5 4 3 2 1

This book is dedicated to those who supported me through the darkest moment in my life.
My husband, who has been my rock. My parents, who have been my strongest supporters. Jess, for being my best friend through it all. And finally, my Lord and Savior, Jesus Christ.
Through Him, all things are possible.

Chapter One

Aliyah loved the smell of the rain.

For once, the cobbled streets of Elwryn smelled of something other than unwashed bodies, horse dung, and the chamber pot contents tossed from windows. Rain had a way of muting the scents she had been forced to become accustomed to these past few years.

Unable to resist, she leaned farther out the carriage to feel the rain. A fat drop landed on her face, and she relished the movement of it down her cheek. Another one landed on her forehead as a gloved hand pulled her back into the carriage.

"It is not proper for a lady to have her face stretched out the window of a carriage like some wide-eyed peasant! To think what Sir Caldryk would think if he saw you like this!"

Aliyah turned to her aunt, an older version of herself, but with fair hair and a pinched nose above her ever disapproving frown.

"Have you ever wondered," Aliyah asked, as she ran her fingers through her chestnut brown hair, "if I don't care what Sir Caldryk might think of me?"

Matylda gasped and Aliyah braced herself for the slap she knew would follow. Her aunt did not disappoint.

"I don't care whether it matters to you what he thinks of you," Matylda breathed, seething. "What matters is that you are convincing as the proper young woman he has been told you are. He cannot have his prized *Wyvanni* looking and behaving like some backwater brat."

Cheek still stinging, Aliyah resisted rolling her eyes. Not at the barb toward her upbringing, but at the term *Wyvanni*. It was not her choice to be an oddity- specifically, an oddity coveted by the nobility this side of the Vendis.

"Yes, aunt," she said, shrinking down in her seat, assuming the mask of the subservient young woman her aunt beat into her over the years.

"Much better. Now, remember, you are to be engaged- the least you could do is act happy about it."

"Yes Aunt," Aliyah sighed as she went back to looking out the window. This time, however, she remained in the carriage.

The rain began to bounce off the roof of the carriage with gusto, drowning out the sound of the horses' hooves. The town gave way to rolling green hills as a tall, peaked roof behind a stone wall came into view.

As they drew near, a wrought iron gate in the wall opened like a great maw of a wild beast. Aliyah shied away from the window and twisted her gloved hands together nervously. She counted each ping of rain on the roof to calm her racing heart.

At last, the carriage rolled to a stop in front of the elaborate mansion. With the help of the coachman who proffered her an umbrella, Aliyah followed her aunt out of the carriage and onto the gravel drive.

The Caldryks do not do anything halfway, Aliyah mused, as she took in the view of what would now be her home.

The two-story house had a gray stone façade interrupted by white columns. The columns rose to the sky like giant sentries. Hundreds of windows reflected the gray storm clouds above them. An enormous staircase led up to intricately carved front doors that were opening.

A blonde-haired man descended the stairs toward them, not bothering with an umbrella. Through the rain, Aliyah noted the crisp general's uniform he wore, and the jagged scar that ran from his right eye and continued down past the collar of his uniform. The smile he gave the pair of women did not reach his cold blue eyes and Aliyah suppressed a shudder as those eyes roamed over her.

"My dear Matylda, you have arrived," Sir Caldryk said upon reaching them. He had a nasal sounding voice that demanded respect. He took Matylda's hand and raised it lightly to his lips. The blush Matylda gave him made Aliyah want to gag.

"And this is the girl?" Sir Caldryk asked, switching his attention to Aliyah. Chills again slithered down her spine at the greed she found staring back at her. Trying to avoid looking at him, she gave a small demure curtsy in response.

"This is my niece, Aliyah... Brandhold." Matylda said.

"Brandhold, you say?" Sir Caldryk said as he appraised Aliyah. "With the gold tint to her eyes... her father was indeed a Myralian?"

"Without a question. My sister brought shame to the family and herself the day she ran off and married that traitorous filth." Matylda spat. Aliyah clenched her fists at her aunt's words and bit back the retort on the tip of her tongue.

"However," Matylda said, as she grabbed Aliyah by the shoulders in a mock embrace "Imagine the surprise when we discovered that the brat my sister and her husband spawned was none other than a *Wyvanni*. When news reached me of my sister's murder, I had to do something. I could not let their child grow up an urchin. So, out of the goodness of my heart, I took her into my own home and raised her as if she was my own daughter."

Sir Caldryk continued to stare at Aliyah as her aunt spoke. "What an... interesting tale," he said, not sounding the least bit intrigued.

"Perhaps you should continue to bore me in my study. Come! We have a lot to discuss." He turned and walked stiffly back into the mansion.

Matylda stood stunned for only a moment before following close behind in a bustle of skirts and heels. With a longing glance at the carriage, Aliyah followed up the steps. A feeling of foreboding settled around her.

***

The interior of the house was as extravagant as the outside hinted. Stopping in the foyer, Aliyah stared, mouth agape, at the grand sweeping staircase and the black marble floors polished to reflect the ornate gold chandeliers hanging from the ceiling.

Absolutely gorgeous, Aliyah thought despite herself.

Noticing Matylda and Sir Caldryk in a room adjacent to the foyer, she hurried to catch up. One of the guards standing outside the study shut the door before Aliyah entered. The sound of the oak door shutting reverberated around the stone manor.

A short, middle-aged woman in a gray dress came and stood next to her. The woman tugged at her sleeve before whispering "Come, Miss."

Shocked by having the door shut in her face, she let herself be pulled away from the door and led up the staircase.

The hallway at the top of the stairs was long but well lit. Aliyah's feet were silent on the red rug running down the center as they passed other oak doors. Detailed paintings of far-off landscapes decorated the walls. Aliyah gave them no more than a cursory glance, worried about where the woman was taking her.

The servant stopped in front of one of the doors and pulled out a key. Upon opening the door, she motioned for Aliyah to enter. Reluctantly she followed, unsure of what would be inside.

It was a bedroom. A giant mahogany bed dominated the center of the room. Its gold duvet and pillows were one of the most inviting things

Aliyah had ever seen. Matching mahogany furniture lined the pale blue painted walls. Across from where they stood in the doorway were another set of doors that led to a balcony. A handful of thick rugs, the color of the walls, lay dispersed around the floor. A stark contrast against the black marble tiles.

"The bathing room is to the left, Miss." The servant said with head bowed. She motioned to an archway and continued, "The master wishes you to be bathed and dressed before dinner."

"What's wrong with the clothes I am wearing now?" Aliyah asked, confusion showing on her face as she inspected the yellow dress she wore. Its voluminous skirts embroidered with dainty silk flowers matched the lace and pearl buttons adorning the bodice.

"Nothing, Miss," the servant said, "The master would prefer it if you wore one of his selected dresses. Please, the bath has been drawn and dinner will be soon." Her voice had a tone of urgency as she motioned again for Aliyah to enter the bathing chamber.

The theme of the bedroom continued into the massive bathing room. Long stained-glass windows lined one wall, letting in light while still giving privacy. A dressing screen was set up in the corner and the servant gave an expectant nod towards it.

Aliyah forced herself to take deep breaths before stepping behind the screen. With shaking hands, she began the tedious process of undoing her buttons. She heard a frustrated sigh as the servant came around the screen to help.

"Allow me, Miss." The servant was efficient and soon Aliyah stood naked before her.

"What is your name?" Aliyah breathed out. She was not used to having anyone see her naked-let alone a stranger. When the woman didn't respond, Aliyah walked hesitantly over to the marble tub set into the floor.

"Linna, my lady." The woman replied once Aliyah was in the water. Her voice a whisper. "But it is not proper for you to address me. The master would not like it one bit if he found us servants conversing with you." She clamped her lips together as if she said too much and refused to participate in any more of Aliyah's other attempts to converse.

Cannot even talk to those around me, Aliyah thought dismayed.

Despite Linna not being allowed to talk, she was efficient, and Aliyah found herself rinsed and dried off sooner than she expected. Linna led her out of the room to an opulent vanity. There she worked with deft fingers and soon had Aliyah's hair styled into an intricate braided crown atop her head.

Once finished, Linna brought her a dress of green silk. Sliding into it, Aliyah spared a glance in the mirror as Linna buttoned up the back.

Her previous dress had been feminine and reserved. This dress was daring and bold with every curve exposed. Only the tightness of the material on her skin kept the bodice in place. A long slit ran from the floor-length hem to the top of her thigh.

Her shoulders and arms were bare, save for the silver bands Linna slid up her arms. Kohl was then applied to her eyelids to complete the effect. Her deep blue eyes, flecked with the faintest of gold, were now a prominent feature.

I look like a goddess from legends, Aliyah thought as she looked at the otherworldly creature staring back in the mirror. *My own parents would not recognize me. I do not even recognize myself.* The thought was jarring and one she would not let herself dwell on. She had not been herself in a long time.

“Come, Miss,” Linna said, eyes cast down. When Aliyah did not respond, she firmly escorted Aliyah out of the room and back to the first level. Soon they stood in front of a large set of doors.

"The dining room, Miss." Linna motioned demurely for her to enter. Aliyah took a breath before opening the door.

Chapter Two

The room was full of people. A band played in the corner of a dance floor while women wearing exquisite dresses were being spun around by men in expensive suits. Other impeccably dressed guests stood in small groups around the room. The sound of their laughing voices could be heard above the music. No one was familiar.

Aliyah took an uncertain step farther into the room. As she did, everything went quiet, and all eyes turned to stare at where she stood. Aliyah had never felt as self-conscious as she did at that moment. She took a step backwards.

Before she could get any further, Sir Caldryk dispatched himself from where he had been talking to a group of men by a massive stone fireplace. He prowled towards her. The fire's heat did nothing to warm the cold pit of dread that formed in Aliyah's stomach as his predatory gaze roamed over her exposed body.

With an effort, she suppressed a shudder and glanced around the room. A group of women near her age stood to her left. She met their gaze, and they stared back with animosity.

"My dear, you look ravishing." Sir Caldryk's voice pulled her attention from the women, and she turned to find him standing directly in front of her. His gaze roamed up and down her body. Aliyah's skin crawled at the compliment.

Wishing her dress contained more fabric, she found herself saying, "I was hoping we might get to know each other over a quiet dinner. I was not expecting so many others. Whatever is the cause of this... celebration?"

"Why, it is our engagement party!" Sir Caldryk motioned around the room as if that fact were obvious. "And you, Aliyah, are the guest of honor!"

The heat of embarrassment rushed to her face as he proffered his arm. Feeling repulsed about being in such close proximity to him, she reached out with a shaking hand. Faster than she could blink, he grabbed her arm and yanked it to his, holding it tight enough to hurt. She grimaced and bit back a cry. She did not miss his look of innate joy in seeing her pain.

He towed her along beside him up to a round dais on the far side of the room. Aliyah had to run to keep up.

Whispers of “who’s that?” And “a Myralian!” followed them as those in attendance stood expectantly and waited for whatever announcement Sir Caldryk was sure to make.

He did not disappoint. “My friends,” he began, his nasal voice filling the chamber, “in our fight against Myral, it is with immense pleasure that I announce our newest strategy for fighting those heathens! They stole magic from us in the past, but now we will reclaim what is rightfully ours!” He paused, looking each attendee in the eye. The anticipation in the room was palpable.

“I have found myself a *Wyvanni*,” he let the last word hang in the air as he motioned toward Aliyah standing next to him. An excited buzz filled the air as the audience turned to whisper among themselves.

“Prove it!” A male voice yelled from the crowd. Aliyah spotted the owner of the voice, a tall middle-aged man standing next to a pale woman in all white. Both wore skeptical expressions.

Sir Caldryk narrowed his eyes at the man as he took a decorative knife out of the sheath at his side. Before she had a chance to react, he held Aliyah’s arm to a straight position and brought the knife down hard.

Aliyah struggled to no avail. The metal was cold as it bit into her skin, and she unleashed a scream. The knife made its path from the inside crease of her elbow halfway down to her wrist. Tears streamed as Aliyah sobbed from the unexpected pain.

No one in the audience moved.

Sir Caldryk smiled wider as he took a step towards her and held a small cup to the wound to collect her blood. Aliyah stared in mute horror as he pulled the cup up to his lips and threw back the contents.

An iridescent aura began to emanate off him before it sunk into his skin. He opened his eyes wide and stared at the crowd. A woman in the audience gasped.

"His eyes! Look at his eyes!" Someone in the crowd shouted. Turning her head, she looked up at Sir Caldryk. His pale blue eyes were now flecked with prominent gold. The gaze he gave her was predatory as he began to address the crowd.

"With a *Wyvanni* on our side, we shall unlock the magic forbidden to us by those so long ago. We can take back what is ours and extinguish those heathen Myralians."

Thunderous applause echoed around the chamber. He paused until it died down. "Think it over my friends. I should like to meet with you individually over the next few weeks to discuss the benefits of swearing fealty to me. Until then... Drink up and think of the rewards we shall reap by conquering Myral!"

With nothing more to say, he turned on his heels as he reached for Aliyah's uncut arm. She resisted the urge to cry out as he dragged her off the stage behind him. The cheers of his supporters echoed in the chamber.

***

Warm sunlight danced behind Aliyah's closed eyelids. She stirred and the events of the prior day shoved her into consciousness. As she opened her eyes, a piercing pain spliced through her brain, and she held back the urge to vomit. She breathed slow deep breaths and waited for the world to right itself.

What had been in those drinks last night?

She tried to remember the party, but everything was fuzzy after Sir Caldryk's speech. Straining, she recalled a servant bringing her a wrap for her arm- only after one of the many guests commented to Sir Caldryk on how it was "such a waste to let a dress like that get all bloodied up." She had not missed the sly smile Sir Caldryk responded with, or the possessive way he hauled her around the rest of the party after.

She had not been allowed to talk- he did all the talking for her. The few times anyone addressed her, he had cut in and told them she didn't speak Gralanthian. She had almost rolled her eyes at that but thought better of it when he squeezed her bandaged arm hard enough to bruise.

A servant walking by offered her a drink and she downed the contents without hesitation, grateful for something to do. The liquid burned going down but left her feeling lightheaded and-

No wonder I was able to get away with so many things after Aunt Matylda had been drinking. A smile tugged at her lips at the thought, but the urge to vomit came back vigorously.

She didn't make it to the washroom before the contents of her stomach surged back up and soiled one of the blue rugs.

"Miss? Miss, are you alright?" Linna's voice sounded far away, and Aliyah jerked as the woman squatted next to her.

Another surge made its way onto the blue rug when she opened her mouth to respond.

"It's alright Miss. It's only a rug. Nothing we haven't cleaned before." She patted Aliyah's back as the last of the contents made their appearance. "There, there, Miss."

Aliyah covered her eyes with her hand as she waited for the world to stop spinning. When she thought she was strong enough to stand, she allowed Linna to help her off the ground. She took a step toward the bed when Linna stopped her.

"Now, let's get you out of your clothes and into something more comfortable."

Aliyah realized she was still wearing the awful dress from the night before. Blood from her arm crusted one side of it, mingling with the fresh vomit. The sight almost made her sick for a second time and she had to force her eyes to look anywhere else as Linna led her to the washroom.

Letting Linna help her out of her dress and into her sleeping gown was hard. The world still spun, and Aliyah had to vomit one more time, this time in the privy, before she let Linna lead her back to the bed.

"You rest. Drink some water. I will be back in a while to check on you and see if you need anything." Linna gave her a sympathetic smile as she pulled the curtains closed and submerged the room in darkness. With quiet steps she walked toward the door.

"Linna?" Aliyah's voice was hoarse, but she was thankful when Linna's silhouetted form paused in the doorway. "Thank you- for your help. It has been a long time since someone has helped me in any way."

Linna went rigid. In a voice just above a whisper she responded, "It has been a long time since there has been someone to help, Miss."

Aliyah did not say a word as the older woman shut the door and left. Her words giving Aliyah something to contemplate.

Chapter Three

The cold mountain air stung as it whipped through the Vendis. Tall trees covered in snow bent and swayed from the force. Josen stared numbly as his friend dismounted his large stallion and investigated the prints they had been tracking. Prints left in the hard packed snow from a similar horse and the nightmarish companions it traveled with.

"They were here no more than a few days ago," Kaino yelled, trying to be heard above the howling wind.

Josen did not know if his friend was using his skills honed as a tracker, or his magical ability to ascertain things others might not. Either way, he was appreciative of his friend's assessment.

"If we push on through the rest of the day, we will be able to make it to Fjorden by sunset." Kaino rubbed his arms against the cold as he looked up at the sky. Dark clouds threatened snow, and even the most experienced traveler would not want to be caught in a snowstorm in the Vendis. "They seem to be heading in the same direction as the town. I would rather sleep in a warm bed instead of our tents if we had the chance."

Kaino glanced toward Josen, who only ground his teeth and gripped his reins tighter.

Calm, he needed to remain calm. It was not Kaino's fault he was on edge. No, it was the hunt that made him sigh in frustration. They had gotten close many times to catching up to the murderous traitor they sought. However, the traitor was always one or two steps ahead of them. Finding ways to leave false trails or slipping away into hidden passes not marked on any map. No, it was not Kaino's fault at all. If anything, it was Josen's.

If I had not gone on that assignment... If I hadn't left her alone... No- it would do no good to go down that path. Those thoughts never led to anything but heartache and pain. He would not think of her today.

He nodded to Kaino, who he realized was waiting for a response. He did not miss the look of pity Kaino gave him. That was nothing new. Relief ran through him when Kaino remounted his horse and led the way to Fjorden.

***

Aside from the snow, the town was exactly how Josen remembered it from the last time he had traveled through here. That had been on an assignment to help settle a land dispute between the town of Fjorden and Holst.

It seemed a lot of assignments the Ringada, the magical protectors of Myral, were sent on lately had been about land disputes.

Ringada of legend had fought mighty battles against the dark evils of the world. As the protectors of light and truth, it was their duty to fight against the dark. After the last Great War, those evils had crawled back into whatever hole they had originated from and had not been seen since. Or at least that was true until a year prior.

In the centuries since the Great War, the Ringada with their once mighty armies had become nothing more than a martial government, with the High Protector at the ruling head. However, the one they had trusted to be the final stand against the Darkness, had now joined it. Darkness had crept back into the world and...

Kaino stopped his horse in front of the town inn's stables. Josen jerked and forced himself to become alert to the world around him as a red-faced man in a thick coat of matted fur rushed out to take their horses. His face lit up when he saw the giant horses and the riders astride them. "Masters Ringada! What a joy to stable horses as fine as yours. They will be well taken care of and warm despite the weather," the man looked up at the flurries that were starting to fall.

"Please see that they are indeed kept warm," Kaino said, throwing the man a silver piece for his trouble.

"Why, Master Ringada, you are too kind," he gave a little bow as he pocketed the money and led their two horses into the stable.

Josen's horse, Ember, tossed her ebony head in frustration and turned to stare at him with dark brown eyes. He tried to give her a reassuring smile.

"You coming, Jos?" Kaino prodded at his side. The snow was starting to come down harder and Josen had not realized he had been staring at the stables. Time seemed to flow differently since that fateful day, and Josen was unaware of the minutes that passed. The horses had been taken a while ago. He shook his head and looked at Kaino.

"Give me a few moments, Kai."

It hurt to talk. How long had it been since he made it through a full conversation with Kaino? He knew he should follow his friend into the warm, inviting building. Settle down at a table and play cards as they once had to pass the time. The part of him that had once enjoyed those things was gone. Burned to ashes like her cold limp body- *Not today,* he thought, stopping the memories from coming to the forefront of his mind. Not today.

***

Swirls of snow entered the room with him. What began as a snowstorm had turned into a blizzard. From the looks fellow patrons were giving him, he knew he must be a remarkable sight. Snow crusted his cloak and coated his eyelashes, hair, and beard. It did not bother him.

There was no need to fear hypothermia when your fire magic kept your body at a continuous temperature.

Kaino sat at a booth flirting with the serving girl. She was pretty, with blonde hair pulled back into a braid and a smile that reached her eyes. It was not the first time Josen had found Kaino in a similar situation- his friend had a reputation. But did it have to be this woman? She looked so much like-

No, don't think her name. Don't imagine her. You don't deserve to remember her. But he did.

He remembered the way her eyes would twinkle at him as she smiled at a funny joke he shared. He remembered the way she felt in his arms as he held her on their wedding day. He had never been so lucky. And yet...luck wore off. Those moments were all that was left.

"This is my brother, Josen," Kaino said, motioning toward Josen with a lazy hand. The serving girl blushed as she nodded to him.

"Hello!" Her voice was too bubbly for Josen, and he inwardly cringed. *She* never would have sounded like that.

Josen nodded toward the serving girl and then glared at his friend, his brother. They were not really brothers. That was a term used by Ringada. However, Josen and Kaino did look an awful lot alike with their black hair and tan skin. They had even developed some of the same mannerisms, having been friends for over twenty years. But where Kaino's brown eyes flecked with gold always shone with mirth, Josen's green-gold-flecked eyes were stern. He had been open once, even friendly. That time had long since passed.

"Can I get you anything?" The serving girl turned her attention toward Josen as if she were appraising him. He hated the attention that came from being a member of the Ringada and he hated how Kaino always used it to his advantage.

"Mead, dinner, and then to be left alone." He threw some coins toward her, his voice harsher than intended.

"Really, Jos?" Kaino threw him a glare before pinching the bridge of his nose. "Just because you choose not to be happy doesn't mean I have to be miserable."

Josen snorted but said nothing as the woman came back with a mug of ale and a bowl of stew.

She slammed the items down in front of him and stormed off.

He eyed her before taking a bite of the stew. It was not the most delicious meal he had eaten, but it was better than whatever he and Kaino would have been able to scrounge up in the snow.

They ate in silence, neither one wanting to talk to the other. Anger rolled off Kaino in waves, but Josen did not care. He couldn’t care. Caring would mean acknowledging something he didn't want to admit to himself. Finishing his stew, he stood up from the table, grabbed his pack and left without a word. Kaino did not bother to look at him as he left.

The room reserved for Ringada contained two beds. Josen took the one farthest from the door. *Let Kaino have less to travel when he comes in wasted*, he thought with a sigh as he unlaced his boots and laid back on the lumpy bed. Despite how he acted at dinner, he did care about his friend. A part of him felt immense guilt at how he had been treating Kaino. He would not have gotten this far without him.

Just because you choose not to be happy doesn’t mean I have to be miserable. Those words plagued him. Kaino was right, it was not fair of Josen to force his own grief and misery onto his friend. To expect him to grieve the same way was not fair. He had not loved her. Had not known what it was like to lose the one good thing in his world. Kaino lost a friend, but he had only come with Josen on this insane hunt because he had worried Josen would need him.

Tomorrow... he would try harder to show how much he appreciated his friend's loyalty. Maybe next time they stopped at an inn he would not chase away his friend's chance at an enjoyable time.

Kaino is right- I am miserable. With Kaino's words replaying in his mind, Josen turned over and covered himself with the thin blankets. Tonight would be bad. He was exhausted and knew there was no fighting the images that would come to him the instant sleep took over.

***

Kaino watched his friend retreat up the stairs. *Oh Josen,* he thought. He remembered a time when they would stay up late playing cards or talking. He missed that friend and his easy-going camaraderie. But most importantly, he missed the light-hearted Josen, the friend who would laugh at Kaino's jokes and crack them back.

Others might only know Josen as the son of the High Protector but Kaino knew Josen better than that. He knew Josen was hurting, and he wished for all the world he could make it better.

Chapter Four

"Calm down Jos," Kaino said, pointing at the flames winding around Josen's fists.

He glanced around the room to see if any of the other patrons were paying attention. Magic was common in Myral, but Ringada usually had better control. It had been snowing for a solid day and Josen had been getting more impatient by the hour.

"We are losing precious ground!" Josen argued back, slamming his flaming fist against the rough-hewn table. Scorch marks remained in the wood.

"I am sure they are losing precious ground as well and are holed up somewhere too, trying to keep warm. It will do you no good to take Ember out in a storm like this." Kaino motioned out the window where great Vendi winds howled, and snow swirled.

Josen knew his friend was right but doing nothing felt awful. It gave time for memories to resurface, things Josen would rather not think about. It had happened the night before.

One moment, Josen was staring at the ceiling of the room he was sharing with Kaino. The next minute he remembered lying in bed next to Ellie.

Her body was soft and warm curled up next to him. Her face was the picture of innocence as she slept. He envisioned pulling her closer to him, pressing a soft kiss into her golden hair. She would stir and gaze up at him with her pale green eyes, the gold in them becoming more pronounced as she was learning to use her magic.

"What is it, my love?" Her voice would be light, and he would be lost staring in those eyes.

"I miss you," he would say. Pulling her closer.

"That's silly, I'm right here!" She would nestle in closer with a giggle.

"How I wish you really were." He had said the words aloud and the image dissolved, leaving him staring at nothing but the cracked ceiling above him. He was glad Kaino had not made it up to the room yet. He had cried as he had not let himself in a long time.

The tears had not been enough. If anything, they had allowed the pains and memories he held at bay to come to the front of his mind. Memories had come unbidden all day and it only frustrated him further.

Memories of their wedding, held at midday on the Summer Solstice. She looked resplendent in a gown of pure white, a long lace train behind her. The dress had been his mother's, as Ellie's family disowned her when she informed them she wanted to marry Josen. Josen had never met a Myralian Nobleman who did not want his child to marry a member of the Ringada. Ellie took it in stride and had always claimed Josen was the best decision she had ever made. He wondered if she still felt that way, wherever she-

"Jos," Kaino's words pulled him back to reality. "We will find them. I know you want revenge, but we need to be patient a while longer."

Kaino's eyes were haggard. Josen knew he had been pushing his friend harder than he had ever intended to when they set out to find his father.

"I know Kai," he whispered. "I have faith in you."

***

The snow let up the next morning. Josen had slept fitfully. His usual dream of Ellie's death plagued him, and he wiped the remnants of sleep from his eyes as he got up to dress. They would have a hard ride in front of them. The horses would more than likely make it through the snow- if they avoided larger snow drifts. Josen tugged his boots on, noticing Kaino doing the same. They got ready to go in companionable silence and then headed toward the stables.

The horses pranced eagerly as the stable workers saddled them. It did not take long before they were ready. Once astride their horses, they took off at a fast gallop out of the small town. They headed towards the last place they had seen tracks of his father. They scouted the area for a while before finding evidence and tracks of a sizable group of creatures leaving a cave and heading south. A horse's prints intermixed with the footprints of the creatures they traveled with. Kaino used his magic to begin tracking the horse.

Kaino had explained his magic to Josen many years ago. Instead of having a physical manifestation of magic, his magic was more of an inward gift. As a tracker he was more observant and prone to seeing things others might miss. The slightest impression on the snow would stand out to him. He had also explained it was easier to track someone or something with which he was familiar. All Ringada were familiar with Raynar, the High Protector's stubborn horse.

They dismounted and searched for more tracks in the snow. Kaino spotted the horse prints farther down a side trail and they ran back to their horses, taking off at a gallop. They followed the path for hours. It started to veer south-east and Kaino stopped, overlooking a familiar ravine.

"They are heading toward Gralanth," Kaino said, looking over the frozen rocky terrain below them.

"Are you sure?" Josen asked.

"Their travel pattern is all starting to make sense. They started off at Ringard and made their way slowly along a south-east route. Yes, they have deviated from it slightly to raze villages along the way and add to their numbers but think about it!

"If your father can get to Gralanth, he will be a free man. No one has the magic to oppose him. He can take anything he wants from the Gralanthians. We have been following him for over a year across the countryside and we did not see it until now!" Kaino held a hand to his forehead, "Maybe I am losing it Jos. I should have seen it!"

"No one is blaming you Kai," Josen whispered as he took in his friend's revelation. "Knowing my father, this was an elaborate plan to throw us off their real intention of getting to Gralanth all along." He started his horse down a path towards the ravine opening. The familiar sound of Kaino's horse followed behind him.

His father. He had not thought of the man who killed his wife with that title until Kaino had brought it up. *Driel, the High Protector, Murderer,*

Traitor, and... Father. Josen pushed the thoughts from his mind as he led his horse into the ravine.

They had traveled this ravine many times in their lives, visiting family that lived in Vendin. They dismounted their horses and Josen let his friend lead. Kaino would have a better chance of spotting the safest path through the icy rocks.

They wound through ice patches and snow drifts. Neither of them spoke as they focused on where they and their horses stepped. They had barely made it halfway through the ravine when the sound of unearthly howls began to echo along the ice-covered stone.

Figures rose from the snow drifts around them. Their ashen skin and dark eyes blended in with the rocks and snow in the ravine. An ambush of grarg. The creatures crawled their way out of the deep snow that now seemed too perfectly placed around the safest path. Josen let go of his horse's reins and drew his Ringada blade from the sheath at the side- not noticing as Kaino did the same.

The first of the creatures had reached them and Josen sent a fireball to its head. It went down screaming, as it tried to put the flames out in the snow. With a start, Josen realized the creature was wearing tattered Ringada gear. The antlered qilin medallion of Ringard was tarnished but identifiable on its cloak. The grarg had been a victim of the battle at Ringard. One of the many victims hauled off and presumed to be dead.

Josen barely had time to dodge before another creature threw itself at him. This one also wore Ringada gear and it circled Josen like a cat waiting to pounce on a mouse. Josen sent flames down his Ringada blade. The creature's black eyes widened with pleasure at the show of magic.

"Delicious. Your magic calls to me, it will be all mine when I am through with you."

The creature's voice was guttural, and Josen shivered despite himself. He had forgotten how disturbing the experience of fighting a grarg could be.

He sent a fireball toward this one too. The creature leapt toward Josen and the fireball shot past it, hitting the wall of the ravine behind it.

Josen barely had time to pull his blade between him and the creature. The grarg impaled itself on the blade. The flames from the sword spread up the creature and it unleashed another unearthly scream before completely igniting. Josen pulled his blade back as two more grarg stalked toward him.

These two wore the simple clothes of a farmer and his wife and they eyed him warily. Josen feigned to the left as they both leaped toward him. Neither of them noticed the blast of flame he sent their way until it was too late. Within seconds they had both been ignited. It was easy to light a living corpse on fire.

Josen looked to where Kaino stood amongst a pile of beheaded bodies. The last two grarg circled him, making strange guttural noises. Josen waited for them to get closer to his friend before sending two fireballs towards them. They went down with ease. Kaino turned to stare at Josen. Long scratches from the creature's nails bled slightly on the side of Kaino's face.

"Are you alright Kai?" Josen asked, breathing hard.

"Those things are unnerving," Kaino said with shaky breaths. He wiped off his blade with his cloak before sheathing it. Giving a whistle to his horse, it trotted over from where he had left it at the start of the ambush. The best thing about Ringada horses was that they were battle hardened and used to combat. Neither horse had left their master's sight.

"That was a perfectly laid trap," Kaino said, motioning toward the snow drifts. "With your father's use of air magic, it would have been easy for him to pile the snow over his entourage of grarg and have them lie in wait for us. I should have seen this!" He kicked a rock, sending snow and ice flinging with it as it soared farther down the ravine.

"Now we know we are headed in the right direction," Josen said, as he stepped around a headless grarg. He sent flames over Kaino's pile, and the creatures were soon smoldering in the snow. "Did you see how many of them were wearing Ringada gear?"

"Yes- I even recognized one of them too. Master Gino. He was always such a good man." Kaino bowed his head in respect toward the flames before heading onward.

"At least we have a better idea of what happened to the victims hauled off during the battle. Jos, if that ever happens to me, please kill me swiftly. Don't let me become a soulless creature set on consuming the magic of others."

Josen shivered at the thought. Being cut off from magic was one thing, but craving it for eternity? Pure hell. His fire magic was a part of him, as much as his arms. It was a tool for helping others and keeping darkness at bay. To think of wanting nothing more than to consume the magic of others the way he might consume dinner after an exhausting day of training... he had compassion for those he had put out of their misery that day.

They continued in the ravine going even slower than they had before. Josen sent blasts of flame at each remaining snow drift in case more grarg lay in wait. None emerged and Josen and Kaino were relieved when they stepped out of the ravine and onto a familiar trail void of rocks. The packed dirt was covered in snow. Noticing fresh tracks of horse hooves, they rode for a few more hours.

Soon the sky grew darker, and they were forced to set up their tents in the snow and prepare for another long day of tracking. It would still be a few days before they made it to Vendin, and they needed to plan before they got there.

Dinner was jerky and bread purchased before heading out in the snow that morning. They ate in silence and Josen volunteered for the first watch. Kaino climbed into his tent without complaint. It was not long before he was snoring.

He was more tired than he let on, Josen thought, as he stared up at the sky.

Only a little sliver of the moon was visible. A somber smile amidst millions of stars that shone down. The frigid air was refreshing and helped Josen stay alert as he focused on his surroundings.

By the time it was his turn to rest, he was tired from trying to keep memories at bay. He shook Kaino awake before stumbling to his own tent and quickly falling asleep. The memories he had pushed down all day came to the surface to wreak havoc in his dreams.

Chapter Five

Ellie sat in the wooden rocking chair Josen had commissioned as a wedding gift. A fire burned in the stone fireplace, warming their small stone quarters, and making her golden hair glow. She hummed a familiar lullaby as she sat embroidering a baby swaddle. This one would have small light blue flowers along the edges. Her slender fingers worked skillfully, and she was so engrossed in her work, she didn't notice Josen staring at her from the doorway.

He loved catching her like that, so focused on her work. It reminded him of the first time he had seen her, sitting on a decorative sofa at her father's mansion. She had been reading a book at the time. He had not been able to look away. Like now, she had not noticed him staring at her. She had not been aware of his arrival until he joined her family for dinner that evening.

They had been seated across from each other and he was aware of her shy glances at him. It had been hard not to return her looks. He had made it through the meal without openly staring at her and Kaino had teased him about it later that night. It was not often that Josen got more female attention than he did. His teasing had promptly stopped the next day when Ellie asked to accompany them into town.

Josen had spent the walk into town getting to know this beautiful woman. She had an amazing mind and was tired of living the life of a noblewoman. She wanted the opportunity to help people- not be cloistered in her father's house waiting for him to find the perfect suitor.

They had talked each day after that, whenever Josen was not trying to make peace between her father and another nobleman who wanted more of their land. Had it not been for Ellie, the assignment would have been tedious.

Josen had been stationed at her father's manor for over a month. During that time, he had grown to love her. He had been awed when she returned his affections and agreed to marry him as he was to return to Ringard.

Her father had thrown her out that same day and Ellie had never been happier. Memories of their courtship ran through his mind as he stared at her. Memories he cherished.

"You know the baby is just going to make a mess in that, right?" He teased from the doorway.

She turned towards him and gave him a smile that brightened up their stone quarters even more than the fire. He walked over to give her a light kiss that turned into something deeper. "I would expect nothing less from our child," she said with a laugh, pulling away. "Especially with how their father always comes in bloody and covered with dirt from training. Kaino was able to knock some sense into you?" She eyed his appearance with a critical eye.

"What makes you think..." he trailed off with a sigh and reached out to touch her growing belly. "Yes, it turns out I have been distracted lately and he used that distraction to his benefit."

Ellie took his face in her hands, her voice soft as she inspected him, "What troubles you, my love?" Her pale green eyes were penetrating, the gold flecks of magic becoming more prominent in them. Josen found himself getting lost in those eyes as he knelt beside her and took her delicate hands in his rough ones.

His voice trembled and he found himself saying, "Ellie... I'm worried. I'm worried for you, for the baby, and..." he gave a slight pause before looking down ashamed, "I'm worried about myself as a father."

He waited for her response. Never had he been more humbled than at that moment.

"Oh Josen," Ellie's voice was tender as she took her hands out of his and again brought them to his face. "You will be a great father. I have no doubt about that."

"How can you be so sure?" He asked, eyes still locked on hers. "How are you certain I am enough? Are you sure this is the life you wanted? A life of danger? Is it worth bringing a child into this kind of life? Your father- "

"When I married you," she said, cutting him off, her voice firm yet tender. "I knew what I was getting into and what luxuries and safety I was giving up. The wife of the next High Protector cannot be someone who shies away from danger. She needs to be someone who can embrace the risks and look at the world, not at what it is, but at what it can become. You are worth being that person for."

Her confidence in him was stunning. She always saw more in him than he ever saw in himself. He held her gaze unblinking as tears began to form in her eyes.

"Josen, I choose you each day- and I will choose you every day after that. This child chose you too, and they deserve to come into a world that can be better because their father will *make* it better. You will be a great father. I would not have agreed to marry you if I thought you would not."

They sat silently as Josen took in her words. Tears formed in his eyes as he stood up, taking Ellie with him. He embraced her, running a hand through her long golden hair. "Thank you," he said, voice full of emotion. "Thank you for choosing me and believing in me. I hope I will someday see what you see in me, but for now, thank you for loving me anyway."

"You will be the best father anyone could ever hope for," Ellie said, face pressed against his chest. They remained like that, his arms tight around her, and Josen found himself clinging to her as if she were the one thing keeping him tethered to the earth.

The scene changed in Josen's dream. The fire had gone out in the hearth and the stone chamber was cold. A body lay in the doorway. A body with delicate features and golden hair. A long cut across the neck had killed her and her hair was drenched in her own blood.

"Ellie- my Ellie." He cried as he pulled her body onto his lap. He held her there, overcome with grief, her limp body a weight he would never forget as he rocked her back and forth.

Kaino put a comforting hand on Josen's shoulder as he sat down next to him. "Shit- I'm so sorry Jos. We should have been fast enough!" His voice cracked as tears filled his own eyes. He stayed there next to Josen, not saying a word.

Time froze in that moment, the light from the small window slowly fading into dusk. Josen was not aware of his tears stopping.

"Something doesn't make sense Jos," Kaino's voice broke the quiet, the first words either of them had spoken in hours. Josen's head snapped up.

"Think about it," Kaino continued, "the guards outside were mauled. Ellie was," he shuddered before pressing on. "Ellie had her throat slit with what looked like a Ringada blade- not claws."

Josen stared unblinkingly as Kaino again began to search the room. "Nothing was touched. Your furniture is intact- we cannot say the same for the rest of the keep...So who killed Ellie?"

Tears formed anew in Josen's eyes as he stared down at Ellie, this time with a searching eye. Her face was a mask of serenity, despite what she had suffered. As his eyes searched the rest of her body, he saw something clutched in her hand. Lifting her wrist, he tugged the item from her grasp. It was the baby swaddle she had been working on.

Kaino gave Josen a long look before continuing with a sigh, "I am going to go search for survivors and to see if anyone else was killed the same as..." he paused, "in the same way." When he did not get a response, he bowed his head and left.

With each step his friend took out of the stone chamber, a numbness began to set in. Josen kissed Ellie's head again and words he had not been able to say in his friend's presence began to pour out of him. Words only meant for her.

"I am so sorry, Ellie. I promised you protection. I promised you they would keep you safe while I was gone. I promised that you would be able to live a peaceful life. That we would raise a family and teach our children to be as sweet and gentle as you, but with the hearts of warriors. I failed you, my love. I am so sorry!" He hugged Ellie to his chest, kissing her cold head before burying his face in her hair.

The light from the window had fully turned to dusk and the shadows in the room lengthened. Time had again stalled at that moment. How long had Kaino been gone?

"I must go now, my love. I have to let you go now. I just... I don't know if I am strong enough. You were the brightest part of my life. A force of good amidst the darkness. I never deserved you, but I am so thankful for the time we had together. Thank you for loving me and letting me love you in return. Oh, Ellie!" He found himself crying into her hair as he lifted her carefully off the ground and placed her onto the bed.

He arranged her so she looked like she was sleeping and caressed her face one last time. He found the swaddle from where it had fallen to the floor and tucked it in his pocket. Grabbing a lantern off the wall, he followed after his friend. His heart tore and ached with each step he walked away from Ellie. Soon, all that was left was a gaping void nothing would be able to fill.

***

He awoke disoriented and sat up with a start. He was not in his stone quarters at the keep with Ellie. He had not just held her limp corpse in his arms. No, he was in a tent in the snow hunting down her murderer. He lay back on his bedroll, the phantom weight of her corpse in his arms. He ran a shaking hand over his face, wiping away the tears that had come unbidden as he slept. With his other hand, he reached into his pants pocket and pulled out a stained piece of fabric.

The blue embroidered flowers were bright despite the dust and dirt that had accumulated on the once white fabric. He rubbed a thumb over a flower before bringing the swaddle close to his chest. With a great heaving sigh, he let the tears fall for what might have been- had he not lost everything.

Chapter Six

Aliyah did not see Sir Caldryk for two days. She spent the first day in bed, recovering from the party the evening before. When she woke up the following morning, she felt much more like herself.

After Linna brought her breakfast, Aliyah decided to investigate her room. The enormous wardrobe seemed like a good place to start. Opening the doors, she was met with a variety of vibrant colors. As she pulled out a dress, she noticed its design matched the one she wore to the party. She pulled out two more. All the dresses were cut in the same style.

She shut the wardrobe and ran over to the large chest of drawers. Aside from night clothes, the drawers were empty. Her chest was tight, and her heart raced as she began to panic. *My clothes! What happened to the clothes I brought with me?* Not that she was particular about any of the items she brought with her. She hated the dresses her aunt often forced her to wear, but at least those dresses covered more.

A knock at the door made her jump. Aliyah rushed to get to her feet as the door opened and an unfamiliar servant entered. A balding man with a wrinkled face. Even though they stood the same height, he still managed to look down on her as he took in her appearance.

"Ah, you are awake," he said in a deep voice. "The master sent me to inform you he requests your presence at dinner tonight. He has important work to begin and expects your full cooperation." He gave a small sniff of disdain, as if he did not expect her to cooperate. When she did not respond, he abruptly turned on his heels and almost ran into Linna in the hallway.

Linna gave a subservient nod to the man before closing the door behind him.

"Who was that?" Aliyah found herself asking as Linna began to make the bed.

Linna did not immediately respond, and Aliyah had to repeat herself. "That is the Archind, the master's Right Hand. He is the one responsible for managing all the servants- and meeting out any punishments. He is not one to cross. It is not my place," she continued, making the bed without looking at Aliyah, "but what was he doing in here?"

"Just telling me Sir Caldryk expects me at dinner and has important work to begin. He expects my full cooperation, whatever that is." She sighed as she went to the wardrobe. "Linna, do you know where my clothes are?"

Linna abruptly stopped making the bed and looked up sharply at Aliyah. "Why, in the wardrobe, Miss."

Aliyah opened the wardrobe doors. "All that are in here are dresses similar to what I wore to the party. Where are the clothes I brought?" She turned back to Linna who was biting her lip and twisting her hands.

Her voice wavered as she answered, "Those are your clothes, Miss. Sir Caldryk ordered your other clothes thrown out."

Aliyah blanched, "He what? Why would he do such a thing?"

"These dresses are ancient cultural Myralian dresses," Linna said, as if that explained everything.

"Does he have something against Gralanthian made clothing?"

"Oh no, Miss. It is all about appearances. You are his Mylarian *Wyvanni*. He wants you not only to act the part but look the part."

"I never wanted this!" Aliyah could no longer keep the hysteria out of her voice. "I never wanted to be a *Wyvanni*. Never wanted anyone to know about it. Most of all, I never wanted to be here in the first place!"

Linna hesitated, as if she wanted to say something to comfort her, but footsteps outside the door made her turn around and get back to her work. The footsteps continued down the hall and Aliyah sat in a chair by her nightstand, exhausted from the outburst.

"Miss," Linna whispered, coming to kneel in front of where she sat. "I have been here for quite a few years and seen things and heard things that have gone on. One thing I am certain about: the Master is a ruthless man with a knack for getting everything he wants. Please be careful in your dealings with him. You are a pawn in this game that he is playing for power. Be on your guard tonight and whatever you do, do what he asks. Your life will depend on it."

Frustrated, she stood up, brushed past Linna, and walked over to the balcony doors. There was no knob.

"Do these not open?"

"Hmmm? Oh, the doors. No Miss, they are bolted shut." She looked sad and Aliyah did not press her for any more information.

Once Linna left, Aliyah continued her search of the room. None of her personal belongings had made their way up to the room, and she suspected they had been thrown out as well. She had about given up on finding anything of interest when she pulled open a drawer on a small hutch below a window. Inside lay a book bound in green leather. It was the size of her hand and had no title to it. She flipped to the first page as she sat down on the blue couch. The book was not a book at all. It was a journal.

I wonder who it belongs to, Aliyah thought as she glanced around the room. Certain she was alone; she began to read.

I cannot believe it! Father found me a suitable match! He is the Lord of Elwryn and has been looking for a wife ever since his father died and left him the title. Father met him while meeting with some other Lords and sent word he was bringing Lord Caldryk home with him. He suggested we might make a suitable match. Can you imagine? Lady Caldryk has a lovely ring to it.

I wonder if he will bring a ring! Lillian said she met him when she went to a ball in Elwryn, and he was so pleasant- and a great dancer. She told me out of spite, but I appreciated the information. Maybe I do need to get a new best friend. That is what Linna is always saying.

Aliyah stopped on Linna's name. *Linna knew the owner of this journal?*

She turned to the next page, an entry from a few days later, and continued to read.

Sir Caldryk comes tomorrow! Father sent a runner to tell us to expect them after breakfast. I do not have the faintest clue what I am going to wear!

Lord Sir Vihan Caldryk is the most handsome man I have ever met. I have also never blushed as hard as I did as he kissed my hand in greeting.

He brought me a lovely cloak from Vendin. It is made of the palest blue and is so soft. He said he loves to go on strolls and was hoping I would join him despite the weather we have been having. You should have seen the jealous look on Lillian's face when he gifted me with the cloak and extended the invitation to take a stroll with him. Apparently, she was never extended an offer during her time in Elwryn.

The stroll was amazing. I showed him around the gardens, and we sat on a bench by the pond for over an hour as we talked. When I got back, he kissed my hand before bidding me good night. I never dreamed I would be so lucky in Father finding me a suitable match that is so charming.

Charming? Aliyah could not fathom the man she was now engaged to was once this charming suitor. She turned the page again.

It has been a while since I wrote. The past few weeks have been a blur!

Vihan is so wonderful! From written notes proclaiming his love for me, picnics by the pond, or strolls through the garden, he has stolen my heart as I hoped he would. He surprised me tonight by taking me out to "our" spot by the pond and asking me to marry him!

I told him "Yes!" He is everything a girl could dream of.

Our wedding is to be held in three weeks in Elwryn. Father has an important deal that will take him to Cerulean for quite a few months and he wants to see me married before he leaves. Linna is to accompany me to Elwryn. I asked her if she was sad to leave the friends she had made here, but she is as ready for a new adventure as I am.

My wedding day is tomorrow. Time has flown by so quickly. I cannot wait to walk down the aisle and marry Vihan. Tomorrow, at this time, I will be Lady Diedre Caldryk, wife of Lord Vihan Caldryk!

Aliyah went to turn the page again when a knock sounded at the door. There was just enough time for her to place the book back in the drawer before Linna entered and headed to the wardrobe. A turquoise version of the gown and matching slippers were pulled out and handed to Aliyah.

Once dressed, she stared at her reflection while Linna braided her hair into a crown atop her head.

Thoughts of what she had read in the journal swam through her mind. Another knock at the door interrupted her musings.

Linna opened the door and Archind entered the room, hands clasped behind his back. "I am to escort you to dinner." He gave an annoyed sigh as he turned and left without another word. Aliyah rushed to catch up as he walked brusquely down the marble stairs. Aliyah had not been in this hall yet.

Focused on where they were going, she ran into him as he stopped in front of an open patio door. Past him stood tall trees and a flowering garden. Interspersed among the flowers were fountains and statues. The mist of the fountains glistened in the evening sunset.

"My Lord, your *Wyvanni*," he motioned towards Aliyah. Never had she experienced such distaste for the word *Wyvanni*. It left her feeling dirty. He shot her a hard glance before going back into the house.

Before Aliyah could think too much about Archind's behavior, Sir Caldryk motioned for her to sit where he was sitting at a wrought iron table under a pergola. The setting sun cast long shadows from the slats on the roof, leaving the unmarred half of his face in shadow. She tried not to stare at the jagged scar on his face as she sat in the chair across from him.

"Good. You are here," his voice was cold and harsh. Nothing like the voice he had used that night at the party.

Not knowing how to respond, she was relieved when a servant brought her a covered dish. The contents smelled wonderful. Another servant brought her a glass of wine and she nodded in thanks before looking back towards Sir Caldryk. He was looking her up and down as if she were a painting hung in a gallery. Embarrassed, she turned her attention back to her food and began eating the way her aunt had taught her.

"Impressive. Who knew Myralians eat with such decorum," he sneered.

Heat flooded her cheeks. Her aunt's words about being a backwater brat came back to her. What did he really want from her? She was no one. A girl born on the wrong side of the mountains with a power she could not control. That is who she was. Someone unfortunate to have been gifted a power in the wrong land.

Aware he was watching her every movement; she took care to dab her mouth gently with a napkin before responding.

"I'm-" she did not have a chance to finish before he leaned over and backhanded her face. Tears formed in her eyes at the sudden pain, and she touched her face gingerly.

"Rule number one," he said as he picked up his fork and speared a slice of fruit with it. "You will not speak unless asked to do so." He held her gaze, as if daring her to make a sound. She did not give him the satisfaction of reacting and he took his time taking a bite of the fruit before continuing.

"Rule number two, you are not allowed to speak to any of the many guests we are to host the next few evenings. As far as they are concerned, you are not from here. You have no ties to Gralanth- other than being betrothed to me. They also are all under the impression you only speak Myralian."

She did not want to tell him that her Myralian was limited. There had been no opportunity to speak the language since she was a little girl. And it was only ever to her father to whom she had spoken. Her father, *what would he think?*

"Rule number three," she forced herself to focus on Sir Caldryk, "you are to do what you are asked, when you are asked and without any complaint. I have important work to begin- work you are vital to. If you do not comply..." he paused to look at Archind, "we have ways of persuading you. Nod if you understand."

She gave a small nod and Sir Caldryk went back to eating. No longer hungry, she picked at her food, wishing she was Gralanthian.

Chapter Seven

Aliyah instantly hated this room.

The study had no windows and was lined with odd trinkets and old books. Maybe once she would have found it fascinating. Might have even spent time lounging in one of the armchairs while reading a book by the fireplace.

Instead, she sat ramrod straight in a wooden chair that faced Sir Caldryk. He leaned against a large polished wooden desk. Papers and stacks of books lay scattered across its surface. She had no idea what he had brought her in here for, only that he had commanded her to follow him after the awful dinner on the patio.

"I have studied a lot about your kind," he began as he motioned lazily to the stacks of books. "From the dawn of the new age, written in a language of the ancients, to the latest writings by Masters of the Ringada.

"It occurred to me while reading one day, there was never any mention of what banished magic in Gralanth. What power so great could take away the power of others? You can imagine my delight when I came across a specific word that answered my question..."

Aliyah's stomach clenched as she waited for him to say it.

"*Wyvanni*," he said the word like a caress. "Imagine my even greater delight when I discovered one living within my domain. It did not take much to get your aunt to agree to an engagement proposal." He held up a stack of letters that had yellowed with age. Aliyah was close enough to see the handwriting. Tears welled up in her eyes as the elegant script of her mother's hand was waved before her face. She longed to reach for them.

"Even though your mother's parents disowned her for marrying a Myralian, she kept in touch with her sister. For years, your mother kept in correspondence with Matylda- and not just the daily woes of women. Oh no! She wrote everything about her daughter and the amazing magical abilities she was showing."

He opened one letter and began to read:

My Dearest Sister,

It has been quite a while since we have enjoyed your company. I hope all is well. I have some exciting news! Aliyah's magical ability has finally appeared! After giving us quite a shock when it manifested, Eldris was incredibly pleased. Apparently, it is an exceedingly rare ability! There has not been one in Ringada history in years. Our daughter is a Wyvanni. Eldris and I plan to move to Ringard as she gets older. They will have to accept her- despite being a half born.

I do not understand how her power works. It is not something she can physically manifest like Eldris' ice. No, it is more as if she can manipulate his magic. Her three-year-old temper tantrums make it interesting for him. Last week she almost froze him solid when he told her it was time to go inside.

I still have a lot to learn about magic. It is so strange, it has become an integral part of life now, when it used to be a shunned subject in our father's house. Nothing we were ever taught about Myral is true. I have seen it. I hope one day you can come to see it the same.

Your Sister Always,
Valeri

Aliyah had begun crying as he read the letter to her. Her vision was blurred, and she cried out as Sir Caldryk tossed the letter he had read to her into the burning fire. She lunged out of her chair, fingers outstretched towards the flames. Archind's firm hands grabbed her shoulders from behind, holding her in place. She had forgotten he was standing behind her. He refused to let go, despite her desperate attempts to escape, and she sobbed as the paper turned to ash.

"Your blood is not the only way one can access your powers and I would like to explore that further." Sir Caldryk looked at her with what she assumed he meant as a pleasant expression. The scar on his face did nothing to put her at ease as it pulled at the side of his mouth.

"I don't know what you are talking about," she cried out. She did not see Archind's hand as it smacked her across the back of her head.

"Hmmm... I think you do." He put the rest of the letters in a desk drawer and locked the drawer before continuing.

"Yes, you do know what I am talking about. Your mother outlined your magnificent use of your magic in her letters to Matylda, did she not? I have read them all. You not only enhanced your father's water magic, but your mother soon developed earth magic after you were born."

"I don't..." the memory came unbidden. A memory she had no recollection of until that moment.

"Papa pretty! Make more pretties!" She was three. Her father stood outside in the snow forming shapes and animals in the snow with just his magic. He smiled at

her and lifted his hand to make more when her mother's voice rang from inside the house.

"Come inside, you two! You have been out there for hours! You will catch a cold!" Her mom stood shivering in the doorway; a purple shawl thrown around her shoulders. Her light brown hair was pulled into a loose braid that hung off her shoulder.

"But Mama! Papa's making me pretties!" She turned back to her father, "Make more please Papa?"

Her father gave her a small grin but shook his head. "Another day, my little love." He bent down to pick her up and haul her inside the house.

"No!" She said, with as much force her three-year-old body could muster. "No, Papa, no! Make more pretties!"

Her father took another step, "I'm sorry but we will have to wait for tomorrow."

"No!" She threw her fists down to the side and stomped her foot. "I said make more pretties NOW!"

Her father stumbled as water began to circle him. He cried out as it started forming into ice and then melted, only to form into ice out of his control. "Aliyah! Stop!" His voice was a gurgle.

Her mother ran for her, shoeless in the snow. "Aliyah!" She pulled Aliyah's arm. "Stop that right now! You are hurting him!"

Her mother's touch distracted her. Something inside of her snapped and released. The water around her father landed in the snow. She turned to stare with wide eyes at her parents.

That had been the last time her father used magic for fun.

Aliyah blinked, realizing Sir Caldryk was talking. "I think you do know. I think you have known all along, and it is only a matter of time until you will use your magic to fuel my own. Your blood may be potent, but it is nothing compared to the information written in your mother's letters."

He caused the faintest of fireballs to form in his hand and looked at her expectantly. "I want you to increase the flow of the flame. Make it bigger."

Aliyah stared at the ball of flame, panic rising within her. *A ceiling cracking above her. Smoke filling her lungs. Two bodies lying together on the floor-*

"Make it bigger!" Sir Caldryk slapped his hand down on his desk, making her jump. "You are not concentrating! I said, make it bigger!" His face was getting flushed as he spat the words at her.

"I don't know how to make it work. I don't know how to fuel another person's magic and bend it to my will. I don't know how to do anything." The words came out of her in a rush. Tears were starting to form in her eyes as she stared at the flame, and her head still swam with memories. Her heart pounded as if it would leap out of her chest.

He brought the flame closer to her face, as if the closer proximity would make her magic work. The heat of it hot against her skin and she pulled her head back until it smacked against the wooden back of the chair. He pushed the flame even closer.

"Do it!"

"Please!" She cried. "Please- I don't know how to- "

He put out the flame and smacked her across the face with his still hot hand. Her cheek burned from more than the sting of the slap.

He lit another fireball. "If you don't know how to fuel it- maybe you can put it out!" She shook her head in response.

"You will do it now or you will experience the wrath of my flames." He edged closer with the fireball. It was next to her cheek now and she closed her eyes from the light and heat.

She tried. The fear of the fire coursed through her, and she tried to will it to stop and flicker out. Nothing happened. She gasped and tried even harder. The heat of the flames kissed her cheeks.

"Do not disappoint me!" He roared at her. "I didn't search all over for you so you could whimper in a chair and tell me lies!" The heat dispersed. For an instant, Aliyah thought she had forced it out but as she opened her eyes, she saw him getting another fireball started.

"Your mother said you can do amazing things! You gave her power and strengthened your father's magic all as a little girl. Now you are nothing more than a weak woman. You will learn to give me what I want eventually." The flaming hand gripped the arm of her chair. A burn mark was left in the wood. "But since you will not give it to me now, I will have to take it by force." He grabbed her arm and dragged his knife across one of her arms.

A blood-curdling scream broke free as the steel bit into her flesh.

"You can make this stop. You can make it stop for good if you will give me what I want!" He yelled the words at her and then grabbed her arm and brought it to his mouth, forgoing a cup. The sensation of his lips sucking on her arm made her want to vomit. When he was done with her, he lit both hands on fire, making her flinch.

"I think this is enough for tonight," Sir Caldryk said, inspecting his flaming hands, the flames now brighter and hotter. "Get some rest. We start working on your power tomorrow."

Archind dragged her out of her chair. Stunned, she did not resist as he pulled her out of the room.

***

Linna was waiting for her when she made it back to her room. "My lady! What did he do to you?"

Linna gasped as she saw the cut on her arm and burns on Aliyah's face before rushing to the washroom to get her bandages.

"He wanted me to will my magic to fuel his." Aliyah's voice was soft, the words forced. "When I couldn't do it, he..." She looked away from Linna's sympathetic expression as the woman began to clean and bandage the wound.

Once Linna left, Aliyah crawled into bed still in the turquoise dress, and sobbed.

Chapter Eight

Aliyah slept fitfully that night. Dreams of her parents intermingled with images of Sir Caldryk. His hands were encased in flames as he shook her. Her skin burned where he touched it, and a scream escaped her lips-

A hand clamped down on her mouth. Startled awake, she opened her eyes to find Linna standing over her.

"Shh." Linna's eyes were wide as she removed her hand from Aliyah's mouth. A set of male voices echoed down the hall.

"Madra is not pleased with how things are going here," a deep voice said. The voice was one of nightmares and Aliyah found herself gripping her sheets tighter as it continued, "you are to be uniting the Lords to swear allegiance to her, not dallying with some new plaything."

"I am not sure what dallying you are referring to," Sir Caldryk's nasally voice responded. Was that fear? Yes, that was fear in his voice.

"Come now," the cold voice tsked. "Surely you did not think you could keep your new bride from her attention… here we thought after the loss of your first wife… well. We all know how well that ended. The laughingstock of the Lords. A man whose wife would rather die than be stuck living to see the monster he was becoming."

"You know nothing about what happened," there was anger now in Sir Caldryk's voice.

"Surely this one will last longer, won't she? Or will she too find a way out… when she sees the monster you really are."

"How dare you come into my home and be so disrespectful!" Sir Caldryk yelled. "I am a lord, not some lowly slave. You may be the Executioner, but we all know she needs me for her cause."

A humorless laugh echoed down the hall.

"You really do believe that don't you? That you are needed for the cause? She is bound to many. Do not think, because she accepted your bond before others in your country, that makes you special. There were many before you and many that will be after you. Thousands serve her."

The voices had begun moving away and Aliyah could hear no more of the conversation.

"Who was that?" Aliyah whispered to Linna.

"A very powerful man," Linna replied, her voice barely audible.

Aliyah leaned over and lit the oil lantern beside her bed. It cast a warm glow in the room and instantly made both women less leery.

"Tell me about him," Aliyah said softly, as she reached over and gripped the older woman's shaking hands.

"He is a man of myths," she began, "someone who should not exist. He is the right hand and consort to Darkness herself."

"Surely you don't mean-" Aliyah could not finish. There was no possible way the stories she had been told as a child were true. Those were fantastical tales told to scare children into obedience.

"Indeed. About a year ago, the master and his wife went to visit family near the Vendi Mountains. During the trip, the master and his father-in-law went on a hunting trip into the mountains. When the master came back, he was no longer the same," she paused and glanced down at her apron.

"And his father-in-law?" Aliyah prodded.

"Didn't ever come back, Miss." A tear fell. "He was a good man, too. Hired me to be his daughter's maid servant at their manor. Her father sent me here with her when she married the master. I was with her from an early age right up until... until she died."

"Oh Linna, I am so sorry! That is awful!" Aliyah put a comforting hand on the older woman's shoulder.

Linna gave her a sad smile and took a deep breath before continuing. "We soon returned to Caldryk Manor, and the Master locked himself in his study for weeks. He did not come out for meals or to comfort his wife as she grieved over her father. Some of us servants think he went mad there in his grief. He was close with his father-in-law. But..."

Aliyah realized she was gripping Linna's shoulder tight and let her hand drop into her lap.

Linna shuddered before looking Aliyah straight in the eye.

"The rest of us," she continued, "the rest of us think he saw something in the mountains. He claimed his father-in-law fell into a ravine, one too deep to bring the body back, but you should have seen his eyes. His eyes were flecked with gold and his skin was ashen. Being caught up in their grief, no one noticed... but I did. His mannerisms were off. There was a hunger in his eye, a look that hasn't left since.

"The Executioner showed up a week after the Mistress died. He came into the Manor and pulled the Master out of his study. The Master had only come out for his wife's funeral before shutting himself in again. We heard the Master screaming before we even knew the Executioner had arrived. When he was done, the Master was left lying in the entryway, blood running down his face from the scar that now mares it."

Aliyah sat stunned as she absorbed Linna's words. Who was this man that everyone feared? He now knew about her, what would that mean for her?

"Miss," Linna's voice dragged Aliyah out from her thoughts, "there is one more thing I need to tell you about the Executioner. There is a reason he has that title. It isn't only because he kills those the Darkness wants killed... he executes ALL her plans.

"I don't know all of Sir Caldryk's plans, but I know he has been desperately looking for a *Wyvanni*. His own *Wyvanni*. He has searched for one of your kind since the day the Executioner came. Whatever happened on that fateful hunting trip has led him to you. If you play your cards right, you may be able to use his desperation to your advantage."

***

Awake due to the Executioner's visit, and wanting to take her mind off her own problems, Aliyah went to the table by the window. Linna's story ran through her mind as she took the green journal back to her bed and began to skim through it. When she found an entry mentioning Vendin, she stopped and began to read.

Father invited Vihan on a hunting trip. I am to accompany them to Vendin and then wait for their return. It will be a lovely opportunity to do some fine shopping and see the sights Vendin has to offer. We leave in the morning.

Aliyah flipped through a few mindless entries about Diedre's shopping trips in the Vendin market, stopping when she got to the entry where Diedre wrote about her father's death.

Vihan returned from the hunting trip this afternoon all covered in blood and clothes in tatters. Father did not return with him. There was an accident on the hunting trip and Father died falling into a ravine. Vihan almost died as well but was able to pull himself to safety. The horror! My heart is broken at the loss of my Father, but to think Vihan had to witness his death. He cared for Father deeply. Vihan hasn't wanted to talk about it, and I don't want to press, but I miss my father!

The next few entries contained minimal details of planning a funeral when there is not a body to burn, intermixed with recollections of memories of her father she wanted to share at the event. Turning a few more pages, Aliyah found what she was looking for.

Something has happened to Vihan. Father's death has badly shaken him. He has been spending a lot of time in the study. He will not come out for meals, or to go to bed. He has begun to sleep in his old room instead of with me when he needs sleep. I miss him. I miss the closeness we once had. I just lost my father- I do not want to lose my husband also!

The next entry was from a few days later.

I confronted Vihan today.

I barged into the study when he refused to come out for lunch, even after I had explicitly invited him to join me in the garden for the meal. I have never seen him so furious. He had a crazed look in his eye and the books! He had so many books with drawings done in blood open on his desk.

He screamed at me to get out and threw an inkwell at me before I could. I have holed myself up in my room for the time being and have locked the door. I do not believe he will come talk to me- he would have to leave the study for that- but I feel safer with the door locked. I do not think I will ever be able to get the image of his crazed eyes out of my head.

Someone came calling and he was forced out of his study to do his Lordship duties. I snuck into the study while he was occupied and stole a few of the papers he had sitting in stacks on his desk. I know he will find them missing but I do not think he will suspect it was me. By the time he does, I plan to be long gone. Linna is going to come with me. She has family in Myral, and she thinks we can make it there safely.

I wrote too soon. He found out it was me who stole the papers. Archind must have seen me. I told Vihan I burned the papers to get a reaction out of him and to get his attention. He believed me and then he beat me. My Vihan beat me. Told me what a wretched woman I am and how he never loved me. How I was a fool to think I was worthy of his love. He said it over and over as he dealt out my "punishment." When he was done with me, he left me on the floor with only Linna to help clean me up.

I cannot keep living like this anymore. I am a prisoner in my own house. Vihan has locked me in my room and allows only Linna to see me. It has been weeks since he beat me. Weeks since I have seen anyone else. My husband has become a monster. I do not want to be married to him anymore. I do not want to live anymore. I wish I could see my father again.

Aliyah turned the page but there were no more entries. She went to close the book when a slip of paper near the back caught her attention. She flipped to that page and found a handful of folded papers. Papers written in blood.

***

Archind was sent to fetch Aliyah before the sun had fully risen. Groggy from the evening conversation with Linna and thinking about everything she had learned, she blinked sleep from her eyes and stifled a yawn as she followed him back into the study. Sir Caldryk sat behind his ornate desk reading a ledger. He had dark circles under his eyes, and he did not look up at Aliyah as Archind forced her roughly into the same chair as the night before.

"My timeline seems to have been moved up," he said, without acknowledging her presence. He stood up from his chair and walked over to a bookshelf before grabbing a book so ancient it looked as if it was one more read away from breaking.

"I have read every single book on why there is a lack of magic on this side of the Vendis. As I said last night, it all has to do with *Wyvanni*." He flipped to a specific page in the book before turning the book toward her. The words were in an unfamiliar language, but Aliyah noted the writing was in red ink. *Blood*, Aliyah realized. Her suspicions were confirmed when her attention was caught by an image on the bottom of the page.

A group of figures knelt in a circle, blood dripping to the ground where they held knives to their arms. An aura had been drawn around them. A group of others in throws of pain and tears sat watching those in the aura. They were drawn darker. Dragging her attention to the next page, the group that had knelt with the knives lay in a puddle of blood.

Aliyah stared fixedly at the book and jumped when Sir Caldryk abruptly closed it.

"By the blood of *Wyvanni* was Gralanth cursed, and only by the blood of *Wyvanni* can it be saved."

A pit formed in Aliyah's stomach at his words. Questions formed at her lips, but she bit her tongue to keep them from escaping.

"You have seen how consuming your blood has granted me powers for a brief time. Imagine what sacrificing yourself would accomplish for all Gralanth." He leered at her as he came closer and gripped her jaw painfully. "But do not fret just yet. We have only begun. Your powers are weak, and we have few moons left to prepare them before the solstice."

Chapter Nine

Josen and Kaino rode with caution through the grassy fields outside Vendin. Snow did not fall much outside the Vendis in Gralanth in late spring. They had left their tents in a secure location and picked up supplies before continuing forward. They did not want to be burdened by unnecessary items when a bedroll would suffice.

Kaino had been scouting the area in front of them for quite some time, looking for signs of Josen's father. They had not found a lead in days and both men were beginning to wonder if they should not have left the Vendis.

They continued toward the main road. This close to the Vendis, people were used to seeing Myralians and they did not fear detection.

As much as the Gralanthian nobles claimed there was a hard boundary line of the Vendis, it was not the case. The closer you got to the mountain range, the more of a melting pot the villages and towns became. Vendin itself had once been a Myralian city until a Gralanthian was given authority to rule over it. Now it was nothing more than a mix of cultures and customs known across the entire continent. It was often referred to as the City of Color, and it was a place dear to Josen's heart.

He gazed back toward the city, now nothing but a bright blob standing out against the brown and gray of the stone mountains. The high peaks were topped with snow and Josen imagined the Vendin houses were dusted with a layer of white as well. They continued around a bend and Josen lost sight of the magnificent city.

He turned his attention back to the road before him. There were few people traveling it today and they would have been able to travel at a faster pace if Kaino was not looking for tracks. Josen willed his friend to find something, anything that would tell them they were on the right path. He would even have prayed to the gods had he thought it would help.

The sun had just reached its zenith in the sky when loud crying came from up ahead. Kaino motioned for Josen to stop. Both men dismounted their horses and crept along the road. Their horses stayed in place, trained to not move, or leave until called.

The side of the road was lined with trees and the two Ringada slipped into them undetected as they headed toward the sound. Peering through a bush, they saw a ramshackle group of refugees heading toward Vendin. Their clothing was soot stained and tattered and many of them were shoeless. The crying came from a small child that had suffered some burns. Many other refugees were covered in burns as well.

Kaino stepped out from the trees, startling many of the tattered folk. "What happened?" His voice was calm as he scrutinized each member of the party in turn. They stared back at him with fear.

"We won't hurt you." Josen's voice was calming as he stepped around the bush. "Please, we want to help."

"Help?" An older man with wisps of hair and missing teeth spoke up from the back of the ragged group. "And what *help* does *your* kind have to offer us?" He spat towards them.

"Our kind?" Josen asked carefully. "And what might that mean? We have done nothing to you and are offering aid."

"Bah! You filthy Myralians and your heathen creatures of darkness tore our village apart! We lost many people in the attack and many others were hauled off. We are all that remains! You ask what your kind has done to us- this!" he said, motioning toward the refugees, "this is what your kind has done to us."

"Your town was attacked recently?" Kaino asked.

"They came in the night," a younger man stepped forward, ignoring the protests of the older man behind him. "They burned our buildings and hauled off with as many of us as they could. Nightmarish creatures with ashen skin and black eyes. They were led by a man all in black. He rode a tall black horse and surveyed the town as it was being destroyed, then rode away with the creatures when they departed."

"And did you see which direction they went?" Josen asked, his impatience getting the better of him.

"Please forgive my friend," Kaino said, sparing a withering look toward Josen. "We have been hunting this man and his army of grarg for quite some time. If you could point us in the direction of your town and tell us what direction he went after that, it would be quite appreciated." He threw a coin toward the man. It landed in the dirt with a thud.

"He..." The man licked his lips, eyeing the coin that had been tossed to him. "He went east. Right over the Knoll hills. We ran in the opposite direction toward Vendin. We are hoping to seek shelter there."

"Shelter you will find," Kaino said, pulling out more coins and distributing them among the small crowd. "Ask for Nettle, she will help. Mind you though," he said, looking toward the older gentleman, "she is one of our kind and does not take too kindly to having that sort of attitude directed her way. Knowing her though, she has already been alerted of your arrival."

The man looked at him quizzically. "Nettle...?"

"Just Nettle. Ask around and you will find her. Everyone in town is aware of who she is." Josen responded impatiently.

Josen whistled for their horses and smiled as the refugees pulled back in fright from the sound of pounding hooves. Both men mounted their horses and were about to leave when Kaino turned back towards the small group.

"Don't forget- you are to ask for Nettle! When she asks who sent you, don't forget to mention it was two Ringada!" He turned and pushed his horse into a gallop.

Josen was about to follow when he heard the murmurs of the refugees. "Ringada? They are Ringada? Heaven help us all."

***

It took them two days to reach the destroyed village. The fires had long since gone out and all that remained were charred remnants of what had once been houses and other structures. Burned corpses lay scattered around as well, telling the story of the last moments of the town's existence. It was not a pretty sight, but they had seen worse.

Armored corpses on the ground. Blood streaked and splattered on the stone walls. Bodies pushed down stone stairs, their necks broken and bent at odd angles. The silence in the keep. Ellie's body in the doorway-

"Are you alright Jos?" Kaino's voice broke through the unbidden memory.

Josen blinked, realizing he was standing in the middle of the town square, looking at where a woman with blonde hair lay crumbled. Her body had been mauled by claws- not slashed through with a blade. He took a step back trying to calm his breathing. Flames licked at his fingers in response.

"We need to find him. We need to stop this before more towns are slaughtered," Josen answered. His voice was devoid of emotion, but inside he felt like he would explode.

Kaino nodded in agreement and began heading toward the direction the surviving members of the village had indicated the monsters had gone. Even Josen could easily see their path of trampled grass up the hill. Josen gave the woman one last look before setting her corpse aflame. He moved on to the next corpse, an elderly man who looked to have been too weak to run. Within seconds he was smoldering. Josen found every single villager and gave them the proper farewell. He imagined their souls being released by the flames, free to travel to the great beyond.

He did not think about the last time he had done something similar- or how it had been Ellie that had been laid upon a pier and it had been up to him to release her soul. He could not think about the pain that had come from watching his dreams turn to ashes. If he did, there would be nothing stopping him from turning his flame on himself and releasing his soul to join hers.

Instead, he worked until there were no more souls left to release. Each body burned to cinders. The flames responded with eagerness, ever willing to obey his command. Caught up in his work, he jumped when a hand fell on his shoulder. He turned to find Kaino standing behind him.

Kaino gave him a sad smile. "I followed the trail for a long way, and it veered off toward the east. Come, let's find your father." With a nudge to his horse, he was gone.

Josen followed more slowly. He glared at the village, at the lives and dreams that had been ruined. Something stirred inside him, something he had been keeping contained. Something that frightened him. Hatred.

Hatred for his father. Hatred for the man who had been cold and calculating his entire life. Hatred for the man who had thrown him into a sparring ring at the age of five and expected him to be able to fight- then was disappointed when Josen failed. Hatred for the man who had told him not to cry or mourn the loss of his mother- one of the only bright spots of his life in the keep. Hatred for the man who had selected him as Heir of Ringard when Josen had never wanted it. Hatred for the man who could watch the slaughter of innocents- command it even. Hatred for the man who had murdered Ellie.

He let the hatred flow into him. It fanned the inner flames, making him brighter. He mounted Ember and in seconds was pounding up the hill toward Kaino, the hatred pushing him on.

I will find you, Father. And when I do, I will kill you. The flames within stirred with glee at the thought.

They traveled the rest of the day through the long grass. The trail was easy to follow, and they pushed on after dark. They followed the trail until it split off in two, one doubling back to the west and one heading north.

"We should rest for the night," Kaino said with a yawn. "They already have a few days' lead on us, and we want to make sure we choose the correct path to follow tomorrow."

Josen sat unmoving on top of Ember.

"I mean, if you want to keep going, I can push through, but errors will be made, and I would rather look at the trails with fresh eyes." He yawned again.

"We will stop for the night," Josen said. He had not spoken since leaving the village. His voice was cold and uncaring. Kaino flinched at the tone but dismounted Maelstrom and began to set up camp.

Josen was more tired than he had been willing to admit. He would have pushed his friend farther on the trail but knew Kaino was right. Fresh eyes would be better. Besides, it would give him more time to contemplate what he would do to his father when he did catch up to him.

With that, he took the first watch. The sky above them was clear and the moon, now at half, bathed the grass in pale moonlight. Josen could hear small animals scurrying through the grass and the sound of lazy insects created a staccato of sound. It was peaceful here in the grass. Peaceful enough to plan without interruption. When it was time for Kaino's watch, Josen laid on his bedroll and fell asleep. The beginning of a smile formed on his face. Revenge would be his and it would be glorious.

Chapter Ten

Aliyah's back ached from sitting on the chair in the study. It had been four days since Sir Caldryk had brought her there and divulged his plans. Four days of pure hell. Each day began with him slicing into her arm and drinking her blood. The gold flecks were becoming more prominent, a reminder of the torture. They faded slower each evening too.

"Again!" He screamed at her, and she nodded tiredly.

When was the last time I was given water? He only let her out of the chair once a day at lunchtime to relieve herself and then eat whatever small portions he gave her. She had determined he needed to keep her alive- just so she could kill herself at the appointed time A sycophantic sacrifice. At least it got her out of his nightly dinner meetings with unknown guests. Instead, he kept her locked up in the study to eat the tiny portion she was given for dinner.

Those hours were spent stretched out on the floor near the fireplace. Most of the time she dozed, dreaming of better times. Times when she thought she would have years ahead of her, a life to live. Now she had weeks at best until-

A searing pain engulfed her upper arm. The smell of burning flesh filled the room as she tried to pull out of his grasp.

"Do it!"

She fought against the pain, trying to calm the part of herself that was fighting against horrible memories. Eyes closed; she reached out with her mind as if trying to find a light in the dark. *There.* The small kernel of magic emanating from him was stronger than it had been before. She focused on it and found herself exhaling as she imagined extinguishing the heat burning her arm. The pain lessened and she cracked open an eye to assess the damage.

On her arm was now another blistered handprint. If he was not trying to burn her arm, he was trying to get her to increase the intensity of his own magic. Stoke and dim, stoke and dim. She was not sure which was worse. Fail on the stoking and Archind would push a knife into her arm, slicing until her pain would force Sir Caldryk's flame to increase. Fail on the dimming and... well... she had his handprints burned forever into her skin.

She panted and gulped for air. The heat in her arm was a constant reminder of the hell her life had become.

Archind came over from where he had stationed himself by the wall and grabbed the ceramic crock of salve off the desk. He was not gentle as he applied it to her arm. The salve immediately took most of the heat away and Aliyah tried not to show how grateful she was for the medicine.

They had not started with the salve right away. Instead, they had pushed her to her limits until she had passed out from the pain that first day. Realizing they could not get anything more from her, they had brought in the salve for the burns, and ash for the cuts. The salve and ash were a double-edged sword. It immediately took the pain away but made sure they could continue hurting her again. Death would be a welcome escape, a forever slumber.

A memory of screams in a burning building flashed before her eyes. No, death would not be welcomed.

Sir Caldryk reached his hand out to her other arm and gripped her wrist. Slow heat began to creep into her wrist and tears pierced her eyes at the pain. "Again!" he demanded.

She had closed her eyes to try to find his magic and end this round of pain when a loud boom echoed inside the manor. Loud footsteps echoed down the hallway before a large gush of wind forced the door open, blowing papers and some books off the desk. The candles at the far end of the study were extinguished in the wind. Sir Caldryk paled, and Aliyah turned to see what had made him so fearful.

In the doorway stood a man dressed entirely in black. His face hidden under a cowl. The light from the hall reflected off the blade he pulled out of an ebony scabbard at his side. The blade had a slight curvature and Aliyah started at the sight. Her father had owned a blade like that. It was a weapon reserved for a member of the Ringada.

The hooded figure took a step into the room and turned his head toward Sir Caldryk, who jolted and let go of Aliyah's arm. She stared dumbfounded at the hooded figure as he came to stand across from them.

"What-" Sir Caldryk began.

"Did you really think news of your plot would not reach us?" The hooded figure's voice was deep and emotionless. It was the same voice she had heard outside her bedroom door those nights ago.

"Plot?" Sir Caldryk asked, a look of mortification on his face. Aliyah had never seen him so powerless. It filled her with pleasure.

"Did you think word of your *Wyvanni* would not reach her?" He said, as he angled his head toward Aliyah. She stared at the hood, trying to see the face underneath.

I should be scared, she realized. She could not feel it though. Anything that made Sir Caldryk terrified was something worth watching. She found herself curious as the hooded figure cocked his head before throwing back his hood and revealing the man beneath.

He had long dark hair that had started to gray at the temples. His complexion was similar to Aliyah's, and she noted the prominent gold flecks in his eyes. Eyes that stared at her in deep thought.

"So," he said, looking away from her to address Sir Caldryk. "This is her... she is young." He gave Aliyah another appraising look and his eyes stopped on the scars and burns adorning her arms. His expression became incredulous and when he spoke his voice was one of a nightmare.

"You thought to take what you deemed as rightfully yours by innocent blood?" He brought his hand to a fist and Aliyah jumped as a glass shattered on the desk. "You thought you would go behind Madra's back and steal from a daughter of Myral?" Another glass shattered.

Aliyah heard a sword being drawn and dragged her attention to where Archind was coming up behind the Executioner. He gave a swing and stopped midair. The Executioner had not even moved. Archind grasped at his neck as if he were gasping for air. Suddenly, a crack sounded through the room as his body went limp and landed haphazardly on the ground. He did not move and his neck lay at an odd angle.

"You thought," he continued, looking now at Sir Caldryk. "You had the right to defile and debase this woman here." He pointed at her and then brought his fist higher. Sir Caldryk rose with the Executioner's fist as if an invisible hand had yanked him out of his chair. Aliyah watched in horror as Sir Caldryk choked and gagged as the air around him was sucked away.

"Madra will deal with you later, but first..." his voice became a murmur as he turned his attention to Aliyah. "What did he tell you?" He asked.

Sir Caldryk floated in the air, inches above the ground. Unlike Archind, his gasps filled the chamber.

"What was he going to have you do?" The Executioner's voice was quieter now as he approached her. As he walked past the desk, something caught his eye. The ancient book lay upon the desk. Without any sign of what he was doing, an invisible wind forced the book to open to the page Sir Caldryk had shown her.

His face turned red, and he stood up straighter as he walked over to Sir Caldryk. With a nod of his head, Sir Caldryk went limp and fell to the floor. The sound of his head knocking against the marble floor echoed in the room. Aliyah was too far away to see if he was breathing. The fear she knew she should have been feeling all along hit her as the Executioner turned his attention back to her.

"You need to leave. Run, as far as you can away from here. Go to Myral. You will be safe there for the time being, and no one will ever do this," he gestured towards her arms, "to you again."

She sat there and tried to understand what he was saying. "Go! Before Madra reads my mind and knows what I have done. Take my horse, he is waiting out front. He will let you ride him if you tell him, 'Ringa-mor.' Please, go now- I do not know how long I can keep her occupied."

Aliyah jolted out of her seat and attempted to bolt for the door. Her legs, sore from sitting so long, refused to support her and she found herself falling. She caught herself on the chair and forced herself to keep moving.

***

Once her legs were steadier, she ran. She turned a corner toward the entryway and ran into something solid and fell backwards. Looking up from the ground, she was surprised to see Linna.

"Here Miss!" She tossed something into Aliyah's hands. Aliyah grasped the item- the straps of a pack. She fumbled to put the pack on her back as Linna helped her off the ground.

"We must leave, Miss!" Linna began to pull her toward the entrance of the house.

They had almost made it to the front door when large shapes leaped from the staircase above and landed in front of them, blocking their escape.

"What do we have here?" The one closest to Aliyah said. The words came out in a hiss, and Aliyah found herself staring into its nightmarish eyes.

"We've been looking for you," the second one hissed as they both turned and stalked toward her.

A feminine yell pulled their attention away from Aliyah as Linna pulled a knife out of the pack she was carrying and threw herself at one of the creatures. She landed on it with a thud and began rolling on the ground with it as she attempted to stab the creature. "Run!" she screamed toward Aliyah.

The attention of the other creature was now on its companion and Aliyah ran out the door. She skidded to a stop as she saw the giant monstrosity of a horse standing on the gravel drive. Surely, he didn't expect her to ride *that*? She gulped as the black horse whinnied anxiously. It stared at her with wary eyes as she turned and ran toward it.

"Shh- it's ok," Aliyah tried to make her voice sound calm as she approached the horse. It shifted uncomfortably and sent loose stones flying with a kick of its feet.

"Please don't kick me off," she pleaded with the horse, as she reached for the reins hanging from its neck. The horse shook its head and pranced back out of her reach. "Umm," What was that word? She tried to remember the phrase she had been told. "Ringa-mor" she said, aware of the precious time it took to remember. The horse stopped moving and bowed its head toward her. She flung herself onto the horse right as more howling erupted from the mansion. For once she was thankful for the high slits in her scrap of a dress.

She glanced back toward the manor. Linna's dark form still fighting with the monster. "Come on!" She screamed.

Linna looked up at the sound of Aliyah's voice. Her attention off the creature, it reached up with claw-like hands and sliced at her throat. Her eyes went wide, and she gave Aliyah a look of horror before falling to the ground.

Aliyah screamed and the two creatures came stalking toward her. The horse, hearing the creatures, took off at a fast gallop down the gravel path. Aliyah was unprepared for the horse's speed and struggled to stay on. Her muscles strained as she fought to regain her balance. The ground gave way behind them and the trees lining the dark road were a blur. Finally righting herself, she held fast to the reins and let the tears come.

Deep guilt came upon her as she thought of Linna. Tears came unbidden and streamed down her face as huge sobs wracked her. Still, the horse kept moving, the howls fading in the distance.

Nowhere in Gralanth was safe. The Executioner had told her to go to Myral, but why? Why give her his horse? None of it made sense.

The horse crested a hill and Aliyah's thoughts were interrupted by screaming. She pulled hard on the horse's reins, and it skidded to a stop.

Looking down, she saw smoke billowing up from burning buildings. Dark distorted shapes moved through the haze, attacking those who were running from the fires. Children cried and women and men screamed, the echoes of it etched into Aliyah's mind. Howls like the ones at the manor began to mingle amidst the screaming and it made the hair on the back of her neck raise. The guttural sounds became louder. Elwryn was under attack. She thought of how angry the Executioner was at Sir Caldryk and how he must have sent some of the creatures from the manor to the town. All because of her.

The horse reared and Aliyah struggled to calm it. Not wanting to continue traveling on the road, she looked wildly at the forest on either side. A trail led off the side, and she turned the horse with a significant effort. With a whinny, it began to trot toward that break in the trees. The sound of screaming was cut off and only howls remained.

Chapter Eleven

The forest was dark, the tall trees a dense canopy overhead that blocked out all but the palest slivers of moonlight. The nocturnal sounds of the forest echoed around her, making her jump at times. The only comfort was the breathing of the animal beneath her, a sign she was not alone.

The path was wide, not a road, but used, nonetheless. The horse moved at a slower pace than it had before, but Aliyah did not mind. They had ridden hard from Caldryk Manor. She knew little about horses, but even this monstrosity of a beast could not keep the pace forever. Ahead she heard the faint trickle of water, and she nudged the horse toward the sound. There, right off the path, was a small stream. The horse stopped inches from the water and bent to drink.

Aliyah fell as she attempted to dismount the horse. Her bare legs were already sore and chaffed, and they shook as she stood.

"Thank you," she whispered to the horse, gratitude for the animal making tears well up in her eyes as she patted its sides. It continued to drink deeply from the stream. Fearful the horse would run off without her, she held the reins tightly. With her other hand she began to dig through the pack Linna had handed her.

It was hard to see the contents with what little light was in the forest. Her hand touched something cold, and she pulled the item out. It was a sheathed hunting knife. She put the sheathed knife under her arm and continued to pull out the rest of the items.

Her hand grasped what felt like leggings and a man's tunic. *No dress, but at least my legs won't hurt as badly when riding.* She grabbed the items and then, seeing the horse was done drinking, led it over to a small tree and secured its reins.

Hoping no one was around to see, she struggled to unbutton the back of the dress. Panic began rising in her as she thought of having to wear this abhorrent gown the rest of her life. Then, taking a deep breath to calm herself, she remembered the knife which she had laid on top of the clothing.

Without hesitation, she snatched it and sliced up the slit. It took longer than she wanted, and she found herself pulling at the fabric which tore the rest of the way up with a huge ripping sound.

She tossed the fabric to the side and quickly donned the leggings and tunic; thankful for the warmth both items quickly brought to her naked body. She picked up the remnants of the dress and stuffed them into the bag, not wanting to leave evidence she had been there in case someone was following her.

“Well, shall we continue?” She addressed the horse as she untied the reins. “Not that we know where we are or how to get where we are going... but I’m free!” She began to laugh, an edge of hysteria to it. “I made it out. I don’t have to sacrifice myself for him.” She laughed again and her body flooded with relief.

“He will never hurt me again. He’s most likely dead,” the thought stopped her cold, cutting off her laughter. If he were dead, so was Linna and that was too hard to think about.

“I wish I knew what your name was,” Aliyah said as she remounted the horse. “It’s not as if you were a willing participant in this escape to begin with. Although you probably are never a willing participant- being owned by someone with the title of Executioner.”

The horse gave a strange whinny that almost sounded exasperated.

She rode in silence, eyes trying to depict movement in the trees. Not that she thought someone was following her, but he had told her to run before Madra- whoever that was- found out. There was that unspoken promise in his words that Madra would make him come after her. She pushed the horse to move faster and was grateful when it obeyed.

They walked through the night. The horse was able to maintain the pace. The sun began to rise, and light began to flicker in through the trees. It was comforting to be able to see her surroundings more clearly. Aliyah began to search for a place to rest. It had been a long night and she struggled to keep her eyes open.

A tight grouping of trees lay to the left. She led the horse to it and tied him to a tree. He began to pick at some of the grass and weeds that grew underfoot.

Aliyah rummaged through her pack, pulled out the dress, and dumped the pack's contents onto it. An apple rolled out and she retrieved it before standing up and offering it to the horse. He ate it eagerly and sniffed her hand as if asking for more. "That's enough for now," she said with a slight laugh as his breath tickled her hand. Still laughing, she went back to looking at the pack.

A fine blue cloak had been shoved into the bottom. Aliyah threw it over her shoulders, thankful for the weight of it and heard a clinking sound as something heavy fell out of the cloak. It was a small purse of coins. Opening it up, she was amazed at the amount of money in the sack.

Linna must have put every spare coin she had in there, and then some, she thought.

Beneath the coin sack lay the green journal from the drawer. *What are you doing here?* She thumbed through the pages, noting the pages written in blood were where she had left them, before putting the book back in her pack, along with the coin purse.

The rest of the items in the pack were food. Apples, jerky, and bread. The bread was only slightly stale. *I wonder when Linna packed this...* She picked up another apple and began munching as she put the items back in the bag. Stopping when she found a belt that had been hidden under the loaf of bread.

She donned the belt and attached the hunting knife to it. It calmed her nerves to have the weapon close at hand. She closed the pack and debated attaching it to the horse's saddle. She was exhausted. Instead, she wrapped herself up in the thick cloak, used her pack as a pillow, and fell asleep.

***

"So easy," a raspy voice said. Aliyah jerked to a sitting position and, blinking the sleep away, found two distorted forms staring at her from a few feet away. "So deliciously easy...."

"But we were to take her alive," the second one said, staring at the first.

"Her magic is... intoxicating," the first one said with a sniff toward Aliyah, who was now awake enough to process what was standing before her. The talking creature, Aliyah was not sure what to call it, had long greasy black hair. Its companion had long greasy auburn hair. Both had ashen skin and were covered in blood that had long since dried. The blood covered clothing and skin alike.

The first creature edged closer, and Aliyah scooted until her back hit the tree behind her. "Now, none of that..." it said as it stalked toward her. "We have been sent to bring you in. She did not necessarily tell us in what condition she expected you though, did she?" it said, with a sneer towards its companion.

"No... I do not believe she did." The other creature said with a smile that sent shivers down Aliyah's spine as it edged toward her.

She fumbled for the knife at her belt, hands shaking with fear. *These must have been the creatures I heard at the manor and in Elwryn.* It was not a comforting realization.

She held the knife up defensively as she tried to stand. They did not wait for her to stand before the dark-haired one sprang towards her. She let out a scream, trying to slash at it as it knocked her to the ground. The horse, having been quiet the entire time, let out a worried snort and began to tug on its confined reins. It pulled free and took off, running back out onto the path.

The second creature was distracted by the sound of the horse. Aliyah tried to push the first creature off her. It held her down tightly, startling her and pinning her arms beneath her. It broke her hold on her knife easily, gripping it instead and bringing it close to her face. Her eyes were wide as the creature brought the flat edge of the blade close to her face. She felt the cool metal run down her skin, and she shivered in response.

"I want a share of it," his companion whined. "You always take more than your fair share!" It knelt next to her. The smell of its rotting breath made her gag. Its spittle hit her face. She pulled hard against the one holding her.

"Tsk, tsk," it said, bringing the sharp edge of the knife to her chin. Her neck stung as it started to bleed. It leaned to slash at her again and she screamed.

Chapter Twelve

Kaino's horse, Maelstrom, drank deeply from the stream. His sides heaved in exhaustion from the hard ride. When they had come across Driel's trail the day before around the town of Elwryn, they decided to push through the night. They had been too late. His army of grarg had already ransacked the town. They had followed his trail up toward the Nobleman's manor. All that was left were the smoldering remains of what was probably once a very fine house. Kaino pitied the people that would have been in there when it burned.

They had seen many provinces that had experienced the desolation of the grarg. They almost did not need Kaino's tracking magic when they could follow the trail of smoldering towns and villages. It was getting exhausting. Always tracking, finding the trail, and then getting there just after the grarg left- Driel with them.

At the beginning, Josen had believed his father was being held against his will. Kaino remembered the weeks they spent hunting the Vendi Mountains for any traces of the grarg. It had been impossible- even for him- to find anything substantial to show which way they had gone. It was as if whoever they were following knew about Kaino's gift and made sure not to leave too many traces behind. It was infuriating.

At some point, long after Kaino had come to the conclusion himself, Josen agreed that his father must be working with the grarg. It was a relief to finally have Josen agree. He had not been the same since Ellie died.

Not that Kaino blamed him. He could not fathom the grief his friend must feel. Nor did he fault Josen for not wanting to converse, or his intense motivation to find his father. He did not even fault him for his short temper, although he could do without that.... He wondered what Josen would do if they never found his father. It was not a thought he liked to entertain too often.

Josen sat astride his horse, lost in thought, again. He absentmindedly ran his hands over the baby swaddle he carried with him. Its once white edges were covered in Ellie's blood and now dirt from long months traversing the continent. Its blue flowers still shone through, and it was those that Josen tended to rub the most.

He never talked about it. Kaino had tried broaching the subject many times since that day. He never got more than a mumbled response. He did not tell Josen that he heard him gasping at night when the grief overcame him. He did not tell Josen that he was worried about him.

He had tried that once. Kaino cringed, remembering how Josen had almost bitten his head off. He had worried Josen would set him aflame with how enraged his friend had become. Never in their near twenty years of friendship-beginning the first day of training at five years old-had he ever seen Josen so angry. It was frightening.

So Kaino did what Kaino knew best. Which was to crack jokes, usually at his own expense, and try to make the best of an unpleasant situation. He looked again at Josen, making his voice lighter than he felt.

"Jos, I am going to go look around and see where the trail goes next. Maybe you should let your horse drink water?" Kaino suggested-motioning toward Ember. He waited for a response. Josen continued staring at the swaddle. With a sigh, Kaino left his friend and began searching for traces he could track.

***

Josen glanced up as Kaino walked away. The motion was almost too much effort. He was not numb all the time, but today was an exceptionally difficult day.

Kaino left his horse with Josen. He knew he should offer to help but he did not have the energy to say anything. Kaino was right though, his horse did need water. He dismounted the horse and pocketed the swaddle, rubbing his thumb over a flower one last time.

He stood there, focused on listening to the sound of both horses lapping water with their tongues. The rhythm was soothing. He forced his breathing to slow. He was getting the beating of his heart back to normal when an ear-splitting scream broke through his concentration. His horse stopped drinking, her ears moving in annoyance. He looked around. Suddenly more alert than he had been in months. He was listening for another scream when Kaino came back, running.

"Did you hear that?" He panted as he leaned to grab his horse's reins. "It came," he breathed, "from there." He pointed at the direction in question. Without a second thought, both men mounted their horses and were soon thundering down the path. They had only gone a little way when the scream sounded again. It was coming from a dense group of trees to the west.

Josen motioned for Kaino to go around. He dismounted his own horse as Kaino disappeared into the trees. His sword slid noiselessly from the sheath as he stalked towards the sound. He pushed aside some foliage and found himself looking into a small clearing. What he saw made his stomach drop.

Two grarg knelt in the middle of the trees. One in the dirt and one astride a woman. She kicked and thrashed beneath the creature which held a knife in its hand. She cried out again as she tried to push it off her. The grarg backhanded her in frustration and the sound of the blow reverberated through the clearing.

Josen jumped into action. One minute he was behind the tree, and the next he was sending a fireball at the creature atop her. He did not recall summoning the blaze, only hours spent practicing in the training room had allowed him to summon fire instinctively. The other grarg turned to stare at him, terror in its black eyes. *Funny,* Josen thought, *a creature like this had feelings after all.* His blade tore through the creature's neck before it even took a step.

Kaino approached the one on fire. It had begun rolling in the dirt, trying to put out the flames. Its howling became shrieks as Kaino kicked in the side, laying a boot on its stomach before stabbing it through the heart. It gave a gurgle before it finally lay still. Fire flickered as it consumed the rest of its body. Josen touched the other one and it too went up in flames.

The woman lay unconscious between the two smoldering corpses. Josen ran to her, hoping he had not hurt her with his fire blast. Blood trickled slightly down her neck. The sight of it brought him back to a different place and time. *A dark room, Ellie lying still on the floor. Blood caked down her neck and into her light hair. The feel of her cold body, once warm. The pain-* he sucked in a sharp gasp of air at the sudden memory.

"Jos, what is it?" Kaino asked as he rushed over to where Josen and the woman were. "Is she...?" He was too afraid to ask.

It would be their luck to show up too late. When he did not get a response from Josen, he went and kneeled on the other side of the woman. Noticing the blood trickling down her neck, he sucked in a breath before ordering Josen to search through the pack next to them.

The urgency in Kaino's voice broke through the haze and Josen reached over, grabbing the pack. Opening it, he found a ripped dress of fine material lying on top. He handed it to Kaino, who grabbed it and pushed it against both sides of her neck. Josen watched numbly, the fear of not being able to save this woman intermingled with feelings of failure that came from finding Ellie dead. The feelings churned together, becoming indistinguishable from each other. This woman *had* to live.

"The bleeding has stopped," Kaino said after a while. He pulled back the dress, blood beginning to crust on it. "Thankfully, those monsters didn't cut an artery, or cut too deeply." He rocked back with a sigh.

Josen watched as her chest rose and fell, subconsciously counting her breaths. He leaned over her to inspect her wound now that Kaino had moved away.

The cut was not deep, but it was long. It started directly below her chin and ended at the top of her collarbone. She was Myralian, that much was easy to see. Her tan skin, a shade lighter than his own, was starting to regain color. A light spread of freckles lay on the bridge of her nose and high cheekbones. He was so focused on staring at her, he jumped when her eyes opened. Deep blue eyes with gold flecks watched him intently as he studied her with tears in his own.

Chapter Thirteen

"Well, hi there!" Kaino said, his voice was annoyingly chipper as it broke the silence. Josen pulled back, suddenly aware of how close he was to her, a stranger. "We took care of the grarg attacking you. Sorry we did not get here sooner, we heard you scream..." he trailed off, noting the confusion on her face.

"Are you alright?" Josen asked, voice soft.

She focused her attention on him and nodded, wincing as the motion pulled at the cut on her neck. She reached for it, eyes wide, before noticing the dead grarg around her.

"We stopped the bleeding, you don't need stitches, although I'm sure it will hurt for a few days." Josen continued.

"Sorry about the dress," he held up the garment towards her. "Although, it looks like it was not wearable anyway." He eyed the garment, noting how little fabric there was to it. "You are safe now," he whispered to her.

"Thank you," she said. Her voice was raspy from screaming and she winced as her neck muscles pulsed.

She tried to sit up and Josen went to help her before noticing how she pulled away from him. Distrust flashed across her face. He stopped, his hand still out to help her, and let it drop to his side before standing up.

"What is your name?" Josen asked as Kaino whistled to the horses. The woman jumped at the sound. "It's only our horses," Josen reassured her, trying to sooth her.

"Sorry about that!" Kaino said. "We don't want anyone else wandering off with them, not that we have seen anyone but you around here."

"Aliyah," she said, as if she had not heard Kaino. Her eyes were still on Josen. "My name is Aliyah."

"I am Josen, and this is my brother Kaino." He gestured towards Kaino, who gave a little bow.

"Brothers?" Aliyah asked, sizing them up. "You look nothing alike..."

"Ah," Kaino said mischievously. "Brothers in the battle of light! Sent out to solve issues among the common folk and noblemen alike."

"He means we are Ringada," Josen said, as he stepped toward his horse. He patted the animal and went to get his canteen out of the pack on the side of the saddle. He offered it to Aliyah. She hesitated before she took a sip. Pain shot down her neck as she swallowed.

"Ringada?" Her eyes lit up as she took another sip from the canteen.

"The very same!" Kaino said with a laugh and another bow. Josen watched Aliyah as she appraised them and handed him back his canteen. He did not miss the way she looked thoughtful as she took in the knives and swords they carried. Her eyes lingered on the Ringada blades, and a wistful look came to her eyes for a moment. Then her eyes found Josen's face again, noticing him staring at her. She looked down at her hands instead.

Just then, another horse entered the small clearing. Its reins dragging the ground. Josen and Kaino both started at its appearance, Josen even going as far as to raise his blade in a defensive position.

"There you are!" Aliyah said, relief flooded through her as she ran to the horse. "Some support you are- running off at the first sign of danger. I do not blame you though," she said, as she grabbed her pack from where it lay and pulled out an apple. The horse took it willingly and she cooed at the animal.

She turned toward the two men suddenly, as if she had just remembered they were there. They stared at her with stunned expressions on their faces. "What?"

"Where," Kaino began speechless.

"How did you come across this horse?" Josen said, voice harsher than he meant. He cringed as she took an involuntary step back at his tone.

"I didn't steal him, if that is what you are asking. He was, well, not given to me.... more like we were thrown at each other." She gave them a quizzical look, "Why?"

"We have been tracking that horse for months!" Josen said, trying to keep his frustration under control. "How did you get him? Where did you get him? How long have you had him?" Each question was thrown at her like a sharp knife, and she cringed at his tone.

"Jos, calm down, let her speak," Kaino shot his friend a withering look before directing his attention to Aliyah, "It's ok, this horse is not just any horse. His name is Raynar, and he belongs to Driel, the High Lord Protector who went missing over a year ago."

She peered at them skeptically. "I don't know who Driel is, but I got the horse from a man called the Executioner," she began. Both men stared quietly at her, so she took that as a signal to continue. "I was a... resident of Caldryk Manor.

Yesterday the Executioner came. Apparently, Sir Caldryk had been working for a woman named Madra-"

Both men started at that name.

"What did you say?" Josen demanded.

"M-Madra," she stuttered, looking even more confused, "He made a deal with her- whoever she is. I never met her. She was only discussed in passing..."

Josen stared at her dumbfounded and Kaino shook his head.

"Madra was sealed up in a stone tomb centuries ago... It cannot be her," Kaino said, looking at Josen. Josen gave a nod for Aliyah to continue, ignoring Kaino.

"So, whoever it was he made a deal with," she paused, as if waiting for them to interrupt her, "she sent the Executioner for Sir Caldryk. When he got there, he saw what Sir Caldryk had been doing... to me."

***

Aliyah did not want to continue. She *really* did not want to continue. To tell what Sir Caldryk had done to her... it would be like admitting the deepest parts of her soul to strangers. She decided to share the smallest portions she could.

Both men stared expectantly at her. The one who said his name was Josen gave her a pitiful look, "And what was he doing to you?"

"He wanted me to bring magic back to Gralanth." There, she'd said it. The horror of what that meant flooded through her and the sudden desire to curl up on herself and become small overwhelmed her. She stepped around the horse, wanting some space between her and the two Ringada.

The one named Kaino let out a low whistle, "You're a *Wyvanni*?'

Aliyah gave a small nod, looking down ashamed. She stood with arms folded and hands on her scars. She absentmindedly traced them as she talked. "He used me to awaken and maintain his magic, but it wasn't enough. It wouldn't last. He wanted me to- well, it doesn't matter. I am sure he is dead; the Executioner was hellbent on hurting him."

"And why did the Executioner let you leave?" Josen asked. "Why did he let you *live*? We saw the mansion, everything and everyone in it was gone."

Tears welled in Aliyah's eyes, and she found herself rubbing her arms as she answered in barely more than a whisper. "I do not *know* why he let me live. All I know is he saw what Sir Caldryk had done to me and he told me to take his horse and run before Madra saw what he was doing."

She threw her hands in the air and brushed away the tears with an angry hand. "Does that answer your questions? I know nothing about him other than he was dressed all in black and carried a Ringada blade he did not use. Instead, he used air magic to torture Sir Caldryk." She was breathing hard now, and her hand shook on the horse's reins.

Josen and Kaino looked at each other. Josen nodded and Kaino nodded back.

"You have no idea where he would go after the manor?" Josen's voice was quiet.

"No. I ran out the door and got on his horse as fast as I could. There was a strange howling inside the manor-howling that also was in Elwryn when it was getting attacked."

"That would be the grarg," Kaino said. "Driel, or the Executioner as you know him, has been traveling with grarg. He uses them to attack and leave no one alive. Well, almost no one" he gave her a knowing look before clasping Josen on the back. "At least we know what name your father goes by now."

"Your father?" Aliyah asked, confused.

"Yes, it seems my father has a new title. Executioner."

Chapter Fourteen

Aliyah dismounted Raynar and braved a glance at where Josen and Kaino had settled on the ground. Their horses munched on some grass by the stream. They were in deep conversation, and Aliyah was able to watch them without their noticing.

I wonder what they are talking about. She found herself mesmerized by the way they talked, like mirror images of each other, mimicking each other's actions in the way only those familiar with each other do.

They had finally stopped questioning her and suggested they ride a little way away from the grarg corpses. "In case there are any more close by," had been Kaino's reasoning, after which he had looked to Josen to see that he had made the right call. Josen had not seemed to mind his friend taking the lead.

Maybe they are always like that, Aliyah thought, not really caring.

She had wanted nothing more than to leave the trees. What she had sought as a haven had turned out to be nothing of the sort. Now the trees they passed felt dark. Despite Josen and Kaino's company, she imagined the spaces between the trees to be full of nightmarish creatures ready to pounce. It was mostly in her head, the after effect of being attacked. But she could not shake the feeling unseen eyes were watching them.

Raynar whinnied softly and nudged her hand, and she shook from her reverie. A blush formed on her cheeks as she realized she had been staring at the two men. "Oh alright," she said as she pulled an apple out of her bag, turning toward Raynar. "These were for me, you know." She teased the horse as he snatched the apple out of her palm. His mouth tickled her hand as he searched for more fruit, and she giggled.

"You are going to make that horse spoiled, you know that, right?" A quiet voice came from behind her. She whirled around, pulling her knife out of her belt with shaking hands.

Josen stood behind her, hands in his pockets, studying her. She had not heard him approach. *Must be a Ringada thing.* It was unnerving.

Face burning, she turned back toward the horse. "I've learned life isn't fair and anything good is worth showing appreciation for."

She tried to sheath the knife and it slipped out of her grasp. Josen caught it with nimble fingers and held it out to her.

"Thank you," she said with a blush at her clumsiness. She was able to sheath it properly and then turned towards him, face still red. He opened his mouth as if he wanted to say something, but then Kaino spoke up.

"So, Aliyah," Kaino asked from where he lounged on the ground, reclining against a towering rock. He kept his attention on the rock he was tossing and catching above him as he continued. "Seeing as you left in the night, on a horse that isn't yours, with no plan on where to go or what to do...What are you thinking of doing now?"

"I," she began, trepidation rising within her. There was no plan. She did not know where she was, let alone where she was going.

"Want to travel with us?" Kaino said, interrupting her thoughts. He caught the rock and stood up in one swift motion. "It gets so lonely with just Josen here," He walked toward Josen and nudged him with his elbow. "You can't believe how insufferable it can be to travel with someone who doesn't want to talk for days."

"I talk," Josen mumbled. "I usually don't have a lot to say."

"I'm only joking, Jos. It's not like I expect you to talk my ear off- you never have been the sort." He winked at Aliyah. "But you seem like you would be mighty interesting to talk to! Also, it would be rude of us to not escort a fine young woman such as yourself to her destination."

Aliyah blinked in response.

"So..." Kaino asked expectantly, "Where are you headed to?"

"I don't think she has decided where she is headed," Josen said, searching Aliyah's face. She stood there, staring unseeingly as the full reality of her situation sunk in. It was too much. Tears welled in her eyes as her breathing became faster. She began to tremble and then shake uncontrollably.

Josen lunged for her, carefully grabbing at her before she collapsed to the ground. She clung to him; hands fisted in his shirt as the sobs began to tear through her body.

"You are safe," Josen whispered comfortingly, sending Kaino a worried glance over her head as she buried her face in his chest. He awkwardly began to rub her back but stopped when she flinched. "Aliyah, you are safe."

The sobs became even harder, and his shirt became damp with her tears.

"It's the shock wearing off Jos," Kaino said, his voice sounded far away from Aliyah.

Safe? What is safe? Her body hurt. Her arms ached from every knife wound; every place Sir Caldryk had touched her. It was accompanied by the panic she had experienced as she raced through the night on Raynar. It was too much. Where could she go? She had no family in Myral. What awaited her there if she did go?

At some point, her hands had dropped from Josen's shirt. He pulled away from her but remained next to her as if to comfort her. She sat there rocking back and forth on the ground, knees to her chest. He did not try to touch her again- neither of them did. She ran her hands through her hair, pulling at it as she rocked. *What is safe?* She kept asking herself. Had she ever known what safe was?

***

"Jos, I don't know what happened to her, but I can guarantee the grarg are not the worst thing she has experienced," Kaino said as he began to set up logs for a fire. It had been midday when they had fought the grarg off Aliyah. They had decided to camp here for the evening since Aliyah was not in any condition to continue traveling- if she wanted to.

"I'm sure she will tell us when she is ready," Josen said as he touched his hand to the logs Kaino had set up. Flames began to lick at the wood, and he pulled his hand back, satisfied the flames would not go out. He then began to unroll the bedrolls. He looked over to where he had left Aliyah sitting on the ground. She had not reacted when he had left to go help Kaino. Now she stared blankly at the fire. He had not realized her tears had stopped.

He turned back to the bedrolls he was unrolling. He was thankful the nights had gotten warmer, and they had been able to ditch the Ringada tents they had left with. He walked to where Aliyah's pack lay and pulled out the blue cloak she had been wearing when they first met, shocked to realize it was of Vendin origin. Ellie had owned one like it, but in green.

He ran his hand over the fabric, remembering buying the cloak for Ellie from a trader he had met in one of the Southern domains. It was a few months after they had been married. He had been sent on assignment to settle a dispute between two domains. The road between the two needed repair and neither one of the domains wanted to pay for and supply men to rebuild the road.

Normally, Ringada would not get involved in such a minor thing as a road, except this road was on the major trade route. Carts were getting stuck, and supplies were getting lost or delayed. It had only taken Josen a few short weeks to work out an agreement between the two domains. Those weeks, and the week and a half traveling both ways, felt like an eternity without Ellie.

He had purchased the cloak for her from a trader he passed on his way back to Ringard. The trader had even given him a discount, thankful that the road had been repaired. Ellie had worn that cloak everywhere, grateful for the warmth it brought her in the stone keep, located high in the Ringard hills.

Josen smiled at the memory before he could help himself. The emotion shocked him. It was not as if he didn't think of Ellie often. She was always on his mind. This one hit differently. Softer.

He ran his hand over the cloak one last time before walking over to Aliyah. He crouched down in front of her as he drew the cloak over her shoulders. She did not respond.

"Aliyah," her eyes focused on his face, the first response they had gotten out of her in hours. He found that a good sign. "Would you like something to eat?"

She continued staring at him, so he repeated the question. This time she gave a slight shake of her head. He knew what that was like. "I know you don't want to talk about it, but if you ever need to..." he was not very good at this- he didn't even want to talk about his own grief. When she did not respond, he got up and walked away, leaving her sitting on the ground, staring at the flames.

***

Aliyah was vaguely aware of dozing off in the night. She had stared at the fire until all that remained were the coals. Her eyelids had gotten heavy at that point, and she had succumbed to sleep, wrapping herself up in her cloak. She was empty inside, after crying all those tears, and her dreams were mercifully void of anything.

The sunlight and the indistinct mumbling of voices woke her. Her eyes were sore, and she rubbed at them as she sat up. *This is not where I fell asleep last night,* she realized with a shock. Instead of the hard ground, she lay on a cushioned bedroll. A thick wool blanket was laid across her. She did not remember being moved and she blushed at the thought of either one of them moving her in the night.

"Ah! She arises," Kaino teased from where he sat across the remnants of the fire. He assessed her as she stretched and stood up shakily. "How are you feeling today?" he asked.

Her voice was hoarse when she answered, "I feel... not better. But, I feel" she stopped and thought, *honestly, how do I feel?* "More myself than I have in a long time." *There, that's true.*

"I am sorry for my behavior yesterday," she continued. "I have not broken down like that since...Well, it doesn't matter. It should not happen again." She winced as she remembered how broken she had been the day before. If she thought about it for too long, she knew she would go right back to crying.

"Don't worry about it," Kaino said, moving his hand as if to brush the matter aside. "We all have days like that- besides, you aren't the first person I have seen fall apart like that." He winked at her, and she found herself giving him an awkward smile in response before taking in their surroundings. The place they had stopped to camp was charming, the light streamed through the trees, and the sound of the babbling stream was a soft noise in the background.

"Where is Josen?" She asked, noticing his absence. His horse was gone as well.

"He went off to scout ahead for more grarg. I went looking last night and found traces of them, but it looks like they wandered off toward the south."

"Are you going to follow them?"

"I am not sure what we are going to do. On one hand, they will hopefully lead us right toward Driel. They tend to be wherever he has been. However," he gave her a sideways glance, "you are an anomaly. *Wyvanni* are not rare, but they have been becoming more uncommon over the past few hundred years or so. Your Sir Caldryk is one in a long line of Noblemen- Myralian and

Gralanthian alike- that have tried to find their own *Wyvanni* and the power that comes with it. They think finding and controlling a *Wyvanni* is the ultimate path to glory, not thinking about the other person in the equation."

Aliyah stared at him, shocked at the direction the conversation had taken. She absentmindedly rubbed her arms and the raised bumps of the scars beneath the thin linen of her shirt. A reminder etched into her skin of what she was, of who others expected her to be. "I never wanted to be a *Wyvanni*, it isn't like I chose this."

"It isn't like Josen chose to be gifted with fire or I with discernment, it just happens," Kaino said, his voice soft. "They say it is based on our personality or traits we tend to show. I tend to do an excellent job at reading people and environments. Maybe I always would have that skill, but the magic in my blood chose discernment, and that skill is amplified. Where I might have always been more observant than others, my observance is heightened. I can see things others do not. Things that do not stick out to others stick out to me. It can get annoying to always see more than would be proper.

"Take you for an example," he nodded to her, "you rub your arms when you are nervous. It only took me to see you do it twice to realize it was a habit. Others, it might take them a few days to recognize that about you." She stopped rubbing her arms, looking at him with a stunned expression.

"Is that how all magic works?" She asked, trying to figure out what to do with her arms instead. It was odd being read so easily.

"Josen's magic is based on his passion. Fire tends to awaken in those that are passionate." She started. Sir Caldryk's magic was fire. *He was passionate,* she realized, *passionate about having power.*

"Magic does not differentiate between reasons for passion. Josen is passionate about many things, things that might be different from others, but the amount of passion he has...that is what makes a Fire Wielder powerful."

Aliyah nodded as if she understood. Her mind was still trying to comprehend the magic she had seen Sir Caldryk wield. "How does...how does other magic work?" She could not bear to ask about her own.

"Other magic works in similar ways; amplifying a trait someone has and putting it into a physical manifestation. Water, for example, is usually for those who are calmer. But do not go assuming it can't do damage," he said. "Many people have mistaken Water Wielders for being serene, but have you ever seen a storm on the ocean?" She shook her head. "Anger a Water

Wielder and you find yourself facing the wrath of angry waves in a mighty storm." He laughed and she suspected he had experienced that firsthand.

"Air magic is found among those who are natural leaders. The ones that feel the need to be in control and have everything their way. It is not as visible as fire and water, but it can be deadly. Imagine having the air sucked out of your lungs just because you annoyed someone."

Aliyah trembled, remembering the Executioner. She did not have to imagine what it was like to have the wrath of an Air Wielder- she had seen it firsthand. She was thankful he had not used that magic on her. She hoped she would never find out.

"Earth magic is a tricky one," Kaino continued, noting her trembling but not saying anything. "Those blessed with ground magic are often very stubborn. They will uphold an ideal and argue it to the ground- no pun intended. Josen's wife, Ellie, was an Earth Wielder. She did not have much experience using it, her parents were an odd sort. A nobleman that does not want his daughter to marry a Ringada? Isn't that the dream of every noble family? Well anyway, she was learning how to control her magic and was getting rather good at using it until-"

He suddenly stopped talking, looking at something behind Aliyah. She turned toward the cause of his distraction. Josen had come back into the clearing. He was leading his horse and his eyes were livid. Aliyah looked down ashamed, feeling as if she had been doing something she was not supposed to.

"Until she died," Josen finished, voice cold.

Chapter Fifteen

Josen's words hung in the air. He turned away from them, leading his horse to where the other horses stood. "I suggest you get ready to move out. I saw no sign of grarg, but if we are to get you to a town by nightfall, now is the time to go."

Aliyah sat there stunned, heat rising to her face. *I haven't done anything wrong. Kaino was only giving me a lesson on how magic works. It was not as if I asked about Josen's wife- I didn't even know he was married!* She avoided making eye contact with Josen.

Kaino, having no qualms about his friend's attitude, studied him with a piercing gaze, as if he knew what Josen was thinking. *Maybe he can...* she thought as she began to pack up the bed roll.

It was hard. Her hands were shaking from being startled and she could not get the roll tight enough. With an exasperated sigh, Josen left his horse and walked toward her. He bent down to help her roll up the bedroll and she pulled back from him, wary of his mood.

"Thank you," she dared whisper, keeping her eyes down. "For letting me sleep on your bedroll," she hastily added. He grunted in response.

"I also need to apologize to you. I have never cried like that before and..." she stopped when he moved away from her to put the bedroll on his horse. She glanced at Kaino, who gave her a slight shake of his head.

Chagrinned, she went to her own horse, storing her cloak in her pack. The day was already warm, and she would not need its weight as they rode. She grabbed her saddle from where one of the men had laid it and Kaino went over to help her. He showed her how to tighten the straps, his voice calm, but she did not miss his apprehension. When their eyes met, he gave her a pitying look.

"I don't have anywhere to go specifically, but I would like to head to Myral," she directed toward Kaino.

Josen's shoulders stiffened in response, and she glanced at Kaino for support. He shrugged, eyeing Josen as well.

"You planned to make your way to Myral on nothing but a horse and the clothes on your back?" Josen asked, not turning from his horse. His voice had an edge of bewilderment.

"I hadn't planned on leaving, ever." Her voice was quiet and the realization she had expected her life to end in a short amount of time almost had her curled up in a ball again.

"Jos, maybe we should escort her?" Kaino said, also watching his friend. "It's not like we can just let her wander off and hope she gets there. She is a magnet for misfortune- no offense," he directed at Aliyah.

Her face burned. *It's not like I did it on purpose.* Kaino was right, misfortune was a great way to explain what her life had been like since her parents had been killed.

Maybe it is just me...

"You don't have to go with me if you don't want to," she tried to sound nonchalant, but her voice wavered, giving her away. "Point me in the right direction and I am sure I will find it- eventually. I do not want to be a burden." She said the last part softly.

"It would be an honor to escort such a fine young lady, such as yourself, to Myral," Kaino said, bowing playfully "Besides- the safest place for you, since you are *Wyvanni* would be Ringard- or at least it should be the safest place."

Ringard? Do they want to take me to Ringard? Aliyah had not thought about going to Ringard. Myral yes, but Ringard was so far away from the Vendis... There was no way she would ever make it there by herself. A plan began to form in her mind as she thought about the journal pages in her bag. She could petition the heir for an audience, show him the pages... it was her duty to notify the Ringada of what Sir Caldryk had been up to. Wasn't it?

"No." Josen's voice was curt. "We need to find Driel. Besides, you cannot get into Ringard without an express invite, and we don't plan to go back there right away."

Kaino opened his mouth to say something but shut it at the look Josen gave him.

"Then drop me off as close as you can if you plan to escort me. I will go petition the heir for an audience. I will go- with or without you. I said I did not want to be a burden and I meant that." She spoke with more courage than she felt.

She knew a little about how the Ringada government worked thanks to her father's stories. There was never a lack of leadership, and she knew an heir would have been named and would be sitting on the throne right now in Driel's absence. It was not always a biological heir. It was possible for anyone to be picked among the masses of Ringada to be the next leader.

An odd look passed between the two men. "You seem oddly familiar with the inner workings of Ringard," Kaino said.

"My father taught me many things. He wanted me to know about my heritage and the country he came from." She forced her voice to be firm.

"And who was your father?" Kaino asked, genuinely curious.

"Eldris Brandhold. He was a member of the Ringada before I was born."

Silence. Both men stared at her. She swallowed, feeling more self-conscious. She did not talk about her parents much, but seeing this reaction made her wish she had never mentioned anything.

"*The* Eldris Brandhold?" Kaino's voice was full of excitement. "He is a legend! His story is told to all new trainees, something to inspire them when it gets hard! I cannot believe it! You are his daughter?" It was not so much a question, more of a shout of excitement.

She took another involuntary step back at his response before answering, "Yes."

Kaino looked at Josen with an odd expression, "Her father was a member of Ringard. That gives her clemency. Express invite or no. It is our duty to help her get to her destination."

"Were that you were born in the ranks," Josen muttered as if to himself.

Kaino stared thoughtfully for a moment before saying, "I don't think we have a choice, Jos. They are going to track her wherever she goes. I can see it. Those first two were the scouts. If it is Madra, back from the dead, she is not going to let another *Wyvanni* live. Not if she sees her as competition."

"We don't even know if it is truly Madra," Josen said with a defeated sigh. He turned around to face them.

"Who exactly is Madra?" Aliyah asked. Both men stared at her with mouths agape.

"Madra, Dark Mistress, entombed for her crimes against Myral and Gralanth alike? She caused the Vendi Wars about four hundred years ago..." Kaino peered at Aliyah to gauge her reaction. She had turned pale and was staring at them wide-eyed.

"You don't mean Madranna?" She gasped. *She was a myth. A legend. She can't be alive!* Aliyah looked around, as if the woman would walk out of the woods with darkness trailing behind her. Stories she had been told as a child swirled in her mind, stories her father had told her.

She could hear the low timber of his voice as he tucked her in at night, telling her the stories of Ringard and their foes. The ones about the giant beasts her father had saved villages from were always her favorite. However, there was one story her father had told her only once. The story had frightened her, and her father had told it to her as a cautionary tale, as she had grown old enough to understand the magical gift she carried.

The story was about a *Wyvanni* that used her power for good. She used it to help others and made the world a safer place, a peaceful place. A world where Myralians and Gralanthians lived together as one, with no divide between them. It was said the Vendi mountains had not even been there- only the river which wandered lazily between lush farmlands. Aliyah did not believe that part about the mountains, but the woman was what had frightened her.

Everything was peaceful, perfect. Then the *Wyvanni* realized she could take whatever she wanted. She had helped build this paradise. She deserved some reward.

With the help of her lover, a man no one remembered the name of, she went on a rampage. Governments were overthrown, and villages were invaded by the army of those she bound to her, bound to her in a way that was a mockery of something sacred.

Those she bound to her became less than they once were. They became beings who thirsted for the magic she had stolen from them through the bond. They would do anything to get it- like attacking a woman alone or destroying whole villages. Once bonded, their animal instincts took over as they did the bidding of their mistress, with no true will of their own.

Her father had followed the tale with a warning. "No matter how strong you become, remember, you must not ever take the will of another away. Letting others decide and act for themselves is true strength when it is easier to bend them to your will."

Nightmares plagued her for weeks. Visions of ghastly beings followed her, waiting for her to give a command before they devoured the magic within her. Her mother had chided her father for telling her that story.

"I thought she was just a myth parents told their children to get them to behave. 'Don't do that or Madranna will come for you in the night!' that sort of thing..." Aliyah looked nervously towards Kaino. "There is no way she might still be, well, alive."

"It seems more things are possible than we realized," Josen said, as he stared at Aliyah. "You know the thing I always questioned about the story of Madra? Why didn't they kill her? Why did they entomb someone so dangerous? Wouldn't killing her have been better? It never made much sense...

"And now, if she is back, what good did the entombing do? Other than hold off her forces for a few generations? Why is she back now? And why does she want my father?" He shook his head. "Like I said, it makes no sense."

"I think we need to go back to Ringard," Kaino said, "we need to ask Moryn and Sleth about things they might know. They have been with your father for ages. I'm sure they might know something. I cannot track him on his horse anymore because Raynar is here. Besides, Aliyah needs an escort to Ringard. You are not going to let her wander through the Vendi Mountains by herself, are you?"

Josen debated within himself for a long while. Long enough for Aliyah to suspect he was going to disagree and indeed let her wander through the mountains by herself. She was shocked when he gave a defeated sigh. "Yes, I think it might be best to go back to Ringard. I do not want to- the ancient gods know how hard Moryn will try to make me stay." He sighed. "Let's ride."

***

They rode in silence for a while. Josen took the lead and Kaino the rear. Aliyah stayed in the middle, her horse falling into a familiar pattern with the other two Ringada horses. They moved nowhere near the speed Aliyah had the night she fled Caldryk Manor. They stayed at a steady pace the horses could keep at with minimal stops. Not the fastest, but it was effective and faster than walking. Aliyah found herself admiring the scenery as the horse made its way through the forest. She inhaled the scent of pine needles, fresh and decaying. The scent was comforting. *It smells like freedom;* she relished that thought.

Kaino moved his horse so it was walking next to Raynar. The two horses kept pace with each other, their hooves sending up dust clouds on the dirt path. "Sorry about earlier," his lips moved so quietly she struggled to hear him. "Josen is particular about certain subjects, and I got carried away. Just know, he was not mad at you- he was upset with me."

She gave a slight nod of appreciation for his insight. "Thank you for explaining," she tried to match his tone. "So, tell me," she said, not caring if Josen overheard, "how long will it take to get to Ringard?"

Kaino laughed, "Oh, only two to three weeks to the Vendi Mountains. Another month after that- if we do not run into any problems- to Ringard. If we do happen to run into problems, it could be a while longer."

"And what kind of problems should I be expecting?" Images of grarg attacks and large Vendi beasts flashed through her mind.

"Oh, the usual... late spring snow in the Vendis... grarg attacks...We have to be prepared for anything."

"I see.... And are we planning on being in the woods the entire time, or will we move to main roads? Not that I mind-" she hastily added. "I am good with whatever gets us there the fastest. I just wondered if we will be stopping at any inns or if we are going to be sleeping on the ground...."

"We will try to avoid roads while in Gralanth. Being Myralian, we stick out easily and we try to avoid that sort of attention. Once we get closer to the Vendi mountains, we can venture into towns and stay at an inn or two if that is what you would prefer?"

"It shouldn't be up to me- I am just thankful for your willingness to help me. I can pay you- if you would like. I feel bad you are going out of your way to help me. Especially escorting me all the way back to Ringard."

"We are Ringada- we don't need the money, but if you would like to pay for a night's stay or two at inns along the way, I am sure both of us would welcome it." He winked at her. "By the time we get to where we can stay at an inn, I am sure we will all need a bath by then anyway." He started laughing and Aliyah could not help but join in.

They rode the rest of the day and Aliyah found Kaino easy to talk to. He did not ask her any of the hard questions she knew he was dying to ask, and she was grateful for it. Instead, he spent the day telling her about the land, the trees they passed, animals, and how it was all interconnected. She was fascinated and the hours flew by quickly.

Josen did not talk to them at all. He rode ahead of them, back straight, all but ignoring them. A few times throughout the day, Aliyah thought she saw him fiddling with something white in his hands, but when she peered harder, the item was not there. She wanted to ask Kaino about it but did not want a repeat of the morning. *It's none of your business. Just be glad he was willing to escort you.* She hoped his silence would not last the entire trip to Ringard.

***

The sun was just starting to set when Josen left them. He had not said anything to them all day so it shocked Aliyah when he addressed them saying he would scout ahead for a place to stop. He was so different from the way he had been the previous night when he had been trying to comfort her. It was difficult to keep up with the mood swings.

"Kaino," Aliyah said, not daring to talk until Josen's horse was out of sight. "Is he always like that?" She gave a nod of her head in the direction Josen had disappeared.

"Unfortunately," Kaino sighed, rubbing a hand over his tired face. "It's been over a year since she died, and he has only gotten quieter and more reserved since."

"How did she-" Aliyah cut off as Josen approached. His horse's footfalls were audible on the bramble. She had kept her voice soft, and she hoped he had not heard. She searched him for any sign of displeasure. He stared back at her with hard eyes.

"There is a place not too far from here that the stream juts back over to. We can camp there for the night," his deep voice was expressionless, and Aliyah looked at Kaino to gauge his reaction. He watched his friend warily before urging his horse to follow. Aliyah let out a breath she had not realized she was holding, then nudged Raynar to follow.

Josen was right. It was not far, and it was a decent camp spot. Aliyah climbed off her horse, shocked at how wobbly her legs were. Her fingers clutched at the saddle for support. They had only stopped for short periods of time to let the horses drink or rest when they came across the stream. Kaino seemed to think the stream was leading toward the main body of the Golyth River. He was probably right.

Who needs a map when you can track whatever you want? Aliyah thought with a wry smile.

It had been a few hours since she had last dismounted Raynar. Her numb legs made it difficult to stand and she walked with shaking legs over to where Josen was placing logs for a fire. The thought of being alone with Josen made her uncomfortable.

“Where’s Kaino?” She asked, voice quiet.

He continued setting the logs without looking up. “He spotted some rabbit tracks a little way back and went hunting.”

“Oh,” Aliyah said, feeling awkward. “Is there anything I can help with?”

“No,” Josen said as he put a hand over the logs. He pulled his hand away and a crackling fire was left in its wake. Aliyah took an involuntary step back, her heart racing. He looked up at her, and instead of anger a look of concern flashed on his face. “Are you alright?”

"Mmhmm,” she squeezed her eyes shut, taking in a deep breath trying to calm herself. His hand was still flaming, and she tried not to think about another hand covered in flames touching her.

“You don’t seem alright,” his voice was soft. When she opened her eyes, he was staring intently at her.

“Fire scares me,” she breathed out. “Nothing good in my life has come from fire.”

He looked at where his hand was burning and made the fire disappear. “Do you want to talk about it?” He sounded as if he honestly wanted to know. She opened her mouth to respond but his actions that morning ran through her mind, and she found herself asking a question in return.

"Do you want to talk about your wife?" She threw the words at him, tired of the way he had been acting all day and trying to deflect the attention off herself. She regretted the words the moment they were out of her mouth. She threw a hand over her mouth as if she could not believe what she had said.

She eyed his now clenched fists and the fire that was forming there. Aliyah took a slow step back. Her throat was tight and the memory of other hands pressing hot flame against her skin. She took another step back and was startled by whistling.

Both of them turned their heads in the direction of the sound. Kaino came out of the trees, three rabbits clutched in his hands. The melody he had been whistling cut off as he inspected the scene before him. His eyes widened as he took in the sight of Josen's burning fists and Aliyah's pale complexion.

He gave a dark chuckle. "I left you alone for twenty minutes and Aliyah has already got under your skin, eh Jos?" He laughed again. "I should have done this earlier." Strangely, Aliyah found the tension dispersed. Josen must have felt the same as he immediately quenched the flames at his fists.

Kaino threw the rabbits toward Josen. “I hunted; you cook.” It was more a statement than a demand. Aliyah was wary of the mood as Josen grabbed a knife and began skinning the rabbits. She found herself clutching at her arms as the knife sliced into the meat and she looked away quickly before walking away to unsaddle her horse.

Chapter Sixteen

Josen was aware of Aliyah walking away as he skinned the rabbits. He had been aware of her since the moment he saw the grarg attacking her. She was so different from other women he had been around. *Or maybe she isn't different, maybe you finally noticed someone outside of yourself.*

He had not been aware of anything other than the need to find his father and get answers about Ellie's death for a very long time. Seeing Aliyah being attacked had broken something within him. A dam that held his emotions back. It scared him.

He did not want to feel anything. Feeling things meant hurting. Being numb was better. He was good at being numb and only letting his emotions out in small increments. Aliyah had caused fissures in that carefully built wall. He could feel the grief ready, waiting. It would come.

He only hoped he could stop the holes before they burst.

"So... what was that about?" Kaino asked, sitting on a fallen log next to Josen. He did not need to specify; Josen knew exactly what his friend meant.

He decided to answer honestly. "She got startled by me starting the fire and so I asked her if she wanted to talk about it. She told me nothing good in her life had come from fire. Then she asked me if I wanted to talk about... Ellie." Her name sent a pain through his heart. He hardly ever said her name. *What is wrong with me?*

"Then you decided to scare her more by showing off your fire magic?" Kaino asked, voice light.

"No, it was a reflex. Her question took me off guard and then the next thing I knew we were staring each other down" He pinched the bridge of his nose. "I'm a mess, aren't I?"

"Do you want the truth?" Kaino said, sounding serious.

"Maybe?" He braced himself as he skewered the rabbits with more force than necessary.

"I think you have been holding on to Ellie long enough, Jos. She would want you to be happy, not this emotionless shell you have become." He said the words gently, but they pierced Josen's heart like daggers.

"I'm not saying you should move on," Kaino continued quickly, seeing Josen's expression. "What I am saying is you need to live- and not the way you have been doing. *Actually* live. Laugh at the funny moments, enjoy the blissful ones. Allow yourself to be happy."

"I don't know if I can be happy, Kai. I don't know if I even deserve to feel that way again. I had never been so happy as I was with Ellie. She was the bright spot in my rather dull life. How can you move on when your sun is gone and all that is left is the dark of night?"

"You look for the stars," Kaino said without hesitating. "They might never be able to replace the sun, but they have their own beauty and light just the same."

"You make it sound so easy," Josen said as Aliyah walked back from unsaddling Raynar. He found himself intrigued by the relationship she was forming with the animal. He knew that creature to be unruly and stubborn- but not for her it seemed.

"Oh, I don't know about easy," Kaino said. "But I know it's possible."

Aliyah joined them in time to overhear Kaino's response. "What's possible?" She asked as she sat down on the log next to Kaino. She took her long chestnut hair out of the braid she had put it in that morning and began combing through it with her fingers. Josen watched, mesmerized at the way the light reflected off the strands.

"Happiness," Kaino said as Josen turned to give him a look of alarm across the fire.

"Happiness is always possible," Aliyah said. "It depends on how much work you are willing to put into it. How much you are willing to fight for it." She leaned forward, elbows resting on her knees and face propped up on her hands staring unblinkingly at the fire. Kaino shifted on the log to look at her and Josen stared at her from across the fire.

"My childhood was happy, blissful even." The words started to pour out of her. "I did not realize we had little money- it didn't matter. My parents loved each other, and my father worked hard to provide for us," she began, eyes beginning to tear up. She brushed away a stray tear.

"You were not always one of the Caldryk's household?" Josen examined her as if she were a puzzle he was trying to solve.

"No, my parents met when my father was on an assignment to see the status of Gralanth. He met my mother in Shalshollow, a province outside Elwryn..." she smiled and gave a little laugh. "He was doing some reconnaissance and was supposed to observe and not be seen. Naturally, my rather observant mother spotted him." She shook her head, smiling.

"He came back to see her over the next few months, and she would leave notes for him in a tree trunk close to where she had first seen him. That went on for over a year. Finally, my father asked her if she would marry him, and to his surprise, she said yes. My mother was happy to leave her father's home. My grandfather was not a kind man, and much preferred his older daughter, Matylda. My mother had a wild streak he had never been able to beat out of her." She paused, looking at them, "am I boring you?"

Both were absorbed in her story. Kaino with pleasure and Josen...wistfully? It was hard to see his expression with the shadows caused by the flickering flames. "Go on," Kaino coaxed, and she took a breath before she obliged.

"They ran away, stopping in the village of Rynsin, right on the Golyth. A year after their marriage, they had me. My father worked as a carpenter. He was proficient at it, and it brought in decent money at times. My mother had grown up a lady, with servants to do things for her in her father's house. She had to learn how to run a house and do the chores herself. She never complained though.

"Despite my father leaving the Ringada and my mother leaving a life that should have been luxurious, they found happiness in each other. They worked hard. Both could hold their own in an argument, but they loved each other enough to build their own happiness." She wiped more tears from her eyes and saw Josen discreetly wipe some from his.

Interesting, Aliyah thought.

"My father used to find any excuse to dance with my mother," she said, not fully intending to continue the story, but it felt right. "He would pull her away from whatever she was doing and dance with her right there. As I got older, he taught me how to dance and he would take turns swinging us both around our small house. He always knew how to make us laugh." she smiled fondly as she trailed off.

"What happened to them?" Josen asked, concerned, from the other side of the fire.

Her smile turned into a frown as a new memory resurfaced, one of pain. She forced herself to say it anyway. "They were murdered."

Both men jumped at that. Kaino's audible gasp beside her caused her to jump as well. Josen gave her a look that urged her to continue the story. "They came for them in the nighttime. Mercenaries, I think. My father heard them coming, years of training in the Ringada kicking in. He tried to get my mother to run with me, but she did not have enough time," her voice had gotten smaller and both men were leaning closer to hear her. She swallowed, bringing her legs to her chest, and hugging them tight.

"My father took me from my mother and hid me in a closet, throwing clothes over me. He told me not to make a sound and I did everything I could to remain quiet..." she looked up, meeting Josen's gaze. "I did not see what happened, all I have are memories of the screaming. They killed my mother first. 'For taking what was not rightfully yours,' one of the men had said. My father's last words were my mother's name. He was cradling her when he was run through." She shut her eyes at the memory.

"They did not search for me. I do not know if they didn't know about me, but one of them set the house on fire." Memories of the crackling of the wooden home inflamed came rushing back. The smell of smoke filled her lungs from a completely different fire than the one they currently sat around.

"I ran out of the closet when I saw the flames. My parents were lying in the kitchen." She wiped her eyes as if to erase the image of her father cradling her mother that she saw now. The glow of the surrounding fire left eerie shadows over them. She paused, caught up in the emotions of the memory. Then began with a shaking breath.

"I ran outside and collapsed. I was found later by those from the village coming to help put out the flames."

She shook herself and lifted her gaze from the fire to meet Josen's eyes. "So ever since that day, when my aunt came to collect me, my life has been what some might consider hell. She was not one to show love or affection- especially when drunk. However, throughout every beating I endured, every..." she paused. She could not get the words to describe what Sir Caldryk had done to her.

"Every hurt I've had to suffer through," she continued, "I always thought about my parents. To know that somewhere there are people who feel happy enough to dance in the smallest of houses despite the hardships of life. That is what I hold onto. That one day I might have the opportunity to feel happy enough to be pulled into someone's arms and dance despite the pain."

Kaino stood up beside her and held out his hand to her. Voice uncharacteristically somber, he asked, "Well, until then, my lady, may I have this dance?"

Aliyah looked at him startled and eyed the hand he held out to her. She met his eyes and he gave her a tender smile she could not resist giving back. She accepted his hand, and he pulled her up, until she was standing right before him.

His hold on her was gentle but firm as he led her through some quick footwork that left her breathless. He twirled and dipped her, the shadows from the fire seeming to bend and twist with them. Kaino threw her into a dangerously low dip, and she giggled, despite herself, as he yanked her back up. He let out a quiet laugh of his own and soon they were both too out of breath for dancing.

He led her back over to the log, giving her a deep bow as she sat down winded. "Thank you for the dance, my lady. Perhaps we might do this again sometime?" He winked.

"Sounds lovely," she said through wheezes, holding her side from the pain, and they both erupted into laughter.

"Are you two done?" Josen asked, voice stiff from where he sat pulling the rabbits off the skewer. Their laughter cut off as they turned to stare at him. "I mean," he said, trying to keep his voice calm, "the rabbits are going to be cooled soon and it's time to eat." He would not make eye contact with either of them.

"Thanks Jos," Kaino said, patting his shoulder before taking a rabbit from him. He grabbed the other one Josen had prepared for Aliyah and brought it to where she still sat on the log. She thanked him as he handed it to her. The logs shifting in the fire and the lazy hum of evening bugs were the only sounds as they ate.

"Thank you for cooking," Aliyah said as she licked the rabbit juices off her fingers. The rabbit was good. She had never tried rabbit before and was shocked at how delicious it was. "And thank you for catching the rabbits," she added to Kaino. He nodded at her, a twinkle in his eye.

"I'm going to go wash up in the stream," she said, standing up. It had been a long day and the desire to clean up was compelling. She left the two men sitting around the fire. She felt their eyes on her back. The stream was only a little way off, just out of reach of the fire's light. She knelt next to the it, putting her hands in the cool water. *Dancing with Kaino was... pleasant,* she thought. *Unexpected but... nice all the same.* She washed her face, not caring as the cool water dripped onto her tunic. It sent a shiver through her, and she stood up to head back to the fire. She patted Raynar as she passed him, wishing him a good night. He whinnied at her, and she gave him a final pat before rejoining the men.

***

"You can use my bedroll tonight to sleep," Kaino said as she approached them, stopping to pull her long blue cloak out of her pack. The day had been warm, but it was cooling off now that the sun had set. She paused; cloak halfway thrown around her shoulders.

"And where will you sleep?" She asked, not looking at him as she continued to fasten the cloak around her.

"I'm on first watch," he said matter of fact. "When I wake Josen for the second watch, I will use his bedroll."

"Oh," Aliyah said before adding, "I don't mind taking a watch."

"We know. We talked about it, and we think it would be better if someone who has training in weapons kept watch. We are not sure what training you may have had, so for tonight, we'll just keep watch."

Aliyah nodded as she lay down on the bedroll, wrapping her cloak around her. The bedroll smelled like him, woodsy with a hint of citrus. It was a comforting scent, a peaceful scent. She found herself quickly drifting off to sleep.

She dreamed she was dancing in her parents' kitchen. The feel of the worn wooden floor was cold on her bare feet. Her father twirled her around, lifting her off the ground as he had when she was a child. He pulled her closer, the pulsing of his heartbeat against her chest. His arms were comforting. She was about to tell him how badly she missed him when he threw her into another twirl, and she lost sight of him.

When he pulled her back to him, it was not her father who was holding her, it was Kaino. The cold floor beneath her feet was replaced with a forest floor and, instead of a kitchen, a fire crackled in the background. He spun and dipped her as he had earlier in the evening. She found herself breathless as he spun her around repeatedly before putting her into a low dip.

He held her there for a long time. So long she felt the rush of blood to her head. When she finally started to rise, she was shocked to find Josen was the one lifting her back up. She stared at him for a moment, appraising him. The fear set in as she realized this version of Josen was somehow wrong. His skin was very pale and ashen, and his eyes were pitch black. She tried to pull away and his grasp on her became tighter, his nails digging into her skin. She tried to scream but no sound escaped.

She tried pulling away again and this time the creature spoke. "So easy. So deliciously easy."

Then the screaming started.

Chapter Seventeen

Josen sat on the log Kaino and Aliyah had occupied earlier. Kaino had long since gone to bed and was sleeping peacefully on the other side of the fire. Aliyah slept in Kaino's bedroll near the log. Josen tried not to stare at her as he fiddled with the baby swaddle between his hands.

He knew Kaino did not understand the comfort it brought him to have something of Ellie and their unborn child with him. Kaino would never say anything, but Josen knew his friend well enough to know Kaino worried about him.

Maybe he would try to find ways to be happy. Kaino and Aliyah had made it sound so easy. Thoughts of Aliyah had him staring at her. She had started twitching in her sleep and a look of discomfort had formed on her features. She flinched and he leaned forward to lay a comforting hand on her shoulder without thinking about it. Before he reached her, she let loose a scream and sat straight up. He pulled back alarmed.

"Are you alright?" He asked, uncertain. He looked her over as she pulled her legs into her chest and began to rock slightly, panting heavily.

"I-I think so." Her voice was quiet and strained. She inspected him from over her knees, thankful to see his normal complexion and green eyes staring back at her. The gold flecks of magic glowed softly in the dim light. She ran her fingers through her hair and shook her head, as if to dislodge the dream. "It was just a nightmare."

"Do you want to talk about it?" Josen asked, wincing as he remembered how well it had gone the last time he had asked her that. He hoped it would not be a repeat of the afternoon.

"It was about the grarg," she said, not wanting to get into too much detail. "Everything was fine in the dream until the grarg showed up. It repeated some things one had said to me before you rescued me." She shuddered, pulling her cloak closer around her.

Noticing the fire had started to go out, Josen got up and threw another log on it. The fire burned brighter suddenly, and Aliyah suspected he used magic to get it that bright that quickly. It did not startle her as it had earlier. The heat and light helped dispel some of the terror the dream had brought on.

"I have a dream," Josen said, trying to distract her. "It is always the same dream really. I am hunting the grarg and must race back to Ringard. I am too late to save them- to save her. I relive that night repeatedly, each time I close my eyes to sleep." He shut his eyes, pinching the bridge of his nose. "Every single night."

"What was her name?" Aliyah dared ask. She did not expect a response and he sat for a long while before answering.

"Ellie," he whispered. The name was like a caress on his lips, and it felt right to say her name. "Her name was Ellie."

"She must have been wonderful," Aliyah said.

"She was my everything. She was graceful and elegant, and perfect. You said you dream about being happy enough to dance for no reason? We were. Our life was blissful. She was my bright star in the dark night of being a member of the Ringada.

"Everyone loved her. She had this way about her, this force of light and goodness. It was impossible to be within her presence and feel down." He stopped, not knowing why he suddenly wanted to talk about Ellie and feeling embarrassed by telling some of his innermost feelings to a stranger.

"She sounds lovely," Aliyah said, meeting his gaze, and her eyes were warm. "You were lucky to find each other. How long were you married?" She looked at him, trying to gauge his age. He appeared younger than Sir Caldryk but still slightly older than she was.

"We were married for a little over a year. Long enough that she was expecting our first child." His gaze fell to where he still held the swaddle in his hand. He had forgotten he had been holding it this entire time.

"May I see it?" Aliyah asked hesitantly. She was surprised when he leaned over and handed the item to her. It was a baby swaddle. She brought it closer to her face to inspect the embroidery along the edges. "It's beautiful," she said as she ran a hand over the intricate design.

"Ellie was working on it the day she died. It is all I have left of her that I could carry with me." His voice was sad as Aliyah returned the swaddle to him.

"I'm sorry," Aliyah said, and she meant it. "She died in a grarg attack?"

Josen hesitated for a moment and looked away before shaking his head. "My father killed her." It was a relief to admit it. Aliyah sucked in a breath beside him, and he turned toward her.

"He," she paused, looking pale, "killed her?"

Josen remembered she had seen Driel do some damage at Caldryk Manor, and he did not have to imagine the horrors she was conjuring up in her mind.

"I wasn't there," Josen said quietly. "I was racing back to Ringard, trying to warn them of a grarg invasion- I was too late."

Aliyah reached a tentative hand out and put it comfortingly on one of Josen's. She stared up at him with her deep blue eyes full of concern. Not for his welfare like Kaino's would have been, but because she was genuinely sad he had lost his wife.

Shock coursed through Josen. It had been so long since anyone but Kaino had tried to comfort him. The action reminded him so much of Ellie he struggled to keep control of his emotions. She pulled her hand back and his thoughts were left a jumbled mess.

"How did he kill her?" Aliyah whispered the question before adding, "If you don't want to talk about it, I understand."

He realized he did want to keep talking about Ellie. "He slit her throat. Did it in front of a group of Ringada too. I was told he said, 'I only did it so she will not get her.'" He stopped and took a breath.

"Apparently there was a woman in control of the grarg. As soon as she walked into the keep my father just... he just stopped. He followed her out without a word and the grarg followed suit- carrying away some of our numbers to fuel theirs."

"He let me go," Aliyah said with a little shiver. "He told me to run because he couldn't keep knowledge of me from her. He said that she would read his mind. What does that mean?"

"I don't know, but I plan on finding him and getting some answers before I kill him." It felt good to admit that as well.

"I hope you get the answers you seek," Aliyah said with a soft smile.

They sat in companionable silence for a long time and Aliyah laid back on the bed roll. Her eyes were tired and began to close. Josen began humming a soft tune. A tune Ellie had often hummed. Within moments she was asleep.

***

Kaino pretended to be asleep. He had woken up to Aliyah gasping and had quickly ascertained she was alright before trying to fall back asleep. He was shocked when Josen began to talk to her- really talk to her. He never wanted to talk, least of all about Ellie. So, instead of joining in, Kaino listened.

He had hoped Aliyah would bring out some new response from Josen. Kaino had been shocked when he had seen how quickly Josen had reacted to her screams when being attacked by the grarg.

He also had been shocked by his friend's reaction to finding her injured. It was not like him. He had seemed different in the day and a half since-like he had a purpose again other than hunting down his father.

They had not been around anyone long enough for Josen to let his guard down, and he refused to talk about things with Kaino most days. It was enjoyable for Kaino to have someone new to talk to, at least. Aliyah was like a breath of fresh air. She was full of questions and listened attentively. She also was not afraid to say things that were on her mind. He had hoped Josen would like to talk to her too. It seemed, once he had let his guard down, he did.

Kaino found he liked Aliyah. Not in the romantic way, at least he did not think so. It was too early to tell and what did he know? He had never been in love before. He left things like that to Josen.

Aliyah reminded him of the little sister he had left behind when his parents sent him alone to Ringard. He usually did not think of his family often, but he did miss his sister. They had been close. Despite not knowing how he felt about Aliyah, he still thought she was fun and did not mind that he had a spontaneous side. He had enjoyed dancing with her that evening. He had not intended to ask her to dance, it had just felt right at the time.

He had rolled over so his back was toward the fire. He continued to listen and was just as shocked as Aliyah had been when Josen talked about Ellie being pregnant. *He showed her the swaddle?*

Kaino had a hard time staying “asleep” and wished his back was not towards them. Now there was no way for him to discreetly watch them. Josen would have known he was faking if he had turned around. *Josen always knows. He probably even knows now,* Kaino thought. He tried to keep his breathing even as he listened to Josen tell Aliyah of Ellie’s murder.

Kaino had never been so happy to hear his friend discuss his feelings.

It was quiet on the other side of the fire for a long time. Kaino had to resist the urge to turn and peek. Then he thought he heard Josen humming. *Jos is humming?* That was new, and it was a Ringada lullaby even. *Interesting....* he thought as he found the lullaby working even on him. It did not take long until he really was asleep.

***

The next week passed in a blur. The second night’s events had helped alleviate some awkwardness among the three of them and Josen was a little more willing to talk as they rode. He had never been as talkative as Kaino, who would find anything to talk about to avoid silence. Aliyah appreciated that the conversation stayed on safe topics such as towns they passed, favorite foods, and favorite childhood memories.

Aliyah found both men easy to talk to and she appreciated both of their company. It was beginning to feel as if she had known them forever, and she tried to picture what it would have been like if her parents had gone back to Ringard after getting married. What would it have been like to train with these men? They were a few years apart but would have been trained together. Would they have been friends? She did not know.

The sky was gray when Aliyah awoke, a little over a week after leaving Caldryk Manor. The first few drops of rain landing on her face were cold caresses that pulled her from sleep. She sighed as she pulled her cloak around her before standing up. She needed to relieve herself. Josen and Kaino were already awake, and she nodded to both as she passed, heading into the woods.

She walked to where she was just out of sight of the camp, hoping neither man would come check on her. She was just finishing when a twig snapped behind her. She tugged her pants back up and whirled around to see a grarg standing behind her. Its two companions, both male, stood on either side of her in a flanking position.

She froze. The dark eyes of the first grarg held her in place and she flinched as it opened its mouth, and a high-pitched feminine voice came out of it. “Trouble, you have been a real trouble to find.”

Chapter Eighteen

Aliyah hesitated just long enough for the two companions of the female grarg to lunge for her. She felt their clawed hands dig into her arms, some of her burns shot pains through her body at the contact.

"She smells delicious" the larger male grarg said, grabbing her arm tighter and taking a long whiff.

"Let me go!" She said, trying to make her voice firm as she fought to get her arms free.

"None of that," the other male grarg said, its nails biting into Aliyah's arm. "The Dark Mistress wants you alive girl, but don't think we are above hurting you if you don't come willingly."

Aliyah struggled once more and the first grarg reached out and slapped her face. "You will come willingly, or we will drag you back to the Dark Mistress," it hissed.

Aliyah let loose the scream that had been building in the back of her throat. The grarg paused before looking at each other, a silent communication. The larger of the two male grarg yanked her up and threw her over his shoulder before running. The two others stood back in defensive positions as Josen and Kaino rounded the corner, weapons at the ready. Aliyah fought and flailed at the one carrying her, but he never slowed.

She screamed again as a deadly fight commenced. Josen and Kaino were lethal, their motions swift and graceful. The first grarg attacked Josen. It lurched towards him in an obvious attack. Josen had her beheaded within seconds. Kaino's fight lasted a bit longer. The one he was fighting had watched its companion being easily taken down and it was more cautious. It dodged and lunged a few times at Kaino before it too had its head rolling on the ground. Both men ran for Aliyah.

Josen got to her first. He sent a fireball at the feet of the one carrying Aliyah and it stumbled. She felt the creature lose its footing and she began flailing even harder. Josen threw another fireball and this time it fell, letting go of her.

She landed hard and rolled away from the creature. The sting of rocks and twigs bit into her exposed skin and left bruises in its wake. She was vaguely aware of Josen beheading the creature with one fatal swoop of his curved blade. Then he was standing before her, pulling her up off the ground and into an embrace. Her head spun from the sudden change of direction, and she did not miss the way his heart thundered in his chest as he held her. He breathed a relieved sigh and gently pulled back from her, hands on her shoulders assessing her for injuries.

"Are you hurt?" He said, his eyes soft as he took in the sight of her dishevelment. His hands were gentle as he touched her face and turned her head from side to side, looking into her eyes. "You don't seem to have a concussion," he said. "However, you do have some cuts. You should wash them out in the stream. Can you walk?"

Aliyah nodded as Kaino came up behind them. He was staring at Josen with an odd expression on his face Aliyah could not read. Josen let go of her and took a step back, and a small flutter of disappointment went through her at the sudden loss of contact. She felt colder, and not just because of the rain that was falling harder through the canopy of leaves above them.

She turned and started walking back toward the stream and was thankful for Kaino's presence as he joined her. The smell of burning flesh hung in the air and she turned to see Josen setting the three grarg on fire. Their forms were ashes within seconds, the fire a rush of power that defied the rain.

Kaino escorted her out of the canopy of leaves to the slow-moving water of the stream. Aliyah was shocked by the reflection that stared back at her. She had a long shallow cut on her forehead from where her head had hit a rock. It stung as she rinsed it out. A bruise was forming on her cheek, and she touched it gingerly. It throbbed beneath her finger. She rinsed the other small cuts she could find, aware of the rain that was now pelting down.

Her slippered feet squished in the muddy bank of the stream as she went over to where Kaino was readying the horses. Kaino gave her an appraising look before coming over to where she now stood next to Raynar.

"Are you alright?" He asked her, as he helped her up onto the giant horse.

"Yes," she whispered back. She was still shaken but thankful the three grarg were dead and smoldering. "Thank you for coming to save me-again."

"We were so careful! I don't know how we did not hear them or notice their presence." He was angry. "We will have to be extra vigilant today. Maybe fires at night are a bad idea," he trailed off as Josen approached them.

He extinguished the remnants of their campfire with a snap of his fingers and grabbed his pack. He snatched Aliyah's from where it still sat next to the log and handed it to her. She took it without a word.

The two men had begun to clean up camp before hearing Aliyah scream. She was thankful for their preparedness as she accepted her pack from Josen. She tried to catch his eye, still bewildered at the embrace he had given her minutes before. He would not look at her as he strode over to his own horse and pulled himself on in one swift motion.

Angry howls erupted from within the forest. The piercing screams were reminiscent of the ones at Caldryk Manor. She looked around and saw Josen give Kaino a nod. Kaino took the lead and Josen kept his horse behind Aliyah's as the horses took off at a gallop.

The howls retreated slowly as the horses' hooves ate at the ground. They rode hard, trying to put as much distance between them and the grarg. Aliyah's heart raced at the sounds. She imagined the creatures lunging out of the trees and tackling her to the ground. Phantom claws bit into her skin.

Focus, she told herself as she paid attention to the way the horse moved beneath her. She was glad when they made it out of the woods and back onto an established road hours later. The howls of grarg had been left far behind.

***

It was a relief to be out of the trees, even though the rain more thoroughly soaked them. Open grassy fields flanked the other side of the road. In the distance, the outline of the Vendi Mountains was visible despite the downpour. Their jagged shapes rose high into the sky. Glittering before them was the Golyth River. They were still so far away.

They slowed the horses after a while, giving them a break. The road was muddy from the rain and there were few people on the road. Aliyah stared warily at everyone they passed. None were grarg. Those they passed peered curiously at the three Myralians. Not because they were Myralian, their cloaks hid any features that would identify them as such. No, they stared because of the weapons peeking out from beneath Ringada cloaks and the giant horses they rode.

Josen thought of the attack on Aliyah that morning. He had not realized how much he had come to appreciate her company and her presence in the week they had been traveling together. He thought of how it felt to hold her in his arms briefly and he felt something stir inside of him, feelings he had locked away with the death of Ellie.

He tried to think of something to say to Aliyah. They had been quiet in the rush out of the forest, but now the road was almost void of anyone. He nudged Ember to ride up next to Raynar. Aliyah looked at him through the rain.

"Are you alright?" He kept his voice low, not caring if Kaino overheard, but wanting some privacy, nonetheless.

"I think so," her teeth chattered as she spoke. "I really d-d-don't like grarg."

He chuckled darkly at that. "I don't think anyone likes them- except maybe whoever makes them." His voice grew somber at that.

"How are they m-made?" Her teeth were chattering even more now.

"That is a mystery I do not know the answer to." He wished he did. He wished he knew how they were made and controlled. He knew it had something to do with the corrupted magic of a *Wyvanni*, but he did not want to frighten Aliyah more than she already was.

"I hope we n-never f-find out," she said with a shudder. "I would be f-f-fine never seeing one ag-g-gain. I don't know what is worse- their eyes or their v-v-voices."

"They really do set one on edge, don't they?" Josen said.

"Have you heard one of them s-speak? Every time I feel like I am staring at death and then it has the voice of a nightmare."

"I can't say I've had many chances to converse with one," Josen said. "They seem to find you more appealing than me. I can see why though."

She eyed him with one eyebrow raised from beneath the hood of her cloak. "Is that because I am a *Wyvanni* or b-because I am f-female, smaller, and easier to haul off?" Her body shook in massive shudders from the cold.

He had no idea how he had gotten to this point. He had meant it as a compliment, and she had somehow thrown it back in his face. "Umm... neither? I was thinking if I were a grarg and I had a choice between two lackluster men and a beautiful woman... I would go for the woman."

Did I just call her beautiful? He blushed despite himself.

"Well, then they must not be around a lot of r-regular women because I am far from beautiful. If anything, I am quite av-v-erage and they need to get out m-m-more." She said it with a huff that made Josen chuckle.

"You think I'm joking?" He asked.

"Listen, no one has called me beautiful ever. Especially when I am s-soaked through, muddy, and smell like a horse- no offense Raynar." She patted the horse fondly.

"Well, there is always a first for everything." Josen found himself mumbling, embarrassed. He looked her over one more time before nudging Ember forward to ride closer to Kaino.

By late afternoon they were approaching a small town. The smoke from the many chimneys beckoned invitingly. "Would you like to stay at an inn tonight?" Kaino asked above the pounding rain. It had turned into a drizzle earlier, but the storm had picked back up again and had started to come down sideways.

Josen looked at Aliyah. She was shivering despite the weight of her cloak and her slippers were soaking wet. *Her feet must be freezing,* he thought. He weighed the benefits of stopping at an inn before responding.

"I think we need to."

Chapter Nineteen

They entered the town just as the sun should have been setting. The dense clouds above them turned from dark gray to black, the only indication the day had turned to night. The small town's muddy streets were empty thanks to the rain, and they had no problem finding its one inn.

It was hard to see much of the inn through the rain and darkness. However, the many windows shone with the warm glow of candlelight, and it made the dark building inviting. A sign flapped above the door. With the help of candlelight from the window, Aliyah could just make out the words painted on the sign.

The Weary Traveler. She let out a soft snort. *Isn't that appropriate?*

They kept their hoods on as they dismounted their horses. The mud squished into her slippers as she stood next to Raynar and she tried not to lose her footing.

They had agreed Josen should go in first to inquire about rooms while Kaino and Aliyah waited outside in the rain. Neither of them spoke. Aliyah wondered if Kaino was as tired as she felt. She was not sure what was worse- the cold or the exhaustion. She suppressed a yawn as Josen came back out minutes later with the hint of a smile on his face.

"I was able to get two rooms," he said over the pounding rain. "The innkeeper even threw in dinner for a small fee." He grabbed his horse's reins and led them around back to where the innkeeper had said his stable was located. The small yard was less muddy than the road and Aliyah had no problem walking across it.

A stable boy rushed out into the rain as he saw them, gawking at the size of the Ringada warhorses. "Oh wow," he breathed. "A true Ringada horse! I have always wanted to see one of these!" He continued staring, moving from one horse to the next.

Josen handed him the reins to his horse. "And now you have seen three," he said, tossing him a coin. "We expect them to be well taken care of." His tone implied how displeased he would be if they were not. The young man looked at them with eyebrows pulled together, showing just how serious he took this job.

"Yes sir!" The boy said, holding the coin close to his chest in a fisted hand. "Will do, sir!" He took Josen's horse and led it into a stall before coming back for the other two. Aliyah patted Raynar fondly as he was led away, and she thought the horse looked sad at their parting.

"Come on," Josen said, touching her on the arm. She turned toward him, and he motioned back toward the inn. Together they hurried through the rain toward its beckoning lights.

Warm air hit them as they stepped through the wooden door, and it was a relief to be inside the large building. The main room was spacious but warm. Delicious scents wafted from the kitchen. Aliyah inhaled the smell of baking bread and stew, and her stomach gave a rumble in response. Kaino gave a small laugh beside her at the sound and she rolled her eyes at him.

Josen led them up a flight of rickety stairs lit by lanterns hanging in the tight stairwell. They followed him down an equally tight hallway before stopping at two rooms at the end of the hall. "We will take the one on the left," Josen said. "You can have the one on the right."

She nodded her thanks and was about to enter her room when he stopped her.

"Also, I paid for you to be able to have a bath and the water is being drawn right now."

She eyed him stiffly, remembering her comment about smelling like a horse. She could not resist the urge to sniff at her shoulder.

"Not because you stink," he said. "I am sure we all do, but because of how cold the rain was. You need to warm up and they will also be laundering your clothing. For now," he said, pausing to undo one of his many packs, "You can wear these."

He proffered her a shirt and a pair of men's trousers from his pack. She took them and was shocked to find they were clean. He threw some socks on top that had been rolled into a neat little ball. "We had these laundered at the last village we stopped at right before we found you."

"Thank you," she murmured, blushing at the thought of wearing the clothes. Not because they were men's clothes, but because they were *his* clothes. Footsteps sounded on the stairs and Aliyah turned to see one of the inn staff coming toward them.

"The bath is ready," she said, face flushed and slightly out of breath. She must have been the one heating the water. "Please follow me." Aliyah gave one last look at Josen and Kaino before following the woman to the bathing chamber.

The chamber was small, lit by a single candle. A metal tub stood in the center of the room. Steam drifted from it invitingly. Aliyah placed the bundle of clothing on a small stool sitting in the corner and grabbed the bar of soap and towel that were resting next to it.

"Stay as long as you like," the woman said before walking out of the room and shutting the door behind her.

Aliyah turned the iron lock on the door, thankful for the secure privacy it afforded. Not wanting to waste more time than was necessary and risk the water getting cold, she peeled off her clothes. They were wet despite the cloak she had been wearing and the skin on her thighs had started to chafe.

The slippers were a muddy mess and, upon further inspection, were barely holding together. Her feet were caked with mud up to her ankles and she threw the slippers on top of the rest of her discarded clothing before stepping into the hot water.

The bath was amazing. Aches and pains, the discomforts from traveling by horseback, all seemed to disappear in the heat. She lay her head back on the rim of the tub, suddenly feeling tired. The previous days- even the previous month's- events piled on top of one another. Her muscles ached and not just from the bruises that had begun to form from the grarg attack that morning. She was utterly exhausted. She soaked in the tub, letting the grime and dirt come off her and scrubbing vigorously when it would not. She paused when she got to her arms.

The latticework of scars crisscrossed up both arms. What had once been smooth skin was now covered in shallow cuts and angry red welts in the shape of hands. She had never been cut or burned in the same place twice. She hated the marks he had left on her. She felt tears start to form as she looked at the remnants of the torture he had put her through.

No! I will not cry, she thought angrily as she stared at her arms. *I am still me. Scars do not define a person.* No matter how much she repeated that to herself, she could not believe it and the tears came anyway.

She lay her head back on the rim of the tub, letting the tears fall freely down her cheeks and neck until they mixed in with the bath water. She lay there for a while, feeling the release of emotion as it soothed away the hurt she felt. When she climbed out of the bath she felt better -cleaner, and not just physically.

She hurried to throw on the spare change of clothing Josen had given to her, inhaling the scent of him despite herself. He smelled different than Kaino. Where Kaino had smelled of woods and citrus, Josen's scent was reminiscent of cedar and fresh mountain air, with the hint of campfire. It was rejuvenating and she blushed as she found herself smelling the collar of the shirt on her way out of the room. The inn staff member walked over to her, noticing Aliyah as she shut the door behind her.

"Here miss," she said, taking the clothes from Aliyah and handing her a pair of slippers. "I will launder your clothes for you and return them in the morning. The men you are with asked if we had any sort of slippers you could borrow. We scrounged these up for you. I hope they fit." She eyed Aliyah's feet beneath the load of clothing.

"They will be perfect. Thank you," Aliyah said as she bent down to slide the soft-soled slippers over the wool socks she had donned prior. The slippers were oversized, but she did not mind. Her feet felt warmer than they had all day.

She walked back to her room and dropped off her pack. She gave a knock on the men's door, but no one responded. Feeling perplexed, she headed down the rickety stairs into the main room. There were few travelers at the inn, but it took her a few moments before she spotted Josen and Kaino waiting for her at a table in the back corner. They waved her over and she walked to them hesitantly. She knew she had been longer than expected in the bath but neither of them seemed perturbed.

"Feel better?" Josen asked her, eyeing her clean appearance. His pants had been too long for her, and she had rolled the legs up multiple times to be able to walk in them. She nodded as she took a seat across from him.

"Well, she certainly smells better," Kaino chimed in, leaning in as if to take a quick whiff of her. "Definitely better," he said. She gave him a shrewd look.

"We ordered some stew a few minutes ago," Josen continued, ignoring Kaino's comment. "It should be here in a few minutes; they just went back to grab some for us." Her stomach rumbled at his words.

"Thank you," she said again. "Not just for the meal, but for stopping at an inn. I can pay."

Josen cut her off with a wave of his hand. "You are the daughter of a Ringada member, our money is your money. Besides, it's not a big deal. We needed to stop for supplies, and it would be enjoyable to sleep indoors for a change."

The food came out at that moment, saving Aliyah from having to reply. The steaming bowls of stew and bread were placed before them, and Aliyah had never smelled anything so wonderful. She stirred her stew, waiting for it to cool, and observed the others in the room. There were few people and Aliyah appreciated the quietness. She had only been to a few inns before, but each time they were loud, raucous places and she much preferred quiet solitude like tonight.

"Are you going to eat that?" Kaino asked, sounding concerned. She had paused, spoon halfway to her mouth, as she stared at a family of three. They were sitting at another table on the other side of the room. The father and mother were talking with their daughter, who looked to be about ten. Memories of meals with her parents came unbidden and she looked away, embarrassed to be caught staring. She took a bite of the stew.

It was delicious. She found herself eating ravenously and even went as far as using the bread to wipe up any remnants left in the bowl. She sat back in her chair, feeling full. Her eyes started closing of their own accord and the thought of an actual bed had her blinking wistfully at the stairwell.

"I think we should turn in for the night," Kaino said, noticing Aliyah's long glances toward the direction of their rooms. The three said goodnight and Aliyah headed up to bed, falling asleep seconds after laying down.

Chapter Twenty

A loud thump sounded outside her room. Light from the rising sun streamed in through the small window above her bed. Aliyah ran a hand over her sleep-filled eyes, stumbling out of bed. She pulled the door open, expecting someone to be on the other side. No one was there.

She blinked wearily as she looked to either side of the hall, still not seeing anyone. She took a step into the hall, trying to see farther. Her foot knocked into something hard, and she looked down to see a pair of brown leather boots sitting outside her door.

She smiled as she pulled the boots into her room and shut the door behind her. Sitting on the bed, she laced the boots and grabbed her pack off the ground where she had placed it the night before. A slight knock sounded at the door, and she pulled it open, expecting to see Kaino or Josen.

Instead, it was the member of the inn staff from the previous night, holding her freshly laundered clothes. She thanked the woman, pulling a silver coin out of her pack and placing it in the woman's hands. The woman gave an appreciative smile as she walked away.

The smell of breakfast cooking had Aliyah placing the clothes on top of her pack before rushing out of the room. The aroma of fresh baked bread made her mouth water. She closed the door behind her and stood before Josen and Kaino's door. She knocked politely and waited. There was no sound from the other side. Shrugging, she headed downstairs to the main room.

The room was entirely empty other than one lone man sitting at a table. Kaino looked up at her as she descended the stairs. His elbow on the table as he propped his head on his hand. She sat in the chair across from him and he gave her a wan smile. His eyes had dark circles under them.

"Good morning," he said, "you're chipper today." There was a hint of jealousy in his voice.

"That was the best sleep I have had in, well... probably years." She laughed. "Who would have thought a place called The Weary Traveler would be so relaxing?"

Kaino did not laugh. Instead, he sighed, closing his eyes. "Sure... if your bunk mate will let you sleep." The serving girl appeared at that moment, a steaming mug of coffee in her hands. She placed it in front of Kaino and he took a long sip.

"Would you like anything?" The serving girl asked Aliyah. She requested tea and the serving girl scurried away to fetch some.

"Where is Josen?" Aliyah asked after the serving girl had left.

"He left early this morning, said he was going to go get supplies," Kaino said between sips. She did not miss the tone of annoyance in his voice.

"Oh," she tried not to sound bothered. "It would have been nice to join him and get some supplies of my own."

"He said he was going to get you a bedroll and boots and pick up some provisions," Kaino said, sounding a little more like himself as the coffee began to take effect.

"Did he now?" Aliyah said, feeling a little less bothered. "Well, he dropped off the boots." She lifted her leg above the table to show Kaino.

He grunted in response, not looking up at her. He nursed his coffee, and she was thankful when the serving girl brought her tea. She stirred it, staring out the window. The day was sunny, a vast contrast to the previous day. She sipped at her tea-it was quite good. She let the warmth of it soak into her. It was as relaxing as the bath had been.

"You said Josen kept you up last night? What happened?" Aliyah was genuinely curious. Kaino seemed the type to sleep through anything- he certainly had quite a few nights ago when Aliyah had woken up shaken from her nightmare. She knew she and Josen had tried to talk quietly and she was sure Kaino had been asleep the entire time.

"It's the nightmares," he said, looking down into his now empty cup. He pushed it away from him and looked at Aliyah with arms folded. A somber expression on his face. "Ever since Ellie died, he hasn't been the same."

"I'm sure that is to be expected," Aliyah responded, putting her teacup down and leaning with one arm on the table.

"Yes, but it has been... bad. You should have seen how panicked and worried he was when he found out Ellie was pregnant. He never thinks of himself as enough." He ran a hand through his hair before continuing.

"He always sees himself as falling short- especially around Ellie's death." He blew out a breath. "I have tried to help him– tried to get him to see himself how everyone else sees him. He just holds onto the fact that he failed her. That he was not there for her, and his father killed her during the grarg invasion."

"Josen mentioned a grarg invasion, but he didn't explain," Aliyah said.

"It was one of the darkest days in Ringada history." His voice was sad as he continued, "over a year ago, Josen and I were sent with a few others to go investigate some rumors of grarg. We did not believe they were back. Few have been seen in the past few hundred years-and never in this many numbers. We traveled for a few days before coming across their tracks. We set up an ambush, but it turns out they were just a distraction. The real force of the grarg had headed around and invaded Ringard."

"I thought Ringard was impenetrable?" Aliyah had been told so many stories about Ringard, it seemed like the safest place on the continent-maybe even the world.

"It's easy to scale walls when you have claws at the tip of your hands," Kaino said. Aliyah shuddered, remembering how one had dug its nails into her the day before. She resisted the urge to cup her hand around her arm.

"They climbed the massive walls and slaughtered anyone they could find. It was a mess." Kaino stared at his hands which he had moved to clasp before him on the table. When he spoke again, his eyes were distant, remembering the horror that had awaited them at Ringard. "We raced back at record speed. We were too late to warn them. We rushed into the keep and Josen ran for his quarters. Ellie was lying in the doorway. Her throat was slashed."

Aliyah felt deep sympathy for Josen. He had already told her much of this and she understood the horrors that plagued him at night. She knew what it was like to have those you loved taken from you.

"We left soon after to hunt down Driel, leaving Moryn, Josen's second in command, in charge. Moryn is the acting High Protector until Josen returns."

She stared at him speechless.

"What?" Kaino said, looking up from the lines on the table he had been staring at.

"Josen is the High Protector?" It came out a squeak.

"Yeah..." Kaino gave her a look like she should have known.

"Why didn't he tell me?" She felt like a fool. She knew his father had been the High Protector, but anyone could be the heir.

"He hates the title and the role his father thrust upon him. His father had trained him since birth to be the next heir- not caring that anyone else might be considered for the title. He pushed him harder than others – pushed him to his limits and then some. Why he didn't tell you is his business.

"But back to your original question," Kaino said, interrupting her thoughts of confronting Josen. "Josen has had nightmares ever since that night. Horrible ones he refuses to talk to anyone about. He just wakes up shaking and, on nights like last night, when he wakes up, he will not go back to sleep. He will pace or work the frustration out through physical exercise. I'm surprised you slept through it all night."

"Sorry," she said, feeling sheepish. "I guess that's the benefit of having a wall or two between us."

"Maybe next time we stop at an inn, you can bunk with Josen, and I will get a room to myself and finally get some peace and quiet." He said that last part as a joke, not realizing the terror that had gone through Aliyah at the mention of bunking with Josen.

She did not know what to say. It was fine sleeping out in the open, but sharing a room with a man- any man...

"I didn't mean like that," Kaino said, rolling his eyes at her expression. "I'm not sure Josen will ever want anything like that again."

"What will I not want ever again?" Josen's voice said from right beside their table.

Aliyah jumped despite herself. Neither of them had paid attention to Josen entering the inn carrying some large parcels.

"To stop at this town again. I know I sure do not want to," Kaino lied, a hint of amusement on his face. "Do you need help, Jos? You know we would have gone with you to purchase the supplies."

"There was no need," Josen said, placing the packages on the table. Aliyah was shocked he had been able to carry all of it. "I was up early anyway and decided I would get a head start before the rest of the townsfolk started doing their own errands. I beat the rush." He had an unusual smile on his face and Aliyah looked at Kaino for interpretation. Kaino looked just as confused.

"Thank you for the boots," Aliyah said, giving him a genuine smile despite wanting to question him right then and there about him withholding that he was the High Protector. "They fit really well and are way sturdier than the slippers I've been wearing." Those had not come back from being laundered and had probably been thrown out.

"You are welcome," Josen said, the smile still on his face. It did not quite reach his eyes, but it was the biggest smile Aliyah had seen him give anyone.

"These are for you as well," he said, leaning over and pushing quite a few packages towards her. She eyed them curiously before looking back at Josen. “I figured you needed a spare change of clothing- or two,” he added.

“Thank you.” She felt shy suddenly. It was odd to have anyone see her needs and help. It left her feeling strange. She hurried to add “And thank you again for letting me borrow yours last night. My other clothes were returned right as I was coming down here this morning. I’ll go change and give these back to you. I’m sorry I slept in them- they're a bit wrinkled now.”

“There’s no need to hurry, and it’s not like they won’t get wrinkled in my pack... But if it makes you feel any better, we'll wait for you here while you go change.”

She nodded as she gratefully grabbed the parcels designated for her and went up the stairs to change.

***

She decided to open the parcels first before changing. She did not expect the contents to be much different than what she had been wearing prior, but curiosity had gotten the better of her.

She opened the first package, peeling back the brown wrapping. It contained two pairs of women’s riding leggings. She held them up, noticing that they had extra support and padding to help alleviate the discomfort that came from riding a horse. She was impressed and knew her aching legs would be thankful later. Without waiting to open another package, she untied her boots and replaced the men's trousers with the leggings. They were wonderfully soft where the trousers had been coarse and itchy.

She opened the next package and was shocked to find a tunic of the finest material. It was a deep hue of purple and had intricate beading along the neckline. Underneath it lay a tunic of equal finery. The color of this one was dark blue. She picked it up and ran a hand along the delicate beading.

The room had a small mirror above a tiny dresser, and she stepped back to see her reflection as she held the blue tunic up to her. It was the exact color of her eyes, making them stand out, the gold flecks in them more pronounced. She turned away from the mirror, shucking off her shirt and replacing it with the tunic.

She eyed her reflection again, pausing in front of the mirror to admire the effect of the tunic. She felt girlish—beautiful even. She had not felt that way in months. Her aunt had forced her into so many stiff gowns as she tried to find Aliyah a "worthwhile" match. Aliyah had not been shocked her aunt had sold her to Sir Caldryk. To Matylda, making money and status off Aliyah was indeed "worthwhile."

The dresses she had been forced to wear at Caldryk Manor had been another thing entirely.

She had felt awkward having that much skin exposed. She had been his puppet, his plaything, and he had dressed her for the part. She looked like the heathen gods Mylarians were rumored to believe in. No, she never felt pretty in those dresses.

This tunic though... she felt more like herself than she had in a long time. She contemplated that fact as she rubbed the soft material of the tunic between her fingers. She had always been a rough and tumble girl. Where other girls had played with dolls and wanted ribbons in their hair, Aliyah would pretend she was a member of the Ringada.

She smiled as she remembered her mother's horror when she had fallen out of a tree, breaking her arm. "I was just trying to sneak up behind the enemy, mother," she had said. Her mother had not wanted to hear "anymore nonsense about imaginary enemies." It had not stopped Aliyah from climbing the tree again.

She also had not lied when she told Josen she had never been called beautiful. No one looked at a dirt-stained girl and called her beautiful. No one looked at a frightened young woman and said the same. But this tunic... it made her feel confident.

She turned toward the last two packages. She opened the smaller one first. Blushing as she saw the contents inside. On the top of the package lay socks but underneath...

Are those undergarments?

She wanted to die of shame as she imagined Josen purchasing them for her. She threw the items at the bottom of her pack, wanting them out of sight. She kept out a pair of socks and relished the fine make of them. They were soft and warm. She put them on and retied her boots. Anything to put off opening the last package- especially after the horror of finding undergarments in the one prior.

She sighed, as she stood up from tying her shoes, realizing she could not put it off much longer. She removed the string around the package and paused before removing the wrapping. Slowly peeling it back, she looked inside. Dark blue fabric the shade of her eyes lay nestled between the folds of paper. *Doesn't look like undergarments*, she thought, feeling relieved. She peeled back the wrapping with more force. It wasn't undergarments, but what she saw made her breath catch.

She pulled the gown out, hands shaking. It continued to unfold until it touched the floor. It was of a modern but modest design. The skirt was not as full as some of the dresses her aunt had forced her into, but this dress was even more elegant despite that fact. The skirts consisted of layers of blue silk, overlayed with dark blue lace that continued up the bodice which was beaded.

The sleeves were bands of blue silk that would fit right over her shoulders. The dress was exquisite, and Aliyah began examining the beadwork. A slight knock came at the door, interrupting her admiration.

"Come in," she said, without looking up from the dress. The doorknob rattled in response. Whoever it was could not open the door, and they knocked again, more persistently this time. She flung the dress on the bed as she went to unlock and open the door.

Kaino stood on the other side. "Josen wanted me to check and see if you are-" he paused, looking her up and down, "ready" he concluded and let loose a low appreciative whistle. "You clean up nicely."

She blushed, "Thanks. I'm almost ready- I just need to finish packing the rest of the items he bought me." She gestured towards the bed and Kaino's eyes widened when he spied the dress. He pushed past her into the room and grabbed the dress gingerly, looking at it contemplatively.

"Everything alright?" She edged closer, grabbing her pack and placing the rest of her clothes inside.

"Mmhmm," he said, not looking at her. He still stared intently at the dress, and she held out her hand for it.

"I don't even know when I will ever wear the thing," she said softly. He handed it to her, and she gently folded it, putting it on top of the other items in her pack. She pulled the pack shut. "It is gorgeous though."

"It matches your eyes," he said more to himself, but Aliyah found herself blushing. "Should we ever need to dress formally, you now have formal attire." He said the last part with his usual mischievous smile.

"And when would I need to dress so fancy?" Aliyah asked, playing along.

"Oh, I don't know.... Maybe when we get back to Ringard-it would be delightful to see something as pleasant as you wander the stone corridors in such finery. You will stop men in their tracks-married and unmarried alike, as they are charmed by your beauty." He ducked out of the way as she swung to hit him. Kaino began to laugh, and Aliyah joined in. They were both still laughing as they headed down the stairs to rejoin Josen.

Chapter Twenty-One

"Are you ready for your horses?" The eager voice of the young stable boy rang out from where he worked clearing out a stall. Josen had just walked into the stable and hadn't noticed the young man working.

"Yes please," he said as he leaned against a post to wait.

The boy rushed about. An older man, most likely his father, joined him as they saddled the horses. He recognized Ember's snort. Soon the tall black horse was led to him, the stable boy's head only reaching the horse's shoulder.

"Thank you," Josen said, taking the reins as the boy ran back to get Kaino's horse. The older man walked forward, a slight shuffle to his gait as he led Raynar out from where the horse had been stalled for the evening. The horse looked around with wild eyes, snorting impatiently.

"She's not here," Josen said to the horse. Raynar stomped his foot impatiently. "I know you are fond of her, you old rascal. Is it the apples? You go from being the grumpiest horse known to man to being quite smitten with her. She has that effect though, doesn't she?" He gave a little laugh, stopping suddenly when he heard Aliyah and Kaino laughing as they crossed the yard towards the stables.

Josen peeked his head around the corner, trying to be inconspicuous. His heart sped at the sight of her. She had chosen to wear the blue tunic and he was not prepared for the reaction it caused him. It brought out her eyes, which were light with mirth.

He went into town, planning to get her a few essential items when he had spied the tunic in a shop window. He could not identify what struck him about the tunic other than it seemed to have the same charm Aliyah had- and it was the exact color of her eyes. The tunic was feminine but functional- different than what Ellie would have ever worn. Ellie had been all about looking ladylike- even when living in a stone keep. She always wore the finest dresses, and Josen had not minded surprising her with a new one every now and then.

Maybe that was why he could not resist the dress. He had not planned to get Aliyah anything of the sort. It was not something one would wear while riding across the continent and sleeping outside. It was not *functional.* However, it was in the same shop as the tunics, and he would never have noticed it had the clerk not pointed it out to him.

That woman sure can sell clothing to unsuspecting men, he thought drily. *She could convince a nobleman to sell off half his land and feel like he got the better deal!* He laughed to himself.

Or maybe I just have an issue saying no to fine clothing and miss doting on Ellie. He sighed, feeling regretful about buying the dress. *What if she thought it was out of line?* The thought made him worry. He did not want to overstep boundaries with Aliyah.

He was not sure how he felt about her, but friends are allowed to buy friends nice things, right? Were they friends? He hoped so.

The sound of their laughing voices drew near. Josen stared at them from the door of the stable, wondering what it would be like to laugh so freely. He had not laughed like that since before Ellie's death. It was an intriguing thought, and he was pondering when Aliyah stepped up next to him, a bundle of clothing in her outstretched hand. He glanced down at it before taking it from her.

"Thank you," she said as he turned away to place the bundle in his pack, "for everything. I appreciate the clothing and the ah- other clothing." She had a nervous hitch to her tone. He turned back to her as she swallowed and blushed.

Oh... That *might have been overstepping a line.*

He had not picked out the undergarments, the clerk had. He had not even looked at what she had picked out. It was his turn to blush. "I- I had the clerk pick them out. I have no idea what she chose, and I never looked at the contents of the parcel. I told her my traveling companion was female and needed some women's things..." The words came out of him in a rush.

"Oh," Aliyah's face instantly brightened. "Then I appreciate your generosity and your... uh... decency. Also," she paused, blushing again.

I knew the dress was a bad idea... he thought as he waited for her to continue. "If this is about the dress," he found himself saying, and she looked up at him, meeting his eyes. "I saw the dress and thought I would replace the one that we used to stop your bleeding." *There, that's something a friend would do, right?* He hoped she did not hear the nervousness in his voice.

"Oh, well thank you then," she said before adding with venom, "I hated that thing."

"It was a little worse for wear when we pulled it out of your pack..."

"He took away my clothing and made me wear something like that every day." Her voice was small, and she was holding her arms again. "It was the costume I was to wear as his pet *Wyvanni*." She spat out the word.

"I am sorry to remind you of it then. I had no idea. I just wanted to buy you something nice to replace something we damaged." He felt embarrassed. *There you go, always trying to do something nice and ruining it instead...*

"I love *your* dress," she said breathlessly, and Josen did not miss the way she emphasized the dress being his. "I wore his dresses far too long. I look forward to the day I have a reason to wear the dress you bought me." She gave him a shy smile before walking over to Raynar. She gave the horse a loving pat on the shoulder before climbing on, Kaino giving her a boost.

Emotions swirled inside him as he watched her. Kaino met his eyes, looking at Josen with a knowing look. Josen turned his back and with one quick movement he was astride Ember. He tossed a coin down to the older man. "Thank you for your generosity and hospitality toward our horses," he said as he nudged Ember toward the exit.

He passed Kaino who leaned over, whispering so only Josen could hear. "You bought her a dress? Jos, I just..." it seemed his friend was speechless for once. "I am glad to see the old you resurface."

The words stirred something inside Josen, something that had been longing to come out for a while. He wasn't ready to deal with it yet. With a nudge of his heel, Ember made her way out of the stable and into the bright sun.

***

Kaino knew he was being uncharacteristically silent. He hated silence, but for now, he appreciated the reprieve where the only sounds were those the horses made or the animals in the trees around them.

They had been riding for a few hours, staying to the road. He and Josen had talked about their traveling plans while Aliyah was getting dressed and felt the safest route would be to stick to the road as much as possible. Besides, Kaino had pointed out, at least they would know where they were going with only minimal tracking on his part.

They followed the main road. It was busier today than it had been the previous day. The rain had kept weary travelers away. Now it was crowded. They had to keep their pace slower due to pedestrian traffic on the still muddy road.

Maybe trying to cut through the woods would be faster, he thought for not the first time that day as they passed a farmer's overflowing cart pulled by a tired pair of oxen. The animals trudged along while the farmer's children ran about the cart. He was glad when they passed them. He did not want one of their horses to accidentally step on a wayward child. It had almost happened more than once that morning.

They were finally ahead of the crowd and the road was peaceful. He was able to think now without the noise of others. *I still cannot believe Josen bought her a dress. What was he thinking?*

He knew Josen used to buy Ellie dresses- he had even helped Josen pick them out on occasion. He had sat through hours listening to that man debate about colors and styles for Ellie. He knew Josen had never bought a dress that shade before. No-this shade of blue belonged entirely to Aliyah.

Does he know what he is doing? Is he doing it because of Ellie or because of Aliyah? I know he knows they are two separate women- I don't know how he could not see it. With some training, Aliyah could probably even hold her own in a fight, whereas Ellie was daintier... It doesn't matter. He shook his head.

Tonight, after Aliyah falls asleep, I will ask him. If he's ready to move on, great! I'm not going to argue with that. But a dress?

"Are you alright?" Aliyah asked, looking at him with a curious expression.

"Yes, just thinking about how much longer we have to travel." He hoped the lie came out sounding smoother than he felt.

She did not seem to notice, "And how much longer would that be?"

"At least another week to the Vendi Mountains," Josen interjected from where he rode in the lead. "After that we will be taking less conspicuous trails through the mountains, but we know where random villages are located, and we will stop there when we can."

"Yes," Kaino said, "those villages are always *very* welcoming," and he began telling a story about the one time the village leader asked him to marry his daughter. "She was only fourteen!" He said horrified.

"You were sixteen if I recall," Josen said, laughing. It warmed Kaino's heart to hear his friend laugh.

"Yes, but I was much more mature than she was!"

"And are you *still* that mature?" Josen said, shooting his friend a sly glance.

"Oh, most definitely not! That was the last day I ever acted that mature! I left my maturity in that village when I left in the dead of night!"

"She was so heartbroken," Josen said, recalling the expression on the poor girl's face when Josen had told her father Kaino had been sent back on an "important assignment."

"So have you ever thought about marriage since?" Aliyah asked, taking Kaino and, from the looks of it, Josen off guard.

“Me? Married?” He laughed. “I've never been the romantic type. I love the freedom to go where I want and not be tied down.” He laughed again.

“So, you have never...” He was not shocked by Aliyah’s question. He had learned she was not afraid to ask and say things on her mind.

“I’ve been with plenty of women,” he said with a cocky grin. “Enough to know I don’t ever want to be married to one.”

He eyed Josen, who was sitting stiffly on his horse. “What about you?” Kaino asked, turning his attention to Aliyah. “Would you ever want to get married?”

“I almost was,” she whispered. “My aunt sold me to Sir Caldryk under the assumption I was to be his bride.” She looked down at the reins she held in her hand.

“I always pictured myself getting married. Even as a young girl. I was never the one to play with dolls or want ribbons in my hair... but I would listen to my parents talk about their wedding day, and I saw how happy their marriage was. It was something I have always wanted- just not with Sir Caldryk.”

“Did he... do anything to you?” Josen asked.

“He did many things to me,” the bitterness was evident in her voice. “Horrible things, but he never did *that* to me.” She went quiet and Kaino thought she was done speaking, unprepared for what she would say next.

"Instead of even faking a romance, he locked me in a room for days... all to train my powers. He did not want me physically. He wanted me dead."

Josen went still at her words. "What do you mean he wanted you dead?"

"He wanted me to sacrifice myself." There, she had said it.

"Sacrifice yourself? Whatever for?" Josen asked incredulously.

"To bring magic back to Gralanth." Her words were no more than a whisper.

No one said anything in response and the silence was unbearable. She looked down awkwardly at her hands and heaved a sigh at the weight of what she had just said.

"I'm sure he is dead," Kaino said, "but if he isn't, would you like us to kill him for you?"

She paused at that, a gleam to her eye. "No, I don't think I would. He does not deserve a swift death."

"Who said anything about it being swift?" Kaino said, cracking his knuckles for good measure before winking at her. "We are Ringada! We are trained in effective persuasion techniques."

"Would it involve knives?" Kaino did not miss the enthusiasm in her tone.

"If you want it to. Any, ah, specific areas we should mutilate?" he winked at her again. "Although with a little training, you could probably take a crack at him first. Sounds like it could be good for you."

She gave an uneasy laugh. "Well, if he still happens to be alive, *and* we happen to see him, I will let you two know about any areas that need to be particularly mutilated. I would not mind training though, you know, in the meantime."

"I think that is possible," Josen said thoughtfully. "You already have a hunting knife. It would be good to teach you some basic self-defense at least."

"Sounds good," Aliyah admitted. They rode in companionable silence the rest of the morning, not feeling the need to talk, just enjoying the scenery.

***

Josen contemplated Aliyah's words. He had not missed the way she had specifically asked about knives. *What did the bastard do to her?* He did not dare ask. She acted like it was a taboo topic, but he had a vague idea it must have involved her arms.

They stopped for a midday rest, having come to the bank of the Golyth. The river was wide enough for barges to move down it and they saw many, along with fishermen in their smaller boats.

The water was clean and smooth. They left the horses saddled as they grazed near the water's edge.

Josen grabbed the pack of food he had purchased in the small town that morning. He had been able to purchase enough jerky and other non-perishable food items to get them to Vendin, the last major town before entering the Vendis. He had also purchased some bread and cheese for their lunch and dinner that day. He was thankful for something other than travel rations. From the way his companions were devouring their lunch, they were as well.

They dug into the food, eating quickly-anxious to be on their way again. The tall grass swayed in the breeze as the sound of insects and birds could be heard. It was a peaceful place next to the Golyth. The Arthom River in Myral was never this calm. It was the wild twin to the river they sat beside now.

"I need to go relieve myself," Aliyah said as she stood and stretched. She had an embarrassed but nervous edge to her voice, "do we, umm... think any grarg are around?"

"I think you will be alright," Josen said. "Just go over to the trees on the other side of the horses. You should have cover there and we will turn our backs so you can have even more privacy."

She nodded as she headed in the direction he had suggested.

That left him alone with Kaino. *Here it comes...* he had purposefully been trying to avoid Kaino. He did not want to have this conversation with his friend. *Looks like I do not have a choice.*

"So... you bought her a dress..." Kaino looked at him with a slight hint of amusement.

"It wasn't like I planned to get her a dress. I was only going to buy her some functional clothes. But the dress reminded me of her- and we did ruin her other one..." His words fell flat as Kaino gave him a shake of his head.

"Jos, we both know the other dress had already been ruined. It looked like she had cut it to get it off. I just do not want to see you get hurt. She isn't Ellie-"

"Thank you for the reminder." Josen snapped. "What? You think I don't realize she isn't Ellie? I am not trying to replace my wife, Kai. It's just... Aliyah just..." he trailed off, not knowing how to describe what Aliyah was becoming to him.

"She makes you feel things, doesn't she?" Kaino's voice was calm, speculative. "She's pulled you out from whatever dark place you have been in since Ellie's death." He looked at Josen and Josen knew he was using his magic to observe what others might not.

“If it makes you feel better,” Josen said slowly. “She did like the dress, but I realized I toed a dangerous line and I promise to not buy her any additional dresses.”

“I don’t care if you bought her a dress, I just wanted to make sure you realize she isn’t Ellie. She has already gone through horrible things, and she will not want to live through someone else’s romance- it's not fair to her.”

“You care an awful lot about her,” Josen said. “Are you intending on-”

Kaino barked a laugh. “No- I have thought about it and no. I don’t want to get involved in the mess the two of you are in. She also reminds me of my sister— she looks like her too. I wish you the best of luck though.” He added the last part with a wink.

Aliyah was walking back to rejoin them just in time to hear Kaino’s laugh. “What's so funny?” she asked as she sat down on the rock beside Kaino. Josen was relieved she had not overheard the rest of the conversation.

“Oh, Josen was just telling a rather inappropriate joke,” Kaino said. Josen shot him an appreciative glance.

“A joke? What is it?” she asked, as she flashed them both a smile.

“It is too inappropriate for a lady as fine as yourself. We would not want to harass your ears with such humor." Kaino returned her smile with a grin.

"Is it as inappropriate as the one about the farmer and the milkmaid?" She blurted. Both men stared at her. She blushed and then began the retelling of the joke. When she was finished, all three of them were laughing, Kaino even going as far as to hold his sides.

It felt good to laugh. Aliyah's joke had been so unexpected. The laughter poured out of Josen of its own accord. He realized he had laughed more in the past few days than he had in all the time since Ellie was gone. The thought struck him, and he reveled in the joy the laughter brought. He laughed again and felt lighter.

"Maybe you are not as much of a lady as we had assumed! Telling jokes like that!" Kaino said, wheezing with laughter before launching into his own inappropriate joke. They found themselves laughing most of the afternoon as they traveled. Each of them taking turns telling jokes more inappropriate than the last. It made the day pass by in a blur.

When they stopped for the night, they ate the leftover bread and cheese before Kaino and Aliyah went to bed. They had forgone a fire, not wanting to draw unneeded attention. The moon was nearly full and gave plenty of light to see by.

Josen found himself looking at the night sky. He admired the stars, their faint glow like small beacons of hope. Kaino's words came back to his mind, and he looked over to where Aliyah lay, a few feet away. She was curled up in the bedroll he had acquired for her that morning. A small smile played on her lips as she stared at him.

"I thought you were asleep. Did I wake you?" Josen asked. He had not done anything or moved but why else would she be staring at him? He gave her a smile.

"I was admiring the stars and turned over to find you doing the same," she whispered. Then she added a little embarrassed, "I love it when you smile. You don't do it often enough, but your smile fills me with hope."

"Hope for what?" He dared ask.

"Hope that you will allow yourself to feel joy again one day." She gave him a sleepy smile and then yawned as she rolled over.

"You've given me hope that one day I just may," he found himself whispering to himself. "Sleep well Aliyah." Her name was like a caress on his lips, and he leaned over to pull the blankets higher up on her. It was a tender move, one that threw him off guard as he did it. She did not seem to mind as she nestled down in them.

He watched as her breathing became more even and he found himself smiling. He pondered her words the rest of his watch and when it was finally his turn to rest, for once he did not dream.

Chapter Twenty-Two

The next two days passed by quickly as well. They continued their banter and joke-telling. An air of camaraderie seemed to surround them. They talked about their childhoods and what it had been like for them growing up with magic. Aliyah had been amazed to hear Josen's account of almost burning down the nursery as a small child. His cries and tantrums ignited the flame within his blood. It was common for this to happen, but his magic had manifested early, and his parents were quite surprised.

Kaino had been born a farmer's son. She had been shocked to hear how his parents had sent him away as a young boy to be trained with the Ringada. "It is an honor to send a child to Ringard," he had said. Still, the thought of the lone boy climbing the peaks of Ringard made her sad.

She had asked him if he missed his family and from the look on his face, she knew he did, but he said it was not the same. He had gone back a few times to visit them, and his family was different. More children had been born in his absence and they treated him with reverence instead of as a sibling. He did not feel like he had a place with his family anymore and had stopped visiting.

So strange, Aliyah thought. She would give anything to be with her family and here he was saying he felt like he had no place within his own.

She had regaled them with stories of her father and even some stories he had told her as a little girl. They were fascinated by each one. "Who would have thought," Kaino had said after one particular tale. "The mighty Eldris let his daughter do his hair."

"Strange, I know," Aliyah had responded, thinking about her father. It was relieving to talk to someone about her parents. They seemed to care, and Aliyah knew they enjoyed hearing new stories about one of their distinguished role models.

Sharing stories helped the days pass with a blur. She was aware of the mountains edging closer each day. Their peaks rose higher in the sky with each step the horses took. The air was also getting colder as they approached Vendin. Aliyah had pulled on her cloak, realizing how essential its weight and warmth would be.

A little over a week since leaving the inn, the city of Vendin became visible in the distance. It was the largest place she had ever seen, and she brought Raynar to a stop so she could take in the view.

"It is a sight to behold, isn't it?" Josen said from where he had stopped his horse beside Raynar. "It never fails to impress me, the ingenuity of the hands that had formed Vendin- and still do to this day."

"It's," there were no words to describe what lay before her. She had never seen anything like it. "Like something out of a story," she breathed. It was true.

The town looked to be carved out of the mountains. The buildings jutted from one elevation to the next and were painted bright hues that stood out from the gray rock of the mountains. The Golyth river ran right up toward a pass between the mountains. Its body bending and twisting out of sight, glistening in the morning sun.

Aliyah kept her gaze on the city as they continued down the road. The road ran parallel to the Golyth river toward Vendin. Aliyah was thankful to travel on the established route- until the road began to get more congested the closer they got to the city. They went frustratingly slow at times, passing trader's carts and farmers coming in from their fields. What could have taken them an hour to travel took three, and they did not make it to the city gates until late afternoon.

They were eventually allowed into the city, passing through gates as unmovable as if they were mountains in and of themselves. The road turned to cobblestone and the sound of their horses' hooves was drowned out by the noise of the hordes of people along the streets. The calls of merchants trying to sell their wares intermingled with the sound of children playing and women gossiping as they shopped. Strange fragrances assaulted Aliyah's nose, along with familiar scents of spices. No one gawked or was alarmed by the presence of the three Ringada horses. However, Aliyah noted the crowd did tend to part in front of them as if without thought.

Vendin was different than Elwryn had been. This was a city of color and light. Smiles shone on faces and the streets were free of any human waste. Music sounded from the market and Aliyah found herself humming the tune as they continued through the city.

Josen steered his horse up a side road that led higher up the mountain. Aliyah nudged Raynar to follow and was relieved to be off the crowded street. This one was not as packed and allowed

Aliyah freedom to take in the beautiful surroundings.

Houses of stone painted bright hues intermixed with trees from the forest on one side of the road. Each house looked roughly the same, their stone exteriors bulging from the mountain. However, the coloring was what set each of them apart. No two houses on the street were painted the same color. She would have expected it to be gaudy, but its strangeness was alluring.

Kaino had pulled ahead of her, and she realized she had stopped Raynar again to look at the houses. She nudged him forward and he obliged, trotting to catch up with the other two.

They had stopped in front of an orange stone house and both men were dismounting their horses. Aliyah followed suit, still gaping at her surroundings. She did not pay as much attention as she should have to her footing and slipped as she attempted to dismount the tall horse.

Expecting to land on her backside, she was shocked when strong, gentle hands caught her under her arms and her back pressed firmly into a warm chest. She looked up confused and found Josen holding her. Too shocked to pull away, she stayed there in his arms, and they stared at each other for a long moment.

"Are you alright?" He asked without letting go.

"I think so," Aliyah said, not moving. She continued to stare up into his green eyes. He was smiling down at her, and his embrace was warm.

Josen opened his mouth to say something when a wobbly voice called out from inside the house. "Is that my grandson, come to visit his Grandmother Nettle?"

"It is indeed Grandmother," Josen called back, sighing as he let go of Aliyah and stepped around Raynar. Aliyah walked behind him, embarrassed and confused, yet warm from where he had held her.

She met Kaino's eyes from where he stood watching them. "Grandmother?" She mouthed at him. He nodded his head, a bemused smile on his face. Aliyah peeked her head around Josen to view Grandmother Nettle.

The woman was small, a full head shorter than Aliyah. Her fine white hair was worn in a long braid, and she wore a comfortable looking tan dress with slippers. She leaned on a russet cane and peered at the three of them, looking at each one in turn. Deep lines were etched into her tan skin, particularly around her pale blue eyes flecked with gold, which widened in surprise when she caught sight of Aliyah peeking around Josen.

"And you brought a guest! How nice of you! You know how lonely old Grandmother Nettle gets up here all on her own. Come in, come in!" She called as she beckoned them forward.

She held the door open for them. "Lovely, just lovely!" She said to herself as Aliyah stepped into the cozy home.

The house was larger than what Aliyah had gathered from the outside. The front of the house did not give away any of the depth carved into the mountain. They were ushered into a front room where the wide window at the front of the house looked out on the rest of the colorful city below. The room contained a small loveseat and two plush chairs. Josen sat on a chair, motioning for Aliyah to take the spot next to Kaino on the small loveseat across from it. Grandmother Nettle settled down in the other chair, her ancient bones cracking as she shifted to get comfortable.

"Now," she said, addressing Josen, "what brings you back here so soon? Did you find your father?"

"No Grandmother," Josen said, bowing his head, "we were tracking his horse- and we were close-until he let Aliyah escape on it." He motioned toward Aliyah with his hand and the old woman stared at her. Aliyah felt as if she was being exposed, laid bare before this wizened old woman.

"The pain you suffered through, starting at such an early age... It shaped you; I see that..." she trailed off. Aliyah turned, looking alarmed first at

Kaino and then Josen. Both men were staring at Grandmother Nettle.

"Such terror and pain for such a long time. It helped you become something more... something other. Something someone would kill over, or in your case, torture over." The woman's voice was soft, and her eyes were sad as Aliyah turned back and met her pale gaze.

"Such a sad life for one so young, and yet," she paused, "there is so much life left to live," Her piercing gaze left Aliyah's to rest on Josen and she cocked her head. "Yes, much of life is left to live, I think." Aliyah shifted uncomfortably.

"And what do you see of me, Grandmother?" Kaino asked, bemused. His voice broke through the stillness that had settled over them and Aliyah looked down at her hands, feeling relieved.

"You, Kaino, are always an open book. Women, lots of women, but maybe I see you settling down-eventually." She sent him a gap-toothed grin and began to cackle.

"Grandmother Nettle is a seer, someone blessed with the magic to know deeply, and intimately, about those around her," Kaino said, sending Grandmother a grin in response.

"It's the reason I moved out of that cursed Keep and into this brightly colored town- no one knows about my magic! Oh, they suspect I have some sort, knowing I am Myralian, but no one has ever dared ask." She cackled again. "Seers are rare, extremely rare. What was once used for military aid and the betterment of Myral turned into lines of besotted suitors outside my door asking me if the person they were interested in felt the same way." She rolled her eyes.

"Bah! It isn't as if you need clairvoyance to see how one feels about another person! Take my grandson, for example- the way he watches you is evidence he-"

"Thank you, Grandmother," Josen said dryly, cutting her off before she could say anything else more damaging. Aliyah had turned bright red at the comment and dared a peek out of the corner of her eye at Josen. He was just as red-faced as she was, and she could tell he was avoiding looking at her.

"We were hoping to stay the evening with you and grab our mountain gear before heading into the Vendis," Kaino said, trying to dispel the awkwardness in the room, "if that isn't too much trouble?"

"Trouble? I would be honored to have you spend time with me." She used her cane for support as she stood up, bones creaking in protest. "I shall start preparing for dinner- you like Myralian fish fry, right?" She directed the question at Aliyah.

She stared at the woman, overcome with emotion. “Yes, it’s one of my favorites.” Her father had made it for her many times, a recipe he had learned from his time in the Ringada. She had not had it since she was a little girl and had never learned to make it herself.

“I thought so,” Grandmother Nettle said softly, and then, “you may be old, but you are not losing it today, Nettle!” She crackled and continued talking to herself as she exited the room, closing the door behind her. Sounds of a stove being lit and pans clanging came from behind the door.

Kaino began to laugh, first quietly to himself before erupting into loud peals of laughter. “That,” he said, wiping a tear from his eye, “went exactly as well as I had expected.”

Chapter Twenty-Three

Josen shot a glare at his friend as Kaino continued laughing. "It's true, Jos. What did you expect- stopping at your clairvoyant grandmother's house? Did you expect her not to say anything?"

He ignored Kaino and turned to check on Aliyah. He had half expected her to run out of the house, escaping on Raynar. He would not blame her if she did. He would not even try to stop her. Instead, she sat there, silent and unmoving with her face a brilliant shade of red.

Now she was standing at the giant window, her form silhouetted against the orange sunset. Her back was to him. Her hands clutching the hem of her tunic in a tight fist. He went to stand by her, unsure of what to say. They stood there silently, taking in the sights of Vendin below. Streetlamps were being lit on the curving streets, and a small portion of the Golyth could be seen- its waters reflecting the evening sky. The sound of the kitchen door swinging shut was the only sound in the room. Josen did not have to look to know Kaino had left to give them privacy.

"Your grandmother is very..." Aliyah finally spoke, and Josen turned to look at her.

"Annoying and meddlesome?" he offered, trying to read her expression. She was still turned away from him.

"Perceptive," she breathed out. "I have never met anyone who saw me as much as she did. It felt like I was laid bare before her." She shuddered, holding her arms. "It was unnerving."

"I am sorry, I should have warned you before stopping here. I did not think about things she might have construed with our arrival and having you here with us. We are just used to staying here when we stop in Vendin. We left our mountain gear with her when we came through last. We can go stay at an inn tonight if you would prefer."

"That's alright," Aliyah said, meeting his gaze. "It wasn't bad, just unnerving."

She flashed him a smile. "Besides, I wonder what other interesting things she will have to say about *you*, High Protector."

Josen's heart began to beat so fast, he thought it would fly right out of his chest. He took a deep calming breath, and he was sure his face showed the horror he felt at her comment. He tried to think of something to say but his mind had gone blank.

"It's fine," she said, taking a tentative step closer and putting a soft hand on his arm. She took a breath before continuing, "Kaino told me a few days ago. I just wish you would have told me yourself." She looked up at him and he expected to see an accusation in them. Instead, she was looking up at him with concern. "Why didn't you?"

His heart thudded in his chest and his breath caught. "I never wanted the title. I never wanted to sit on a throne and deal out judgment or send others in my place. It gets tiring always being the center of attention. When you met me, you had no idea who I was. You had no idea my title or station. You saw me as someone who could get you to Ringard. Someone who could keep you safe. It had been a long time since someone saw me that way." He paused, taking a shuddering breath.

"You did not treat me any differently and I was afraid you would if you knew. Or even worse, you would walk away- clemency or no." He had taken a step towards her, putting both hands lightly on her shoulders.

"Aliyah, you make me feel things I believed I would never feel again. You told me you hope I will feel joy again, but you are helping me find it. I will admit, Grandmother was not wrong. I do enjoy being near you. Not because of your power or whatever else you might think. You make me happy, Aliyah."

He half expected her to pull away. He was shocked when she stepped closer to him, throwing her arms around him in an embrace. He embraced her back. It was better than holding her outside.

"Josen?" she said, pulling back to gaze up at him. "You make me happy too." She smiled at him, and he went to pull her back into the embrace. He had not felt this elated for quite some time.

"But" she continued, and he felt his heart immediately plummet with that one word. He looked down at her and she put a shaking hand to his face. He looked back at her, fearing the worst.

"I know you still grieve over Ellie," she said softly, lovingly. Pain ran through him at hearing her name and he winced despite himself. "And I am trying to work through my own issues." She took a deep breath and nodded before continuing. "I would like to be friends first. Then, when we both feel ready, I would like to have this conversation again- but only if you still want to."

She looked at him sweetly and he found himself getting lost in her dark blue eyes. From this close he could count the gold flecks in them. She still had her hand on his face and his skin tingled from where she made contact.

Friends. He mulled over the word. It seemed right. “I would very much like to be your friend, Aliyah.”

She gave him an exquisite smile that had his heart racing all over again. “Thank you.” She sounded relieved but then shocked him as she moved closer and placed the softest of kisses on his cheek. She pulled back and walked toward the kitchen.

“I am going to go see if your grandmother needs any help with that fish fry,” she said and she moved through the door, leaving it open behind her.

Josen remained where he was, shocked at her forwardness. He placed a hand over his face where she had kissed him, feeling warm for once in what had been a long time.

***

What did you just do? Aliyah kept asking herself, shocked at her own bravery. *You call him out for not telling you he is the High Protector and he all but professes his love for you. Then you tell him you want to be friends first? What kind of response is that? And then you kissed him?* She was mortified. *What if he does not want to be your friend and your kiss ruined any chance of any form of a relationship?* The thoughts plagued her, and she did not notice Kaino until she had walked right into him.

He steadied her. "Whoa there. Are you alright?" he asked her, giving her a penetrating look.

"Yes, why wouldn't I be?" She tried to sound nonchalant. "Josen and I were just talking, as friends do." She added, unsure why she felt the need to make the distinction.

"Mmhmm..." Kaino said, "and do I need to go check on our *friend*?"

"You can do whatever you would like," she said, tone flippant. She took a step around him and waved at Grandmother Nettle, who had looked up at her arrival.

"Would you like any help?" she asked, ignoring Kaino as he sighed and stepped out of the room to find Josen.

"I thought you might like to help me, I didn't want to presume though," Grandmother Nettle said, handing Aliyah some vegetables to slice before going back to gutting the fish. "Your father used to make this for you quite often, didn't he?"

"Yes, almost weekly," Aliyah said, shocked. She concentrated on the work before her. "He used to let me help cut the vegetables, actually." She smiled now, thinking fondly of the many times she had done this as a youth.

"He was a good man, your father," Grandmother Nettle said. Aliyah realized she must have lived at Ringard when her father had. "I was never shocked he left to be with your mother-

I foresaw it." Her wrinkled hands had made expert work of the fish and she was now slicing them for frying.

"I was the one who had told the elders he should go scout in Gralanth. I knew your mother was Gralanthian, but I didn't know where exactly in Gralanth she resided," she sighed, a slight smile on her face. "Your father had no idea I had meddled with his love life. I could not resist though. I love a happy ending and your father deserved one more than anyone."

"I see..." Aliyah said, trying to comprehend that this woman was responsible for her parents' meeting. "And did you see him dying in a fire?" She asked, the words coming out harsher than she meant for them to be.

"No, I did not. I saw you though." She gave Aliyah another penetrating stare. "I saw that he would have a child, a child that would help bring peace and healing to the world. A child born of both Myral and Gralanth. A child to unite both peoples- but only if she chooses to. It would never be forced upon her; it must be her choice just as it is anyone else's choice and right to make the world better. I just saw she would be more motivated than others in her desire to fight the darkness.

"Imagine my surprise," Grandmother Nettle continued with the broadest gapped-toothed smile Aliyah had ever seen, "when that child I had foreseen over twenty years prior, showed up at my door with my grandson. That I had not foreseen." She shook her head, "But my dear, I am thankful he brought you to me. I am so glad I got to meet you at least once."

"I am glad to have met you too, Grandmother." It was true. Despite what she had told her about herself, Aliyah liked this crazy old woman. It was also comforting to meet someone who knew her father well enough to remember him. They continued preparing the meal in a companionable silence, allowing Aliyah to contemplate Grandmother Nettle's words.

My choice, it will be my choice. So little in life had ever been her choice. She wondered what it would be like to have to make that decision and hoped she would not have to make it anytime soon.

She helped Grandmother Nettle prepare the rest of the meal and set the table. She was sent to "fetch those troublesome boys for dinner" at Grandmother Nettle's request. She found the two men outside taking care of the horses. Neither of them was paying attention and she was able to watch them. Both of their guards were down, and she was pleased to find them joking with one another.

She stood in the doorway, a slight smile on her lips. Kaino noticed her first. He nudged Josen, who turned to look in the direction he pointed. He met her gaze and she found herself blushing and was barely able to get out, "Dinner is ready." She turned and walked stiffly back to the kitchen. *That is going to be a problem. Pull yourself together!*

Talking with Grandmother Nettle had taken her mind off the conversation she had previously had with Josen. She was not ready to have to sit at a small table and converse with him. Something had changed between the two of them and she was not sure she was ready to handle it. Grandmother Nettle was already seated, and Aliyah hurried over to sit next to her. Kaino sat down across from Grandmother Nettle. That left Josen to sit across from Aliyah, where she could stare at him. She tried not to blush, thinking about how she had admitted her feelings to him earlier.

Friends can look at each other, right? They just cannot stare... she caught herself staring at him as he sat down, still in conversation with Kaino, and hoped he hadn't noticed. She tried to stay occupied as she scooped some vegetables on her plate before passing the dish to Kaino. She took a fish off the platter Grandmother Nettle handed her. It smelled delicious.

Aliyah kept her attention down on her plate, listening as Kaino and Josen retold stories of times they had come here as young boys and the trouble they had gotten into- especially in the lake. She was intrigued as they recounted getting caught swimming. They were not in trouble for being in the lake, they were in trouble because they had been caught swimming *naked*.

They laughed, remembering how Grandmother had scolded them, before telling them the next time they wanted to swim naked in the lake, they needed to do it at night when unsuspecting girls were in bed.

"And now, it is their tradition to bathe and swim each time they come to visit me," Grandmother said with a broad grin.

Aliyah blushed thinking about the two men sneaking off to go bathe and swim in the lake. She caught Josen staring at her and it made her blush even harder.

"The fish is delicious, Grandmother," Aliyah said, trying to change the subject. It seemed to work as Kaino and Josen both began praising Grandmother's cooking. Grandmother just smiled and chuckled.

"You two always did like my cooking, almost ate me out of house and home too when you were growing up." She gave them a fond smile.

"So, Josen is your biological grandson...yet you speak of Kaino as if he is also your grandson." It was not a question, but the three of them took it as if Aliyah had asked one.

"Kaino hardly saw his family," Josen began, and she looked up at him, staring into his green eyes. She tried to focus on his hands instead, which he used while talking.

"We began training as Ringada at the same time. He was new and I... well... I needed a friend, someone who did not just want to be my friend because of my father. My parents all but adopted Kaino because of how often we were together." He chuckled. "My mother even referred to him as her 'second son.' My grandmother," he motioned toward Grandmother Nettle, "took him in as well. Every time I was sent here, Kaino would come too."

"It was not right to separate you two lads. Who knew what trouble the two of you would get up to apart? At least if you were together you would get into the same trouble. Much easier to discipline that way," she added, with a wink before using her cane and standing as if intending to clear off the table. Aliyah jumped up to help her.

"No need, my dear," she waved her off with a wrinkled hand, eyes crinkling in delight. "The rule at my house is the women may cook, but the men... the men get to clean up!" She pulled Aliyah away from the table cackling and spoke over her shoulder to the two men. "Have fun cleaning up boys! We enjoyed making a mess!"

The door shut behind them and Aliyah heard Kaino mutter a profanity in Mylarian. "And watch your tongue," Grandmother yelled as she led Aliyah down the hall.

Despite the hallway being stone, it was homey. Sketches and portraits of loved ones hung haphazardly on the walls. It was only wide enough for one person to walk down, so Aliyah followed behind Grandmother Nettle. There were five doors in the hallway, each painted a different color. They stopped in front of a door painted the color of pine.

"This is where you will be staying," Grandmother said, as she opened the door and ushered Aliyah inside.

The room was small but cozy with no windows as it was one of the many built inside the mountain. A bed was pushed up against the far wall, its blankets thick and inviting. A dresser leaned against the wall next to it. The floor was dominated by a plush green rug, a shade lighter than the door.

"It's wonderful," she told Grandmother Nettle, and she meant it. She continued looking around the small room, fascinated by some intricate designs carved into the stone walls.

"This is Josen's room. He will be bunking with Kaino tonight," Grandmother said, pointing at the bright yellow door across the hall. "Now, I know those boys are probably planning to leave early. However, they will not leave until they have had a proper breakfast. Sleep as long as you like. I am assuming you do not plan on swimming with the boys?"

Aliyah shook her head, mortified at the thought. "I think I'm good."

"Well then, I will have them draw you a bath before they leave. They could use the exercise after eating all that food!" She cackled again, turning towards the door.

"Oh no! They don't need to do that. I can draw my own-"

"It is not about whether you are capable, girl. It is about those two doing what their grandmother asks!" With that, Grandmother Nettle hobbled out of the room, closing the door behind her and leaving Aliyah alone with her embarrassment and feeling like a burden.

She sighed and sat on the bed. It was comfortable and she laid back on it. She did not intend to fall asleep, but sleep overtook her anyway. A slight knock sounded on the door sometime later and she bolted upright.

"Come in!" She said, rubbing sleep from her eyes.

"We finished drawing your bath," Josen said, as he poked his head into the room. He gave her a smile as she yawned despite herself. "Grandmother's food has that effect on people."

"You didn't need to draw me a bath," Aliyah said apologetically through another yawn. "I appreciate it, but I could have done it..."

"It was no trouble," Josen said, "and it was an honor. We learned long ago not to argue with Grandmother. She will get her way, no matter what- and for you it was worth it." He gave her another smile and this time she returned it.

"Well then, thank you. I guess I will go bathe and... You have fun swimming." She meant it. She was thankful she would not have to bathe in a nearby lake.

"Will do," Josen said before adding softly, "Good night, Aliyah."

"Good night, Josen." She whispered as he shut the door.

She grabbed her pack from where one of them must have placed it for her on the dresser. She rummaged through it, pulling out fresh clothing to change into. She would sleep in the long shirt Linna had packed for her all those weeks ago. It seemed like another lifetime.

***

The bath was warm and felt amazing. Aliyah relished the heat on her tired body as her aches and pains were soothed. Grandmother Nettle had a variety of soaps to choose from, and Aliyah spent quite some time trying the different scents before deciding on a peach blossom soap. She stayed there, relaxing in the tub, until the water was cold. She grabbed a towel that had been left out for her and dried off before dressing in the long shirt and wool socks she had grabbed from her pack.

Sleep tugged at her as she shuffled out the door carrying her dirty clothes. She nearly dropped them when Josen and Kaino's voices could be heard down the hall. *That was the fastest swim anyone has taken. What did they do- jump in and get out?*

She eyed her door, judging her ability to make it into the room before they saw her or if she should run back to the bathing room. She debated too long, sleep making her thoughts sluggish. Before she had decided, they turned the corner.

"I always find that so refreshing," Kaino was saying. "Nothing like a dip in the lake to-"

Both men stopped and stared at her and her choice of sleepwear. She felt naked standing in front of them.

She flushed. "I was just..." She pointed at her door and they both nodded at her. Neither of them saying a word.

She walked more confident than she felt down the rest of the hallway and only slightly fumbled with the doorknob as she opened the door. Back in the safety of the bedroom, she shut the door behind her and leaned against it, breathing hard.

"Did you see those legs?" Kaino said, with a whistle.

"I thought you weren't interested," Josen responded coolly.

"Just because I'm not interested doesn't mean I can't *appreciate-"* A smack resounded across the hall.

"Ouch!" Kaino yelped before laughing. The sound of his laughter was cut off as the door across the hall closed shut.

Chapter Twenty-Four

Aliyah slept soundly, despite the night's events. It had taken a while for the beating of her heart to slow, but the bed was warm and comfortable, smelling somewhat of Josen. That led her to remember what it had been like to be embraced by him. Their conversation replayed through her head, and it took her awhile to fall asleep.

She rolled over and enjoyed the softness of the bed beneath her. With the room having no windows, it was hard to tell what time of day it was. She could lie all day in this plush bed. She sighed when she heard footsteps outside her door, followed by a light knock.

"Aliyah," Kaino's voice called out. "Breakfast is almost ready. Are you awake?"

"Now I am," she grumbled as she sat up and ran a hand through her hair. It had gotten matted as she slept, and she would have to ask Grandmother

Nettle for a brush. She stumbled out of bed and toward her pack and quickly donned the other set of riding leggings and the purple tunic. She ran her hand over the deep blue dress inside her pack then threw the rest of her clothes on top of it. Pulling the pack tight, she headed out the door and down the hall to the kitchen.

They were already sitting at the table eating. She sat down in the chair she had occupied the night before and began loading food onto her plate. The bacon was delicious. She half listened to what they were discussing. It had something to do with mountain passes in late spring and villages they might want to stop in- especially with the solstice coming up. That caught her attention.

"The solstice?" She tried counting how long it had been since her escape from Caldryk manor. It could not already be the solstice, could it?

"The solstice is a time of great celebration for Myral," Josen said from where he sat across from her. He leaned back in his chair, already finished eating.

"Yeah- it's a time for parties and celebrations. Many people also choose to get married that day," Kaino interjected around a mouth full of food.

"I know," Aliyah said quietly as she fiddled with the hem of her tunic. It took every ounce of restraint to avoid holding her arms.

"Josen, weren't you and Ellie married on the solstice?" Grandmother Nettle asked. "I wasn't able to make it, but I heard so much about it..."

Josen had gone stiff at his grandmother's words, and Aliyah could see he looked pained. She tried to ease the tension, saying the first thing that came to her mind.

"It was supposed to be my death day," She lifted a glass of water to her lips and took a sip, aware of the looks each of them were giving her. Kaino looked perplexed, Grandmother Nettle curious, her eyes seeing more than Aliyah was saying. Josen... Josen looked like he was going to be sick.

"He had a ceremony planned for that day. He did not tell me much, just that I was to... kill myself on behalf of Gralanth. If I did not... well, he had ways to persuade..." She dared meet Josen's eyes. Pure horror filled his features.

"Considering I am not planning to end my existence, I would like to celebrate being a free woman on the Solstice. If that is alright?" She continued to eat, acting as if she had not revealed anything about herself. Josen's gaze was piercing as he took in her words. The silence was palpable, and she was beginning to regret saying anything. She forced herself to swallow another bite of bacon.

"Well, that settles it then," Kaino said, breaking the silence. "We need to get to Ylen by Solstice."

***

They left Grandmother Nettle's in the late morning and headed back down the mountain toward the heart of Vendin. This time Aliyah was prepared for the overwhelming sounds and smells of the city. The streets were less crowded than the day before and she found herself gawking at the wares being sold. Beautifully woven rugs and brightly colored cloaks and headwear were intermixed with pottery, jewelry, and food. It was a remarkable sight.

After deciding to go to Ylen, Kaino had teased her about her hair, which she had completely forgotten about. He had been chided by Grandmother, who then sent Josen into her room to fetch a brush.

It had taken Aliyah all of five minutes to comb through the snarls, yanking the brush hard through her long locks. The two men had winced as they heard the bristles catching, the hair pulling free. Now they waited by the horses as she ventured into the market.

She found a stall that sold brushes and combs, buying one of each with the money Linna had given her. An aching sense of longing filled her as she thought of her friend. She put the money and the items into her pack, fully intending to return to where Kaino and Josen were waiting when the stall across the market caught her eye.

She moved toward it, pushing past people to get closer. It sold several types of weapons. She had seen them gleaming from across the street. It was not the swords that had caught her attention, however. It had been knives. They were of fine workmanship, with elegant sheaths and were in pristine condition. They looked exactly like the knife that had tortured her, the sheaths just a variety of different colors. She would have recognized the elegant design anywhere.

The stall merchant cleared his throat. “Hello! Can I help you find something?”

Aliyah looked at him, wondering if she dared buy one. “How much for the knives?”

The merchant told her the sum and she pulled the money out of her pouch. “I will take two, please.” She indicated the one with the gray sheath and then debated between a green and blue one. She settled on the blue one- it matched the tunic.

After thanking the merchant, she put the items into her pack, hiding them towards the bottom. It was not that she was embarrassed to buy them, she just didn’t want to explain why she had bought them. *They are going to open a conversation I am not sure I am ready to have yet.* She pondered when the right time would be and realized there might not ever be a good time.

Still, today was not the best- not after she had told them what Sir Caldryk had planned for her.

The market was now more crowded, and she worked hard to get back to her friends. They both smiled when they saw her, and Josen looked relieved to see her emerge from the crowd. She mounted Raynar, patting the horse gently on the neck once she was on. She loved this creature.

“Did you find what you needed?” Josen asked.

“Yes. Thank you for waiting.” Her heart sped up as he gave her a smile before leading the way down toward the gate. She urged Raynar to follow. When they passed through the giant gates, she was sad to leave the colorful streets of Vendin behind.

Josen urged his horse to leave the road. There was a trail through the long grass that suggested others had taken this path before them. The path followed the Golyth toward the mountain pass in the distance. There were few others on the trail, and it only took them until midday to reach the pass.

They paused outside the pass before entering. “The path ahead is going to be dangerous,” Josen warned. “We must be on our guard. The grarg could be anywhere, as well as giant beasts. We must proceed with caution.”

Aliyah nodded, afraid to speak. She had heard rumors of the wild beasts that lived in the Vendi Mountains. She grabbed at her hunting knife, wishing they had shown her how to use it. *Maybe I should ask when we stop for the night. Yes, that would be good.*

The horses stepped with trepidation between the mountains. The sunlight, which had been so bright before, did not reach into the pass. It was cooler here. Aliyah pulled her cloak tighter over her shoulders, glad Josen had suggested she wear it before leaving his grandmother's house.

They followed the Golyth as they traveled and stopped for the evening along its banks. The temperature, which had been cool throughout the day, began to plummet as night approached.

Kaino went off in search of firewood and to scout the area. Aliyah and Josen saw to the horses' needs with companionable silence. It felt pleasant to be alone with Josen and not feel the need to say anything. She shot a glance over at him and found him smiling at her from where he was untying some bundles off his horse's saddle. She blushed and fumbled with a knot holding the bundle on Raynar's saddle.

Josen came over to her then, his presence warm beside her. She wondered if he ran warmer naturally because of the fire in his veins.

"Here, let me help you," he said as he undid the knot. The pack fell free and he handed it to her, their fingers brushing as she accepted it from him.

She stared at him wide-eyed, wishing she had not told him she only wanted to be friends. She remembered what it had been like to kiss his cheek the day before and wondered what it would be like to *actually* kiss him.

It seemed Josen had the same thoughts. His green eyes held hers and he reached a tentative hand toward her cheek, tucking a stray strand of hair behind her ear. She leaned into the motion, resting her face on his hand. They stood like that for a moment, and he ran his thumb across her cheekbone where her bruise was fading. It was a gentle touch and it sent shivers down her spine. Josen pulled back.

"We should probably set up the tents before Kaino returns." His voice was full of emotion, and he still held her gaze. He looked like he wanted to do something other than set up tents.

Aliyah had a feeling she knew exactly what that something might entail. *You said you wanted to be friends first and now you are acting like this?* She shook herself and sighed in agreement before walking to where they had deposited the tents.

They would be sleeping in the canvas tents while in the Vendis. It kept away some of the chill and one never knew when it might rain- or snow.

She helped Josen set up the two small tents and he designated one for her to put her bedroll and pack in.

As they were finishing setting up the tents, Kaino appeared with an armful of firewood. He set the load down with a crash and dusted off his hands. “That should be enough for now,” he said, as he walked over to a large rock. He sat down and took a sip from his canteen.

“For now? That is your third load of firewood. How much are we going to need?” Aliyah eyed the substantial pile at the edge of their camp.

“It gets foggy here in the mountains, and fires help keep animals like wolves away,” Josen answered as he began to pile some of the wood. “We will need to keep it burning all night, and you will also appreciate the warmth.” He touched the wood and Aliyah watched the flames from his fingers lap against the wood before catching. It did not startle her as much as it once had.

“What about grarg? Will it give away our position?” She looked nervously around as if expecting one to come lunging out of the mist that was starting to form.

“I would rather deal with the grarg than with wolves,” Kaino piped in. “Wolves and other creatures can be quite vicious. The grarg are some of our least concerns.”

"There really is no other way to Ringard?" She had not thought about asking before, but now, being in the mountains... she wanted out.

"Not without going months out of our way, and that could be even more dangerous as it requires traveling through the Alenth Desert. Miles of dry hot earth and little water. No," Josen sighed, stepping back from the now crackling fire, "this is much safer and faster."

"Oh." She could not think of anything else to say and found herself mesmerized by the flames.

She was less wary of Josen's flames now that she had seen him use his magic often during their travels. It still sent a painful memory through her, but she was getting accustomed to his flames. He did not hurt people for the enjoyment of it. He used his flame for warmth and of necessity- not just because he could. Aliyah had the sense Josen would not mind being without magic if given the choice.

"I was wondering..." Aliyah said between mouthfuls of food Grandmother Nettle had sent with them. Both men turned toward her. "Could you teach me some basic self-defense? I don't want to get caught off guard again if the grarg were to catch up with us."

"We mentioned it earlier, and I am sorry we haven't gotten around to it yet," Josen said contemplatively. "We will have more time each evening now to practice, since it gets darker earlier in the mountains and we don't want to be traveling during the night."

"I can start the training tonight," Kaino offered. "We can work on breaking someone's hold."

"Sounds lovely," Aliyah said, turning back to her food. "Anything I need to know in advance?"

"Be ready to be sore and dirty the next few days."

He was not joking. That evening Aliyah lay on the bedroll sore and exhausted from repeatedly trying to escape Kaino's grasp. He was strong and it was harder than she thought it would be. Her muscles protested as she stretched, a reminder of how badly she had failed. She sighed, trying to get comfortable, knowing tomorrow would be the same.

Chapter Twenty-Five

"Again," Kaino called out, voice demanding. Aliyah's arms shook from trying to break free of his grasp. Her scars burned and pulled with each motion. Kaino had not gone easy on her, and she was grateful for it. However, she was utterly exhausted from kicking and attempting to break his hold.

"I can't." Her arms wobbled again, and she pulled weakly against him. They had been at this for hours.

"Humor me." Kaino's voice had gone from its usual joyful banter to one of stoic instruction. Aliyah missed her easy-going friend as he gripped her arms tighter. "You can do this- even when tired."

She pulled against him again and tried to break his grasp and throw him to the ground. Her muscles locked up and tears formed in her eyes. A gasp escaped as she went down.

"Are you even trying?" Kaino snapped at her as he let go.

Aliyah took a step back, shocked. She *had* been trying. The past few days of training had been rough. Kaino had been showing her how to not only break free of an attacker's grasp, but also how to use the attacker's weight against him and throw him to the ground. Not to mention the elbow jabs and perfectly placed kicks he had her practicing.

Her arms, which had mostly healed on their journey, were still weak from Sir Caldryk's torture. She knew she should be able to continue- she just physically could not. Kaino's frustration took her off guard and she let her exhaustion get to her.

"I'm sorry," she snapped back, having had enough of Kaino's attitude. "I am sorry my lack of arm strength is impeding your ability to teach me. I am sorry that, for reasons outside my control, my arms do not work like they should anymore. I am sorry that I let someone use and abuse me until my arms are practically useless to you.

"It wasn't like I asked him to do it! It is not like I asked for my arms to be mutilated until they are so weak! It is not like I asked to be reminded of that torture each time I try to lift them today!" She had not intended to yell, and horror washed through her as she realized what she had admitted.

"Kai, I didn't-" she said, but he had already turned on his heels and walked away, shaking his head. From the set of his shoulders, she could see he was angry. He did not look back at her as his dark form was soon shrouded in the constant mist.

She sat down on a log with a frustrated sigh, putting her face in her hands. "I'm an idiot," she said to herself and was shocked when Josen came and sat down next to her. Not close enough to touch, but she could feel the heat of his body beside her. He had been keeping watch, letting Kaino instruct without interruption. *Great... he probably overheard.*

"It takes a lot to upset Kaino like that," Josen said conversationally. She did not look up at him. "The only time he gets frustrated like that is when he can see the potential in someone, and they cannot see it themselves. I should know," he gave a dark laugh. "He has been upset with me quite a bit over the past year."

"I wish I could be the way he expects me to," she said, lifting her head up to look at him. He sat closer than she realized and she, once again, found herself staring into his eyes. "I just...It's complicated." She said, forcing herself to look away. She stared at the orange embers of the fire instead.

"Well, we have lots of time tonight since Kaino cut the lesson short. Knowing him, it will take him a while to cool off, but he'll come around. By morning he'll be back to his usual chipper self."

"Are you sure?" Aliyah was worried. She had never seen Kaino that upset before. She had not meant to yell at him- or to make him storm off. He was always so upbeat and kind, but now he felt like a stranger.

"Positive. I have known him for twenty years. He's not one to hold a grudge." He nudged her with his elbow, "and if you want to talk about it in the meantime, I'm here."

She looked at him again and saw immense concern in his eyes. *Well... here goes nothing*. She had wanted to tell them for a while, but how did one explain what she had endured at Sir Caldryk's hand? She opened her mouth as if to say something and then closed it again and began to fiddle with the hem of her shirt.

He moved his hand over tentatively and put her hands in his. She instantly stopped moving. *Breathe*, she had to remind herself to breathe.

He eyed her with compassion and when he spoke his voice was quiet and sincere. "Whatever it is, I want you to know I will not think less of you."

"Do you remember," she began slowly, hands still in his, "about how I said he would make me wear his dresses and be his pet *Wyvanni*?"

He nodded his head, brows furrowing as if trying to piece things together.

"There are a few ways a *Wyvanni* can use their power. We are not like you or Kaino, with magic that can be used at the snap of our fingers. There are very few ways a *Wyvanni* can access their magic." Josen lightly rubbed the back of her hands with his thumb. It was nice and she found herself distracted.

"The first way a *Wyvanni* can use their powers is by boosting or dimming the magic of those around him or her. Sir Caldryk would torture me in what he called 'experimentation' of my power." She looked at Josen. She did not want to go into detail about what the torture had entailed and was grateful when he didn't ask.

He was looking at the fire with her hands still in his. She moved one of her hands away to fiddle with her braid and he entwined his hand with the one he was still holding.

"His experimentation was horrible," she whispered, staring at their hands.

"The other way is more horrible" she paused, and Josen gave her hand a tight squeeze, urging her to continue. "*Wyvanni* can boost the magic of those around them, and for those whose magic lies dormant, it can be awakened. If the *Wyvanni* is unable to boost or awaken someone's magic..." she paused, looking away from their intertwined hands and into his green eyes. When she continued, her voice was less than a whisper. "It can be taken by force." His hand gripped hers tighter as her words sank in.

"How does one take magic by force?"

"The blood of a *Wyvanni* is very potent. If someone were to drink said blood..." she could not continue.

Josen's grip on her hand was painful. She clenched his back, despite the pain. Relieved to have told someone. She waited for him to say something, anything. He did not speak for quite some time, and when he did, his voice was cold. "And how many times did he drink your blood?"

"Almost every day." Flames started to lick at Josen's fingertips, and she flinched, afraid they would burn.

"Josen!" She tried to pull her hand back, alarmed.

He looked down at the flames. Taking deep breaths to calm himself, he was at last able to put them out. It was all in a matter of seconds and Aliyah was shocked to find her hand unscathed. "I'm sorry," he choked, taking steadying breaths. "He drank your blood daily?"

"Yes," she closed her eyes at the horrid onslaught of memories. "He used me to gain the power he craved. For days he locked me in a room, depriving me of necessities, barely letting me sleep. Slicing and burning me to get me to utilize my powers. I would have open wounds and he would make new ones or burn me. Crisscrossing previous ones and never caring how deep he cut. He told me it would all stop- told me the pain would stop if I chose to use my power."

“He would burn you?”

“It was his preferred sort of torture.” She looked down at where their hands were intertwined, as if she could see the flames beneath Josen’s skin. She moved her attention from their hands to his face.

Josen looked back at her, meeting her eyes. With a tentative hand, the one not holding hers, he reached over to tuck the stray piece of hair behind her ear. His hand lightly brushed against her cheek. “I am so sorry you had to endure that,” he said, his voice emotional. He put his hand back in his lap, but Aliyah’s face tingled where he had touched her.

Kaino came stomping back into the camp at that moment. He stopped just outside the ring of light and stared at their clasped hands. Feeling self-conscious, they let go at the same time.

“Leave you alone for a few minutes and you start getting all romantic,” he mumbled, his tone still gruff. He stomped over to where his tent lay and began to go inside.

"Kaino, I-" she began, but he cut her off with a shrewd look.

"Aliyah, I don't want to talk about it right now." His voice was not angry, but it was resigned. She flinched at his response, and he closed the tent flap behind him.

"He's more than disappointed in me, isn't he?" She asked Josen with a sigh. "I really was trying."

"He knows," Josen reassured her. However, he eyed his friend's tent warily before turning back to face Aliyah, who was in mid yawn.

"You should get some rest," he said, nodding toward her tent. He stood up and offered his hand to her. She accepted it and let him pull her up off the log. Neither of them let go immediately.

"Thank you for listening- and for caring," she breathed, looking up at him through her lashes. Feeling suddenly brave, she put her other hand to his face, and then ran a hand through his silky black hair. He closed his eyes at her touch. When he opened his eyes again, she had already extricated her hand from his and was heading toward her tent.

"Aliyah?" Josen called after her. She whirled around.

"Yes?"

"What kind of magic did you awaken in him?" He did not want to say the name of the monster.

She paused, “Fire. I awakened fire.” He could see the pain in her eyes as she turned and ducked into her tent, leaving him alone with nothing but her words and the fire blazing behind him.

***

Fire, of course it had to be fire, Josen fumed. She had mentioned she was burned as part of their experimentation, but he had hoped it was not by the magic she had awakened. He thought of the monster she had been sold to, the many horrors she had endured, as well as what she probably witnessed. It made his blood boil.

He could feel the magic in his blood, calling to him, begging to be used. It pulsed and drummed with every beat of his heart, a staccato rhythm to match her name. *Aliyah, Aliyah, Aliyah,* pulse, pulse, pulse. He felt like he was burning inside. It needed a release, or it would consume him.

He looked around, making sure his two companions were in their tents before approaching the fire. It was not a large fire, in fact, it had even started to go out. He bent over, grabbing more of the firewood and throwing it over the charred remains of the other logs. The logs crackled as the flames licked at them. He put his hand into the flames until it was flat against the log he had thrown in. The fire did not burn him, it never did. He owned the flames.

He closed his eyes, letting the magic pour out of him. It blasted out, a white-hot flame of fury. Anger at what Aliyah had endured was consumed in the burning. With it came something else, a part of him that had been kept shut released.

Feelings for Ellie poured into the flames. Feelings of incompetence, failure, and anguish over her death. The things that ate at him, that fed the nightmares each night mixed with his feelings for Aliyah. The guilt of wanting to move on, despite his love for Ellie. They were released at once.

The flames soared high into the sky, a mighty burning wall. They looked like lithe dancers reaching toward the heavens. It was too much. His pain was too much. The enormity of it forced him to his knees. He sat there; head bowed as the flames raged above him.

He pulled the baby swaddle out of his pocket. Its once white fabric was now stained with dirt from the many times he had touched it. He ran a hand over the delicate embroidery. Everyone had told him he was not to blame for her death. Yet he always felt that had he been there, she would still be alive. He had not been fast enough to reach her, and she was gone. *She is never coming back.* The thought ate at him, and the grief threatened to consume him.

A new thought emerged, one that had been forming and waiting at the back of his mind the past few months. One he had not been willing to consider until meeting Aliyah. *Ellie never expected me to be "enough." She just wanted me to be... me. Broken and all. Now that she is gone, would she want me to be happy? Can I be happy? Can I let go of the guilt I have been holding and find some semblance of peace?*

He knew Ellie would never have wanted him to beat himself up over her death. Grieve her, yes, but she would want him to be happy and still live life. *Happy enough to dance for no reason?* He thought back on Aliyah's words so many nights ago.

Yes, he and Ellie had been that happy. Their love and the life they shared for that brief time was wonderful. He continued to run his hand over the embroidery, remembering the joy he had once felt.

Could he feel it again? Would he allow himself to feel it again? He let out a breath he had not realized he had been holding. It released the last remnants of pain, and with it, the flames diminished until they were nothing more than small embers. He rubbed a hand one last time over the baby swaddle. Then, without hesitation, he stored it away deep in his pack. It was time.

Chapter Twenty-Six

"So," Kaino said, looking at Josen as they put away the tents the following morning. "Holding hands! That's a good first step." He gave his friend a wink.

"Shut up, Kai," Josen growled. He did not want to deal with his friend, who was suddenly chipper despite his attitude the night before. Josen knew Kaino had reasons for being upset the previous night- reasons that had nothing to do with Aliyah but with another trainee. Josen hoped Kaino would tell her.

Josen yawned, exhausted from the night before. It was not that he hadn't slept well. He had not even dreamed. What wore him out was the amount of energy and pain he had released. He yawned and fought to keep his eyes open.

"Hey!" Kaino called, throwing a pair of rolled-up socks at him. Josen's reflexes were too slow, and the socks bounced off his head.

"What-" Josen turned to glower at Kaino. "Why are you throwing socks at me?"

"It got your attention, didn't it?" Kaino said with a self-satisfied smile. "I could have thrown a rock instead. You are lucky my socks were what I saw first."

"What do you want?" Josen's voice was a low growl.

"You sure are touchy today," Kaino tsked before whispering. "What was that about with Aliyah last night?"

Josen looked over to where Aliyah was taking care of the horses. "And don't say you don't know what I mean, because I saw you two." Kaino added.

"Are you going to tell her why you were so upset last night?" Josen countered.

"I will if you tell me about you two." Kaino folded his arms across his chest, eyebrows raised as if waiting for Josen to start talking. Josen knew his friend would never relent and so he launched into a shortened version of the night's events.

"She was just telling me some things about herself- her life at Caldryk Manor. It was awful for her. The things she had to endure..." he glanced at Aliyah again.

"I heard all that. I wasn't that far away- and you two talk louder than you think. But how does that kind of conversation warrant hand holding?" Kaino was genuinely curious.

"It just felt right in the moment. You have been with plenty of women. Haven't you ever just felt something and gone with it?"

"I've felt plenty of things regarding women! The desire to hold hands has never been one of them." He gave a laugh and Josen reached over to smack him.

"One of these days," Josen said with a resigned sigh, "a woman will come into your life and then maybe you will finally realize there is more to her than just her breasts."

"Most women are more than just their breasts," Aliyah piped in, standing behind them. They whirled around, embarrassment shading their features. She shook her head at them as if she were disgusted. "A woman can get a lot of things with her décolletage, but she can't go far without a brain."

Josen tried not to stare at Aliyah's chest but failed. He thought she had a nice one. Not too voluptuous but still evident beneath the blue tunic. He found himself staring and realized that Kaino was doing the same next to him.

Aliyah crossed her arms, a deep frown forming on her face. "Seriously? You two are pigs," she snapped.

"You," she pointed a shaking finger at Kaino, "I am not surprised. However, you," she said, moving her finger to point at Josen, "I assumed you would have at least a bit more decency than to ogle a woman's chest!"

He looked down, shame and embarrassment heating his face. He was shocked when Kaino spoke up, voice light, "Sorry Aliyah, we had just started to see you as one of us- one of the guys. We did not realize you had breasts underneath that tunic."

Josen went cold at Kaino's words. He looked at him, eyes wide with horror and shook his head, willing him to shut up.

"You. Are. A. Pig." Each word was like a white-hot knife. "I hope you meet a woman one day that views you as nothing more than an object of desire and you realize just how hurtful your way of thinking is." She turned and stomped away, picking up her pack and mounting Raynar without waiting for help.

"Smooth," Josen murmured to Kaino, who was looking at Aliyah with wide eyes of his own.

"She knew about my life choices! I can't believe she called me a pig— the nerve!" It took a lot to get under Kaino's skin, and for Aliyah to have done it two days in a row was astonishing.

"I don't think she was judging you," Josen said, as realization dawned on him. "She is speaking from a place of deep hurt, from being seen as nothing more than an object. She already knew about your life choices and has never said anything like that before." He pulled the tent tight and went to attach it to Ember.

"And to think I was going to apologize to her for last night," Kaino huffed under his breath as he mounted Maelstrom. He urged his horse forward, pointedly ignoring Aliyah. She refused to look at him in turn.

Josen eyed her warily as she urged Raynar to follow Kaino. There was a hard set to her shoulders. *This is going to be lovely,* he thought. He hoped at some point the tension would break, but until then, he would let it be.

***

No one spoke for hours. They rode toward Ylen, and they suspected it was another day's journey at least. Solstice was in two more days. Kaino took the lead, trying to find the safest path through the same ravine they had been ambushed in on their way out of the Vendis. Josen did not want to bring it up. Instead, he kept a wary eye on his surroundings as they led their horses carefully through slick rocks and frozen puddles.

Josen also kept a wary eye on Aliyah, making sure she did not fall. Aliyah's mood was still sour, and she refused to acknowledge either one of them. Breath caught in his chest as she slipped slightly on a frozen rock. He began to lunge for her before she righted herself. She heaved a great sigh and shot Kaino a frustrated look as if this was his fault.

Kaino did not notice. He had stopped with his back to them. His horse whinnied nervously at the sudden halt of movement. He looked from side to side, and then turned back to face Josen. A shocked expression on his face. "I can't see," he said, sounding frightened.

"What?" Josen asked, "you can't *see*? You went blind?"

"No- I can see, but I can't *see*. I do not know where to go, I cannot use my magic to lead us. It is there but it's... inaccessible." He tried to sound calm, but Josen knew better.

"How is that even possible?" Josen dropped his reins and pushed past Aliyah to take his friend by the shoulders. "Has this ever happened before?" He knew the answer. Nothing like this had ever happened before.

He tried to draw up his flames and was discouraged when nothing happened. He tried again. Nothing- not even sparks. Like Kaino, he could feel the magic beneath his skin. It called to him. Yet there was something blocking it, a magical dam.

He turned to look at Aliyah. She was standing next to Raynar, an expression of boredom on her face. Her clenched jaw was the only tell she was frustrated.

"Aliyah," Josen whispered, taking a tentative step towards her with palms raised. She looked up, hard eyes meeting his. The gold flecks had fully taken over the blue. She was stopping their magic.

"I know you are mad at us- and you have every right to be," he added. "But we cannot get out of here safely without our magic." Her now golden eyes looked at him skeptically.

"Please," he continued as he took another step toward her, "if we were to get attacked down here, our swords might not be enough. It happened last time we went through here. We were ambushed by grarg." He had reached her now and stopped just short of where she stood.

"Please Aliyah. I know you are more than a pretty face or a *Wyvanni*. You are worth so much more than that. You are funny, and brave, and intelligent. Any man can see that- even Kaino over there," he motioned toward his friend.

"And I am thankful to call someone such as you a friend." He looked at her and saw her trembling.

"I don't know how I did it, I don't know how to let go," she whispered in terror. "I don't know how to make it stop."

He reached for her then and drew her into an embrace. She did not fight him but remained in place. "It's fine," he whispered, face in her hair, as he ran a hand down her back.

"Breathe it in and let it be, accept it as part of you. Then breathe it out, letting it diminish." He repeated the words of many Ringada trainers before him. She melted into him as she did as he said. "It's alright," he said again, pulling her tighter.

He rested his chin on her hair, looking toward Kaino. He felt his magic become more responsive and he saw his friend nod, a relieved smile on his face. "It's fine," he kept repeating to her, and marveled at the fact she was allowing him to hold her.

It was not a romantic embrace, but it stirred something inside of him. The feeling of connection he had been missing since Ellie's death. He had felt it stirring slowly the few other times he had held Aliyah, and now it awakened in full force. He realized he cared about her more than anything else in the world.

He pulled back reluctantly, and she threw her arms around him as if she did not want him to let go. He brought his forehead to hers so he could see into her eyes. The gold was nothing more than small flecks and the blue was deeper than it had been before. She stared up at him, trembling.

"I'm sorry we upset you," he said soft enough for only her to hear. "Not because you were upset enough to dam our magic, but because we hurt you." She stared up at him, and he realized she had stopped trembling.

"Are you well enough to continue traveling?" He asked. Aliyah nodded and stepped back releasing him. She mumbled somewhat of an apology to Kaino before grabbing Raynar's reins and waiting for Kaino to continue leading them.

Kaino shook his head in disbelief before leading them on. They moved with trepidation through the treacherous ravine. It was the fastest way to Ylen but also one of the riskiest. The slick rocks could fell a horse, and they were required to go slow.

Josen flexed his hand, letting flames dance between his fingers not holding onto the reins. *What an experience*, he thought. Magic had always been a part of him. To be cut off from it was like losing a limb. Functional, but you would always know what you were missing.

He watched Aliyah make her way across the ravine, thankful that the worst had seemed to pass. She was lost in thought, and it made her slip a time or two. However, her shoulders were not as stiff, and she didn't seem to be ignoring them any longer. If anything, she looked tired. He knew that tiredness.

He breathed a sigh of relief when they made it out of the ravine and into a grassy field. The air around them was full of fog but the footing was much safer.

"It's about another half a day to travel to Ylen," Kaino said, looking up at the sky. It was too foggy to gauge what time of day it was. "With this intense fog, I suggest we set up camp and wait for tomorrow. I can see the path through the fog, but I cannot watch for danger at the same time."

They agreed to move off the path a little way before making camp. They had left the river behind when entering the ravine, and now their water skins were all the water they had until they made it to Ylen. They gave some to the horses before taking a few sips themselves. They were just beginning to unload packs from the saddles when an ear-splitting howl erupted in the fog.

Josen felt the hairs on the back of his neck stand up as the howl was answered by another, and another. He tied the pack onto his horse, noticing Kaino doing the same. Aliyah had frozen in fear, hands just above the pack. "Aliyah," he whispered from where he stood. She did not look at him. She continued staring at the fog around them as if expecting to see the howling creatures emerge from the fog.

"Aliyah, look at me." This time she obeyed and turned toward him. "We need to run. Get on your horse and run back toward the ravine. When you get there, dismount and search for shelter among some of the bigger rocks. Can you do that, please?" He gave her a pleading look and relief rushed through him as she nodded before climbing swiftly onto Raynar's back.

She nudged the horse back the way they had come, pushing him into a hard gallop. The horse obeyed, fear of the unseen creatures urging it on.

Aliyah had just about made it out of Josen's vision when a dark shape lunged out of the fog at the horse and rider. The horse bucked, bringing its feet down as if to attack the creature. Fear went through him as he saw Aliyah lose her grip and fall off the horse to the ground below. She rolled out of the way of the horse's hooves but came face to face with something out of a nightmare.

Chapter Twenty-Seven

Aliyah stared at the great gaping jaw of the wolf in front of her. Its carrion breath hit her face and she gagged at the stench. She began to back up slowly and was aware of Raynar as he bucked and stomped next to her. Fear of being trampled by her own horse was nothing compared to the fear of the creature before her. The wolf watched each of her movements and its eyes glinted with an awareness Aliyah did not know was possible for an animal to have.

The giant paw of the wolf took a step towards her, matching her movements. She continued to scoot back until her back hit something hard. A boulder- she was trapped. Panic started to rise within her. *So this is how it ends. Devoured by a giant wolf.* The wolf loomed over her now and drool dripped down her tunic. She closed her eyes, bracing for the first bite and the pain that was sure to follow.

Heat rushed past her face. She flinched back as a growl of pain echoed above her. The smell of burning flesh and fur assaulted her nose and she opened her eyes to find the giant wolf on fire. It ran from her, trying to put out the flames trailing up its body. It made it a few steps away before crashing to the ground, a smoldering corpse.

More howls of pain echoed through the fog. Kaino rushed in front of Aliyah, sword drawn to fend off another wolf that had come up to the side of her. He swiped at it, his curved blade a blur. Fireballs shot past her at other wolves that had surrounded them, and Aliyah turned to see Josen fending off wolves with a flaming sword. The wolves began circling him, angry at what he had done to so many of their pack.

The wolves took turns lunging, as they attempted to get through his defenses. Josen met each one head on. The deadly dance continued. Aliyah sat mesmerized. The wolves were starting to edge closer, making a tighter circle around him. Each lunge of a wolf made her stomach churn.

She heard a low growl from her left. She looked up to see a lone wolf stalking toward her. It was bigger than the other wolves, if that were possible. Its gray fur was peppered with white and its eyes glinted red. It was more frightening than the one that had knocked her off her horse.

She stood up, stepping back and grabbing at the knife from her belt. The wolf continued stalking forward, seeing it had an easy quarry. It was only a few feet away from Aliyah when a howl of pain came from one of the wolves circling Josen. He had made contact with one of them, cutting it down. The wolf stalking Aliyah turned its mighty head, a low angry growl emitted from its chest. With a great shove of its feet, it began running toward Josen. It crossed the distance in mighty leaps.

"No!" Aliyah screamed "Josen! Watch out!" She reached toward him, as if to pull the wolf back, preventing it from attacking him. Josen turned towards her, and his eyes went wide as he took in the sight of the wolf. He opened his mouth to say something and then cried out as his whole body erupted into flames.

***

The fire did not hurt- it never hurt. However, Josen was just as shocked as the wolves when his body was completely immersed in flames.

It only took him a moment to get accustomed to the flames before he lunged at the nearest wolf. It yelped as he willed the flames to engulf it. The flames responded as if being urged on by another source. He lunged for the next wolf, and it also was engulfed in flames with hardly a thought. He whirled around to where he had heard a loud growl.

The wolf that had attacked Aliyah was standing behind him, hackles raised, and teeth bared. It lunged for him, dodging his flames. The rest of the wolves backed off, letting their leader fight the burning being who had taken out most of their pack.

It circled Josen and he held his sword up in a defensive position. He dodged out of the way as the wolf lifted its paw to swipe at him. The wolf lunged for him, and he rolled onto the ground to avoid the giant beast.

Standing back up, he spared a brief glance toward Kaino. His friend had just finished off the last of the wolves he had been fighting. Kaino gave him a nod before glancing to where Aliyah stood free of any wolves. She had a look of concentration on her face that neither of them understood, arm outstretched toward him.

Josen turned away from both, making sure the wolf kept its back toward Kaino. *Come on, come on! Look at me.* He baited it. The wolf responded, lunging, coming closer and closer.

Kaino crept forward, low to the ground with his blade held out in front of him. He was lethal. In one swift motion, Kaino leaped from the ground, jumping over a wolf barring his way and landed beside the alpha. His blade slid home and a great wail came from the mighty beast.

Josen rushed the wolf at that moment, shooting flames from his burning arms. The wolf tugged away from Kaino's blade, just as a blast of fire hit it in the face. Disoriented from the pain, it shook its head trying to see. Another blast hit it from the side where Josen had circled around. He sent more blasts at the creature as Kaino kept circling on the other side. Huge crimson drops of blood dripped onto the trampled grass below.

The wolf took one more step before crashing to the ground, nothing more than another smoldering corpse. The rest of the wolves, seeing their alpha taken down, fled through the mist. Josen was aware of them through the flickering flames. He shot a few blasts of fire toward them, not intending to hit any but wanting to ensure they kept running. Soon they were out of sight, melting into the mist.

He looked at where Kaino was panting beside him. It had been a difficult fight— not as hard as some— but creatures like Vendi wolves were tough. He looked to where Aliyah still stood in the same position, arms outstretched toward them, and brows furrowed as if she was concentrating hard on something.

"Huh," Kaino grunted, standing upright, and walking around Josen. "Never seen you go full flame before."

Josen tried to speak but the flames were too thick. He took deep breaths through his nose, trying to will the flames to calm. They resisted. He tried again, imagining the flames winking out like a candle. They did not even flicker in response. He tried a third time, using something he had not done since he was a kid and was learning how to control his magic. He had not thought about the practice in years.

Your magic is an extension of you, it was as if his father was speaking to him once more. *Clear your mind and imagine you are pouring it back into a pot. This pot is where you will keep it until you need it. There, breathe in nice and slow. Do you feel it sliding back into the pot? Keep breathing.*

When you feel every drop of magic is back in the pot, put the lid on it. That will keep it contained until you decide to let it out. You should always be in control of it-not the other way around. Is the lid on? Good. Now open your eyes.

Josen imagined the pot he had kept his magic in all those years ago. He willed his magic to listen, to rest for a time. He pleaded with it to go into the pot as he had as a child. It resisted for a moment before consenting to enter the pot. It was sluggish. It moved slower than it ever had.

He concentrated harder, urging it and shoving it into the pot. When the last drops had receded, he mentally slammed the lid closed. His magic pushed against the lid from the inside.

It was different than when Aliyah's magic had kept it locked up. This was where he stored it, where he imagined it lived inside of him. He was in control. He was also very cold. He opened his eyes and looked down, shock going through him. His clothes were gone. They had been burned away from the flames that had engulfed his body.

Aware of his indecency, he used his hands to cover himself and moved behind Kaino. Aliyah was still watching them but had turned a deep shade of scarlet on seeing him naked. She met his eyes and hurriedly turned away, trying to give him some privacy.

Kaino whistled loudly for their horses before saying, "You usually have better control than that Jos. I cannot believe you burned your clothes off, that hasn't happened in what, fifteen years? And in front of a woman no less!" He laughed, trying to ease the tension.

Josen had gone still- despite the adrenaline coursing through him. He shot a glare at Kaino.

"Oh, calm down Jos- I don't think she saw much. It's not like you were standing there naked for a while. Besides, " he gave a slight laugh, "think of it as more of a... sneak peek."

"Not funny Kai." Josen's voice was hard. "Just turn around and shut up."

The jingling of the horse's reins became louder, and Josen was relieved to see Ember rush over to him.

He grabbed his pack, keeping himself hidden behind Kaino and their two horses. He pulled out the extra set of clothes he had once lent to Aliyah. He pulled them on, noting the way they still smelled faintly of her. Cinnamon and lavender- an invigorating and comforting scent.

Aliyah was still standing with her back to him while she patted Raynar. Was she comforting the horse? He had seen the horse almost trample her in his attempt to escape the wolves.

He pulled thick socks over his feet, realizing with dismay that his boots had burned up with his clothes. *Well, this will be an uncomfortable trip to Ylen.* The thought put him in a sour mood. He put his pack back on the horse and walked over to where Aliyah was tending to Raynar. He waited until he was behind her and then cleared his throat. She avoided looking at him.

"Aliyah, you can look now," he whispered to her. She turned around, keeping her eyes carefully on his face, as if she didn't believe him. The gold was still fading from her eyes, and she had a faint blush to her cheeks. When she spoke, her voice was soft and timid.

"What were those things?"

"Those were Vendi wolves. One of the enormous races of creatures that dominate the mountains. They, and other beasts in these mountains, are attracted to magic. Judging from these, they must have thought we would make a fine meal large enough to feed the pack."

"I see..." she looked away from his face, eyes venturing down the rest of his body. She frowned when she found his feet bootless. "And where are your shoes?"

"I was hoping you could tell me." He eyed her. "I haven't lost control of my magic like that since I was a child."

"I-" she cut off, looking ashamed.

"I'm not mad," Josen said, taking another step towards her and putting a hand on her arm. "You did nothing wrong. In fact, you probably saved us."

"I didn't- I don't know- I was just scared you or Kaino would be hurt." She looked down. "I didn't mean to take control." She shuddered.

"I definitely see the appeal of having a *Wyvanni* around when it comes to combat." He smiled at her before continuing. "Stories say *Wyvanni* were often sent out with groups of other warriors. They would stand back and use their power to boost the magic of those around them. They were also said to be highly trained fighters, but their true worth in battle was in those they saved through use of their power. They shaped it and looked at the bigger picture." He paused.

"All the same, I would prefer to have some advance notice next time." He gave her a slight smile. She looked at him and he was relieved the gold was back to normal in her eyes.

"I made a promise once," she began, voice small. She gripped her arms. "It was to my father when he realized what I was- what I could do. He made me promise I would never, under any circumstance, take full control of another person's magic...and now I have done it twice today."

"I'm sure your father would understand- these were extenuating circumstances."

"Yes, but I liked it," she whispered, looking down. "I liked the feeling of being able to do something when it came to combat."

He brought a hand to her chin, lifting it so she was looking at him. "That is how most of us feel. Magic is addicting. It gives you a rush. It feels like you are-"

"Whole," she finished. He nodded.

"We can work on it some more- when we are both prepared for it. We do not want to get caught off guard like that and I only have so many changes of clothing." He said it as a joke, but he saw her hesitation. "I think it would be good to train, it's only by practicing that you learn to gain control."

Something flashed across her face he could not identify. However, he did not miss the step she took away from him, or the way she curled in on herself.

Kaino had not either.

"Hey Aliyah, if you want to train with something other than fire before we reach our destination-my magic is much less *revealing*. Unless that is what you're going for," Kaino interjected with a wink. He had walked up to them, the reins of Ember and Maelstrom in his hands.

"In my experience there are lots of ways a woman can get a man's clothes off. But burning them off is a new one."

"Thanks Kai," Josen said dryly. Noting the way Aliyah was looking down embarrassed. "Should we make camp? I don't think those wolves will come back and it would be nice to get settled before even more fog rolls in."

They moved apart, pulling items off their horses, and beginning to set up camp. Josen watched Aliyah set up her tent. It had taken him a few nights of showing her how to pitch the tent, but now she could successfully take it down and put it up by herself. He was proud of her. He smiled fondly to himself as he began to build the fire with logs Kaino had gathered. He stopped before setting the wood aflame, remembering what it had been like to be engulfed in fire.

He barely touched a finger to the log, willing his magic to come slowly. It responded with more eagerness than normal, and the flames took with a great whoosh. Aliyah and Kaino looked over to where he knelt in the dirt shocked.

"I think we may need to work on controlling your powers before Ringard, Aliyah."

She grimaced at him. "I thought I had completely let go."

"Maybe I will just avoid using my magic for a while- unless absolutely necessary." He shot her a grin he hoped was reassuring and she gave him an embarrassed one in return before continuing to set up the tent. He dusted off his hands as he stood up. The horses had been seen to, the tents were assembled, and he was exhausted.

"Are you alright Jos?" Kaino asked, noticing Josen's lack of energy. "You don't look like you feel well."

"I think I need to lay down for a little. That fight with the wolves was...draining." He tried to keep from yawning, but one escaped anyway. Aliyah and Kaino nodded to him without speaking as he stumbled into the tent. Sleep overtook him instantly.

Chapter Twenty-Eight

It was his usual dream. The one he had told Aliyah about a few weeks prior. He hated this dream.

Let's just get to the end, get it over with, he thought. He felt like a puppet and the dream some grand puppeteer pulling the strings. It started as it always did, with the ride back to Ringard. He nudged Ember with his heels, willing her to go faster. Froth flew from her mouth as he edged her almost to her breaking point. He pulled ahead of Kaino on the mountain trail, leaving him in the dust.

Ember halted just outside the keep doors. The stone walls surrounding them were covered in blood splatters. Contorted bodies were scattered around the walls. With panic rising within him, he entered the keep, sword drawn and held in front of him. It was dark and the halls were empty of bodies- different than how it had been that night.

His feet moved silently as he made his way up the stone steps. He stopped on the landing at the level his quarters were on. His door was ajar. Light poured out of it, lighting the hallway. It beckoned him forward. He moved, knowing full well what would be in that room. He tried to brace for it, but the dream wouldn't let him close his eyes.

In a few seconds he was at the doorway. He had tried everything to avoid going into this room. Nothing ever worked- the dream would push him in. With a resigned sigh, dreading the sight of what he would see, he took a step into the room.

The room was the same as it had been when Ellie was alive. A vase of fresh flowers sat on the wooden table, their scent mixed with the scent of Ellie- strawberries and fresh linen. It hung heavily in the air, and he breathed it in, relishing something that was distinctly her.

He took his time looking around the room, avoiding the bed. The small window displayed a beautiful sunset outside and the curtains around it blew lazily from a breeze. It stirred the scent around the room. The windows were usually closed in this dream, and he reached up to shut it. The window closed with a clang.

"It's a beautiful day. Why did you shut the window, my love?" He stiffened as warm feminine hands circled his waist. He turned around, not sure what he would find.

She was there with him, breathing and alive. The candlelight reflected off her golden hair. He pulled her into his arms, resting his head on her hair and breathing her in. He relished the feeling of her breath against his skin. She was wonderful and very warm. He pulled her tighter, tears forming in his eyes and whispered in her hair, "I've missed you so much!"

"That's silly," Ellie teased, "I'm always with you!" He stiffened at that.

"No Ellie," Josen murmured into her hair. "You are dead, and I was not enough to save you." The tears came in full force.

She pulled back from him, putting her hands on the sides of his face, so he was forced to look at her. Her pale green eyes looked at him as astutely as they ever had in life. "I know I'm dead, my love. I wouldn't be here if I weren't." He stared at her dumbfounded.

"We only have a little bit of time, Jos. I want you to know," Ellie's voice was emotional, and she ran a delicate hand through his hair. "I loved you and still do with every fiber of my being. Even death cannot change that. But you need to be happy. You need to let me go- you need to let us go." She held a hand to her belly where the baby would have been.

"I don't want to," Josen said, pulling her back into his arms. "I want to stay with you forever."

"You will- but now is not the time. You need to live and where I'm at is not a place for living." Her voice was tender, and she gently pulled back from him.

"My place is wherever you are," Josen whispered, repeating a line from their marriage ceremony. He refused to let her go.

"That might have once been, my love, but there are others who need you."

An image of Aliyah smiling under the stars flashed into his mind.

"She is very lovely and smart," Ellie said, giving him a knowing look. "I like her."

"What?" Josen asked.

"Aliyah. I like her." She gave him one of her brilliant smiles. "Since you can't be with me, I'm glad you can be with her. But don't mess it up!" She said, jabbing him in the chest with a finger.

"Ellie, this is highly inappropriate- wait, you like her?" He gave her a skeptical look.

"Weren't you listening? I want you to be happy! No more moping around. No more self-blame." She took a step closer. "I don't blame you, Jos. My death was not your fault and I want you to know you were enough and you *are* enough.

"No more holding yourself accountable for things that are out of your control! You," she said, pulling his face down as if to kiss him. "Are enough" she breathed against his mouth and then began kissing him passionately.

He held her tightly, aware of every inch of them that touched. He had been on fire earlier but now he felt like he would combust holding her once more.

He had missed her so much. Her tears mingled with his own and he couldn't kiss her fast enough. She clung to him, her small frame holding him steady. For that one moment, everything was right in the world. He had told Aliyah that using magic made him feel whole. Holding Ellie and kissing her made him feel complete.

She was his perfect other half, they fit together like pieces cut from the same wood. Yet...Aliyah was also cut from the same stuff. A different cut than Ellie, but a piece of the same tree.

He felt confused thinking of Aliyah while holding Ellie. He knew Ellie sensed it as she began to pull away. She looked him deep in the eyes.

"Be gentle with her, my love. You must be patient and gentle. She has suffered so many things- things she may never tell you of, and more things will come for her in the future. But she already has feelings for you. I don't know how any woman would not." She sighed, giving him another smile. "You are just that irresistible."

"Ellie, I don't know if I'm ready for that," he could feel her pulling away, she seemed more distant than she had moments before.

"My love, you never will be if you keep holding onto me so tight. Don't be afraid to let go. We will always be with you." She patted her stomach again.

"Ellie, were we going to have a boy or a girl?" He had to know.

"A boy," she sighed, a dreamy look on her face. "He has the cutest dimples and looks a lot like you. I couldn't bring him; it could only be me." She reached up again to run a hand through his hair. "I love you for forever, and even after that."

"I will always love you," he breathed, and pulled her close once more. They held each other for a time, not saying anything. He felt her stiffen and then sigh.

"It's time, Jos," she said, tears forming anew. "My time is up and it's time for me to return. But," she said, putting a finger to his lips to stop his objections. "This was longer than what I expected, and I am thankful for it. I missed you Jos and I'm glad I got this moment with you. Be kind to her and remember, you *are* enough."

She kissed him once more before taking a step back. He didn't stop his tears from falling as she faded out of sight.

The pain of losing her again hit him like a wave and he crumpled to the ground in the chamber.

Tears began to form in his eyes as heat rose within him. His pent-up magic escaped its containment. He let it go fully as he had a few nights before. The heat mirrored the anguish inside of him and he started to shake uncontrollably.

A loud smack rang in his ears. With a start, his eyes opened, and the image of the chamber dissolved. Long hair tickled his face and he realized he was sobbing.

"Josen!" Aliyah's voice was panicked. "Josen, wake up!" He sat upright, knocking his head into hers as she leaned over him.

"Ouch!" She mumbled, rubbing her head, and shooting him a glare. "Now I know why Kaino said to be careful if I ever had to wake you."

"Sorry," he said, rubbing the sleep and tears away with his hands. "What's going on?" He asked, remembering she was panicked.

"Kaino let me take the first watch and I heard you crying out. I wasn't going to wake you, but then your tent lit up and you were on fire again. Well, not completely on fire," she admitted, looking at his pristine clothing. "More like you were beginning to be encased in fire."

He looked around, noting the bedroll was gone, its charred remains beneath him. "I tried calling your name, but you wouldn't respond. So, I..." she held up her shaking hands. Josen's mouth went dry at the sight of them. Her hands were bright red with heat, but not as bad as if she had stuck her hands into flames. These were the burns one might get from touching a hot stove.

"I tried to command your magic to rest," she whispered, "it didn't want to respond, and I had to... I had to," she took a deep breath, trying to calm herself. "Once I reached through the flames, it obeyed. I may have gone a bit heavy on subduing it, though."

He reached inward for his magic at her words and found it slumbering. It was strange. He could feel it there, but it was resting. He gave a mental tug and it responded sluggishly. He stopped before he could make a flame. "Let me see your hands," he demanded, reaching for them.

She let him hold them and he tried to look at them without having to touch them. He didn't want to cause unnecessary pain. He looked up to see her trying to hold back tears. "Does it hurt?"

She nodded, biting her lip.

"I want to try something, it may hurt in the beginning, but it should make your hands feel better. I'm going to have to touch your hands for quite some time though." He looked up at her for approval. She nodded again.

He scooted closer, laying her hands on her lap and placing both of his on top of hers. He sucked in a breath and willed the heat from her hands to enter his. It took longer than normal for his magic to respond, but soon he felt the heat from her hands move into his. She grunted in pain and tears leaked from her eyes, but she held still, letting him continue.

He gently flipped her hands over and continued to pull the heat from them. She watched him through teary eyes. The grimace on her face slackened as the heat diminished. "How does that feel?" He asked, carefully lifting her hands over to inspect them. They were still red, but they felt cooler to the touch.

"Better," her voice croaked, and she gave a shaky laugh.

He didn't let go of her hands and he was surprised when she gave a light squeeze.

"Do you want to talk about it?" She asked, looking up through her long lashes. He knew she wasn't talking about her burns.

"I had my dream, but it was... different," he found himself saying. "It was better than most but just as heartbreaking." The smell of Ellie was still in his nostrils, mixing in with the smell of Aliyah and the charred bedroll. Aliyah gave his hands another squeeze.

"I just realized," she said, horror washing over her. "The swaddle- it must have burned up with your clothes." She pulled her hands away in horror. "I didn't mean to take that from you!"

Josen gave a small jolt of surprise mixing in with fear. The swaddle it had been... *no, I put it in the bottom of my pack.* He reached over, digging through his pack. His hand touched the smooth fabric, and he pulled it out. "It's safe," he whispered. He held it out toward Aliyah, and she touched it gingerly.

"Oh!" She said and gave a relieved smile. "I was so worried it had burned up. I didn't know you had started keeping it in your pack." She cried now in relief and eyed him curiously as he placed it back in the pack. He grabbed one of her hands again in his. She didn't pull away.

"It just felt like it was time." His voice was thick with emotion at the memory of holding Ellie again. Could he do it? Could he be happy?

He gave Aliyah's hand a little squeeze and she intertwined her fingers with his. "Thank you," he told her. "Thank you for everything but thank you for being here with me at this moment."

"Jos, of course I would be here! I wouldn't let you burn everything down without at least trying to wake you first." She smiled at him, and it pierced his heart. It was so much like Ellie's smile. He returned it with a small one of his own before standing up. She stood up with him, their hands still intertwined.

He pulled her out of the small tent. "Want some company on your first watch?"

"It wouldn't really be me watching, would it?" She asked with a laugh, wiping away the remnants of tears. He laughed with her.

They walked over to a spot on the other side of the fire near her pack. He pulled two apples out of his pack, which he had carried with him, and offered one to her. She gladly accepted, biting into the delicious fruit, and he found himself mesmerized by her mouth.

"What?" She asked with a mouthful of apple. It was so unladylike it caused him to laugh. It was a different laugh than the one he had been using. This laugh broke past the barriers he had built around his heart after Ellie's death. It startled him and he laughed again for the sake of it.

"What is so funny?" She said, swallowing.

"You- but just because you are so unlike anyone I have ever known. It's nice."

"So, you're laughing because I'm abnormal?" She gave a mock look of disgust.

"No," he said between laughs, "I'm laughing because you make me happy. Being around you brings me joy."

He felt her stiffen beside him and he turned his head to find her staring at the fire. *Be gentle with her,* Ellie's words rang in his mind. He realized just how close they were sitting and how her hand had become limp in his. He let go of it and she brought her knees to her chest, resting her chin on top of them.

“I didn’t mean to sound so forward,” he said slowly. He turned his body so he faced her. He waited for her to say something, but she just rocked back and forth staring at the fire.

“It’s been a long time since anyone has told me I bring them joy and meant it,” she finally said. “I’m not used to it- being appreciated because of who I am and not because of what I am. It’s... nice.” She wiped away a few stray tears.

He moved closer and put a tentative arm around her shoulders. She hesitated for a few moments before leaning on him, letting her arms and legs relax. Her head rested against his shoulder, and he put his face in her hair, daring to plant a kiss there. It was different from their other embraces. This felt more intimate, more special as he held her in the firelight.

She turned her face upward to look at him and he could see the question in her eyes. He gave her a small smile and pulled her tighter against him, not wanting to answer those questions tonight. She melted into him, and he began humming. It was a soft tune, one his mother used to sing to him as a child. He didn’t notice when she fell asleep, but he continued holding her throughout the night.

Chapter Twenty-Nine

Despite sleeping on the ground, Aliyah was quite comfortable. At some point in the night, she had shifted so her head was in Josen's lap. He stroked her hair, and she smiled, pretending to still be asleep.

"I know you are awake," he chuckled. "Your breathing pattern changed about a minute ago."

She shifted to look up at him from where she lay. "There's no fooling you, is there?" She gave her own laugh.

"Not often," he murmured before shooting her one of his dazzling smiles. She liked this smile- it had become more pronounced over the last few weeks, and it was usually only directed at her. It made her heart skip a beat.

"I'm sorry I fell asleep- I guess I'm not good at keeping watch..." she gave an embarrassed grimace. *Way to go Aliyah. Now they will never ask you to keep watch again.*

"I didn't mind," Josen said, and he seemed sincere. "It was enjoyable to have company."

Kaino stumbled out of the tent at that moment, blinking at the daylight beginning to peak over the mountains. Aliyah sat up, feeling embarrassed at being caught lying next to Josen. She hoped Kaino hadn't seen them.

He looked around befuddled before noticing Aliyah and Josen on the other side of the fire. "Aliyah? You let me sleep all night? What happened to waking me for the second watch?"

Aliyah gave him a nervous smile. "I umm... fell asleep- but Josen was awake by that point and he... kept watch." There was a slight hitch to her voice she hoped he wouldn't notice.

"And why does it look like you slept on the ground?" Kaino asked. With his keen eyes he had indeed noticed the dirt and debris clinging to Aliyah. She flushed.

"Because I burned up the other bedroll last night.," Josen said from behind Aliyah. "She had to wake me before I could burn down the tent or any of our surroundings."

"And why were you burning up?" He gave them both a hard stare, as if expecting something had gone on between them while he had been sleeping. Something had gone on between them, but not what Kaino was imagining.

"Just the usual...my dream. This time it just took me off guard." Josen began, walking over to disassemble the tents. He had his back to them when he continued. "I don't think I will be having that dream again." He nodded as if to himself.

"No one is blaming you Jos- I just haven't ever seen you be this much out of control." Kaino put a comforting hand on his friend's shoulder.

"It's fine Kai. Like I said, I don't think I will be having that dream again." Despite his firm tone, he sounded saddened by that prospect. She shuddered, imagining having to wake him up again. Those flames had been hot. She looked down at her hands. They were still red despite the heat having left them.

"We should get going," Aliyah said from where she still sat on the ground. "You said we would be able to get to Ylen by this afternoon, right Kai?"

As nice as it was last night, I would much prefer to sleep in my own soft bed.

Kaino looked at both of them before nodding. "If we ride hard, we will get there by lunch. Slower than that, we will get there by midafternoon."

"The sooner we get there, the sooner I can get more shoes." Josen said nonchalantly. They all erupted into laughter and agreed it would be worth getting there earlier. In minutes, the camp was disassembled, and they were on their way toward Ylen.

***

Ylen lay below them, nestled among rolling hills. It was more a village than a town, but the small wooden houses looked inviting with smoke curling from chimneys. The fog had dissipated once they entered the Ylenin Valley and Aliyah could see a lake glistening near the village. Small fishing boats were black blobs that cut through its waters.

As they neared the village, the sound of children laughing echoed in the streets. Women and men were hanging solstice decorations on different buildings. Garlands of late spring flowers were intermixed with ribbons hung on doorways. Bright yellow and orange flags hung from second story windows. The smell of baked goods wafted through the air from open windows and somewhere music was playing.

The streets themselves were little more than cleared ground, but Aliyah could tell these villagers took pride in them– they were kept leveled and clean. Many of the villagers stopped and stared at the three Ringard horses and their riders. Aliyah was shocked when many of the villagers began bowing in deference and cries of "Ringada- the Ringada" and "the High Protector! He's here!" were heard through the crowd.

She looked at Josen and Kaino, who were riding a little way ahead of her. They sat up straighter in their saddles as they smiled and waved at those they passed. They had a different air about them she had never seen before.

They seemed larger than life at that moment and she wondered what people thought of the disheveled woman riding behind them. No one paid her much attention, as all eyes were riveted on the two men before her. They rode toward a large building at the end of the street. The crowd had gone silent and followed them with their eyes as they stopped in front of their destination.

The inn was a rotund building with two floors. It had been painted white, but the paint had faded over the years. A wooden wrap-around porch ran along the front of the building with rocking chairs and tables set out on it. A few patrons lounged in the shade, enjoying the summer breeze, and an older woman hung some floral garland around the windows and railing.

A red stable sat across the small yard from the inn. Two stable men leaned against posts just inside the shade of the building. Upon seeing the three Ringada horses, they jogged out to meet them.

The older of the two, a man with graying hair and matching beard, called to them. "Ho there! It is a pleasure to serve the Ringada. Your horses will be well taken care of!" He reached up to secure Josen's reins and his face broke into a wrinkly smile. "High Protector Master Josen! What a pleasure to see you again- and Master Kaino! Always an honor!" He swept them a bow.

"Always good to see you, Ryan," Josen said, dismounting his horse and clapping the man on the shoulder. "Always a pleasure!"

Aliyah and Kaino dismounted as well. "And who is this?" Ryan asked, noticing Aliyah. He reached over to take her hand and placed a kiss on it. "Why, aren't you just lovely, my dear! Such a delight to have a lady such as yourself here."

"This is my sister, Aliyah," Kaino said, throwing a lazy arm over her shoulders. "She is joining us on our travels- said she wanted to see the world." He threw a wink at Aliyah, who was standing stiffly.

"Yes, it's been quite an adventure, traveling with such an exciting group as two Ringada." She managed to say as she gave the stable man a wide smile, trying to change the subject. "Ylen is lovely- I have never seen anything quite so beautiful!"

"Aw Miss- you honor us! Our village is small, but we do know how to throw a party. Will you be staying for the Solstice?"

"That's the plan," Aliyah said with a smile, "as long as the High Protector and my brother don't decide to leave before tomorrow." She threw them a pointed look.

"Leave before the solstice? Why Miss, they are Ringada! The solstice is a big day for them." He leaned conspiratorially towards her and whispered, "it's said their magic is the strongest on that day- the most potent. It's a wonderful day of celebration for them and an honor for our village to host fine men, such as these." He gave her a smile as he pulled back and began to walk away with Josen's horse.

Aliyah watched him go. "I'm your sister, huh?" She turned to look at Kaino, who still had his arm draped around her shoulders. "Anything else I need to know? Any other relations?"

"It's not common for a woman to be riding with someone who is not her betrothed or her family. Also, it will stop people from assuming you are also a fully trained Ringada. That could get... complicated. You truly could pass for my sister- you even look like her!"

"We didn't care about what people thought in Gralanth," she pointed out.

"No, but people in Gralanth generally don't care. Here people assume things and the reputation of Ringada are important to uphold, especially when traveling with the High Protector." Kaino tugged on her braid. "Now come on, sis, we should go inside and get out of this sun.

What would mother and father say if I let you get sunburned?"

Aliyah let Kaino pull her along toward the inn, aware of Josen moving beside them.

"And is it true magic is stronger on the solstice, *my Lord, Master Josen*?" She asked.

"Yes, it is indeed a day when magic is the greatest. And you need not refer to me in such formality unless there are others present, please." He gave her a chagrined smile.

"I had no idea I was to call you that at all- until just moments ago." She gave him a long look. "Should I also bow down to the High Protector? I can get down right here if you prefer." She had stopped walking and was looking at them with both arms crossed. "Listen, I just feel way out of my depth here. Are there any other things I need to be aware of? Any Myralian customs I may not know?"

The two men looked at each other. "Well..." Kaino said, "this is going to be a solstice to remember."

Chapter Thirty

Miraculously, they were able to acquire two rooms at the inn. Aliyah figured it was because she was traveling with the High Protector and another member of the Ringada.

The villagers loved them and gave them the respect one would give royalty. Many people bowed in their presence, and she felt it unnerving. She just hoped no one had been kicked out of a room on their behalf.

The inn was busier than usual as many from outlying settlements had come to the village for the solstice celebration. At least that's what the serving girl had told her when she had shown Aliyah to her room.

Due to the crowded nature of the inn, her room was nowhere close to the one reserved for Ringada members. She didn't mind, at least that's what she had told them.

She hadn't been this alone in weeks. The absence of their presence on the other side of the wall felt odd. *Get used to it Aliyah. Once they drop you off at Ringard, who knows what they will do? They'll probably go off galivanting across the continent looking for Josen's father.* The thought made her sad.

With a flop, she lay on the bed. A sound in the doorway made her sit up.

"Umm, Miss," the serving girl said, her hand raised as if she was unsure of what to do with it.

"Yes, Anne?" Aliyah said, remembering to refer to her by her name. The girl's face beamed when she said it.

"Will you be requiring my services at the moment, or may I be dismissed to go about the rest of my duties?"

Woah! Who does she think I am? Is this the kind of treatment being associated with Ringada brings? Aliyah dismissed the woman politely and was relieved to hear the door click shut.

With a sigh, she stood up and began to survey the room she would be sleeping in for the next few days. It was cozy. The bed was pushed up against the wall below an open window. Pale green curtains fluttered lazily in the warm breeze. A small fireplace was on the other outer wall with a small pile of logs stacked next to it. A dresser rested against the same wall as the door. A porcelain bowl and a pitcher of water sat on it. A mirror was hanging on the wall above that, and Aliyah's haggard appearance reflected back at her.

She was appalled by what she saw. Had she looked like that for days? Never had she felt so dirty and unkempt. She washed with the water from the pitcher. The dirt had caked itself thoroughly onto her face and it took a lot of scrubbing to reveal the skin beneath.

What she saw made her smile. The bruise from weeks prior was completely gone, as were the cuts from when the grarg dropped her. Once she finished removing the grime from her skin, she decided to brush out her hair. It was tangled and she winced as the brush pulled at the snarls.

Once combed through, she decided to leave it down. Her hair had grown long and had a nice wave from the braid it had been in earlier. She also changed out of her tunic and replaced it with the purple one. The blue one desperately needed a wash.

Dressed, she lay back on the bed and was pleased to find it relatively soft. It wasn't the comfiest mattress she had slept on, but it would be far better than the ground. *Would it though?* Aliyah found herself asking. *Last night was rather... comfortable.* She blushed at that, thinking of how enjoyable it had been to curl up next to Josen.

She stood up from the bed, already anticipating lying in it that night. She left her bag in her room before going in search of the men. She found them in the main room, a large space that occupied most of the first floor. A small door led to the back where she assumed the kitchen was located as she saw a few different serving girls haul steamy meat pies and mugs of ale through the doorway.

The room had twenty or so tables that were all occupied by families and friends. Some tables contained games of cards or dice. Aliyah watched fascinated as she scanned the room for her two companions. They were sitting in a corner, watching the other patrons with wary eyes. Neither of them noticed her right away, but both of their faces lit up when they spied her standing at the foot of the stairs.

She moved toward them and was shocked when both men stood up from the table at her approach. She hesitated, wondering if she shouldn't have come to find them. Josen stepped out of the booth, waiting until she was sitting on the other side before taking his seat.

"Let me guess, another Myralian tradition?"

"Not necessarily. It is a great pleasure to show a lady respect," Josen said with a slight smile before leaning over to whisper, "As Ringada, we are expected to show the best manners."

"Ahh...So you did it less for my benefit and more to keep the Ringada reputation secure?"

"More the other way around," Josen said, sending her one of his heart-stopping smiles.

Kaino gave an exaggerated sigh. "Are you two done? I would like to be able to eat our meal without gagging- whenever it gets here," he said, folding his arms with a sour expression.

"Tell me *Brother*, what should I expect of the solstice tomorrow?" She hoped it would shift his mood and she was right. With detail, Kaino began telling her about the Solstice festivities- continuing even once the food had arrived.

"Wait..." Aliyah said, interrupting. "People believe dancing all night long will bring a bountiful harvest come fall?" She had already listened to him tell of the small fair that would be held in the town square and even some different competitions the men would compete in. Apparently, it was a great honor to have a woman you were interested in cheering you on as you competed in log throwing or barrel jumping.

"If it doesn't bring a bountiful harvest, it may bring other things, eh, Jos?" Kaino said, nudging his friend.

"Like what other things?" Aliyah asked.

"Oh, like weddings... births. After a night of dancing and alcohol, things can happen." Kaino said with an odd grin.

"As you know, some people even get married that day," Josen said with a whisper. "It is said those who wed on solstice will have a long and happy life together," he took a breath before continuing, "apparently that is false."

Aliyah reached over to place her hand on his in a comforting gesture. He pulled his hand out from under hers and placed it in his lap under the table. She tried not to take it personally. *Say something clever.* She could not think of anything to say so she took a sip of her ale.

"Well," she said, finally having come up with something to break the silence. "I am glad this girl gets to live to see another day after tomorrow."

"We're glad you aren't planning on dying anytime soon," Kaino said with a laugh. "Instead, we get to see you dance the maiden dance."

"The maiden *what*?" She hoped she had misheard him.

"The maiden dance," he gave her a sly grin.

"What is that?" She had a feeling she didn't want to know.

"All eligible maidens dance a certain dance near the start of the Solstice Ball. It's tradition." Kaino answered. "It's not hard, you dance in a circle and the rest of us watch. The men barrel jump earlier in the day and the women dance in the evening. Sounds fair to me."

"But what if I don't want to do the dance? Can't I just sit out?" The thought of dancing with strangers watching made her feel sick. At that moment, Anne, the serving girl from earlier, approached their table.

"High Protector Master Josen, Master Kaino," She gave them both a flirtatious look. "Will you two be attending the maiden dance tomorrow? It would be a pleasure to dance for the two of you." She gave a flirty laugh.

Kaino gave her a laugh of his own. "We would be delighted to watch you dance. Also," he said, motioning toward Aliyah, "my sister is planning to join but is concerned the dance might differ from where we grew up. Would you have time to show her the steps before the dance? We would be ever so grateful." He shot her a smile that showed her just how grateful he would be. Anne's breathing accelerated and Aliyah looked at her, worried the woman would hyperventilate.

"It would be an honor," Anne said, her voice breathless. She continued looking at the two men. "I will show you this evening after my shift, if that works for you?"

It took Aliyah a moment to realize she was addressing her, as the woman still stared at Kaino.

"Yes. That would be great. Just come up to my room." She watched as Anne nodded, then blushed when her name was called out by another serving girl.

"What was that?" Aliyah shot an angry look at Kaino as Anne walked away. "I don't want to dance in some silly Maiden Dance. Why would you do that to me?"

"Because, my dear sister, I think you will quite enjoy it. It has certain... benefits. Especially if a member of the Ringada were to seek you out after for, say, a later dance?"

Just then, another girl about Aliyah's age walked up to the table. She had blonde hair and was very voluptuous. "Masters Ringada," she said as she nodded to both men. "I was wondering if you two will be attending the Maiden Dance tomorrow?"

Aliyah suppressed a groan. She tried to ignore the woman and was shocked to find Kaino flirting with this one even more. The woman had just barely turned to leave when two more women showed up at their table. The blonde shot the two of them a glare before walking away.

This cannot be happening, Aliyah thought. These two women stayed longer than the blonde and Kino even went as far as to invite them to sit with them. The two girls pushed Aliyah over to the far corner of the booth, so they were sitting across from both men.

When Kaino introduced Aliyah as his "sister" she didn't miss the glance they gave each other as they realized the lack of competition. Apparently, they were sisters, and they had the same annoying laugh. It grated on Aliyah's nerves.

Josen at least seemed to be as uncomfortable as she felt. He would reply when spoken to, but he didn't join in any of the laughter. The two women acted as if they didn't notice. What Josen lacked in cordiality, Kaino more than made up for.

After listening to them compliment Kaino on just about everything, Aliyah had had enough. "Excuse me," she said, trying to get their attention to let her leave the booth.

"Not now dear," the one closest to her said with a dismissive tone, "your brother is telling us a story of how he killed some Vendi wolves."

Aliyah looked at Kaino, who was so enraptured with his story, he probably hadn't even heard the exchange. "Brother," Aliyah said with as much malice as she could muster. "I would like to go to bed. Would you please tell your guests to move out of my way before I *make* them move?"

The two women gave her frightened looks. She gave them what she hoped was a menacing smile and when she spoke, it was through gritted teeth. "Now that it seems my brother is done telling his story for the moment, would you be so kind as to *let me out?*"

With a tangle of skirts, the women slid out of the booth. They breathed heavily and watched her with wide eyes as she took her time to slide as elegantly as she could out of the booth.

Standing, she turned to look at Josen and Kaino. "Masters," she said with a slight bow of her head she had seen others give them. "I bid thee goodnight."

She went to move up the stairs, "Ladies," she addressed the two as if she hadn't just threatened them. "I will see you tomorrow at the Maiden Dance." She moved past them and walked up the stairs without looking back.

A hand pulled on her arm halfway up the steps. She looked back to find Josen staring up at her. "Allow me to walk you to your room?" He asked before adding so only she could hear, "I hate when Kaino decides to entertain."

"That would be delightful, Master Josen." She gave him a smile before taking his proffered arm.

All too soon, they stopped at her door. It felt strange to be doing something so normal with Josen and she wondered if she should invite him in. Not to do anything but talk- it wasn't as if they weren't used to sitting around a campfire talking or... whatever it was they did last night.

She looked down hesitant, trying to get the courage to invite him in, wondering if he thought it would mean something different if she did. Did she want it to be something different?

He shuffled his feet and she realized she was staring at boots. "When did you get more boots?"

She asked, looking up at his face. *So much for my plan.*

"I bought some from one of the merchants here setting up for the fair tomorrow. You sound disappointed- did you like me going shoeless?" He teased.

"I just had this marvelous plan of waking up super early to go buy you boots and leave them outside your door..." She gave him a wan smile. "But now it seems I can sleep in a bit."

"I can let you burn these ones too if you feel the need to buy me boots." He chuckled as he took a step towards her. Aliyah found herself getting lost in his eyes.

He ran a tentative hand down the side of her face and her breathing hitched. *I sound like those blubbery girls downstairs,* she thought.

"Josen," she said softly, trying to keep her thoughts straight. She began wondering again what it would be like to kiss him and realized she did want to kiss him.

He put one hand behind her back, pulling her close. His other hand had moved toward her chin and was tilting it up toward his. "Yes Aliyah?" Her name was like a caress on his lips.

"Are you sure? I know what tomorrow means for you and I don't want you to regret anything. I also don't want to be a distraction. I need to know it's real and I will not be cast aside."

Before he could answer, Anne appeared at the top of the steps. “Lady Aliyah,” she said before realizing what she might have interrupted. Josen immediately let go of Aliyah and took a step away from her. Aliyah felt herself go cold immediately with the loss of contact.

“I’m sorry- I didn’t mean to interrupt,” Anne said, keeping her eyes averted.

“That’s alright,” Josen said in a calm voice. “I was just wishing Lady Aliyah goodnight.” He dipped his head toward Aliyah before walking away towards his room. She reached out a hand and grasped his arm gently.

“I will see you in the morning, Lady Aliyah,” he gave her another dip of his head, this time with a small smile, before he walked away. Aliyah wanted to chase after him and demand to know what he was thinking. She took a step after him when she remembered those women downstairs... she had a job to do.

“Alright Anne, show me your ways.”

***

By the time Anne said she needed to leave, Aliyah thought she was going to pass out. The dance steps weren’t complicated, but they went over them so much that Aliyah’s legs couldn’t take another step. Anne hesitated in the doorway before leaving.

"Lady Aliyah, it's customary for women to wear dresses during this dance." She eyed the riding leggings and tunic Aliyah still wore. "Do you have one or do you need one? I don't want to presume anything- especially of someone who travels with Ringada." she flushed when she mentioned the Ringada.

"Oh yes," Aliyah said, digging through her pack. She ignored the girl's blush, knowing full well the woman had found both men quite pleasing. *Aren't they though?*

Aliyah found herself pondering her latest interaction with Josen as she pulled the deep blue dress out of her pack. The dress was in a sad state. Dust had gotten into her pack at some point and had collected on the silk skirts, which were also wrinkled.

"Oh! That is a gorgeous dress- I mean gown, Miss," Anne said. "I will have it washed and prepped for you tonight. It will be in your room before the Solstice Ball." Aliyah nodded her thanks, handing the woman the dress.

Anne backed out of the room, carefully. Holding the dress as if it would break it by being gripped too tightly.

Aliyah closed and locked the door behind the woman. She debated going to find Josen and figuring out whatever it was between them. She thought back to their conversation in

Grandmother Nettle's living room. She had told him she wanted to give him time, but what if he didn't need it? What if he was ready to move on and she was holding him in place, afraid to get close?

She imagined what it would have been like tonight had she not said anything. He would have pulled her towards him and held her as delicately as Anne had held the dress. She imagined him bending his head down to meet hers until their breath mingled. He would have paused for a moment to look into her eyes and make certain she wanted the kiss.

Impatience would have gotten the better of her and she would have closed the distance between them, taking him by surprise. He'd have pulled her closer then, holding her to him as they kissed. Josen would be gentle and never take more than was given. He would never hurt her.

She felt a tear slip down her cheek and the image of what might have been slipped from her mind. She sighed, walking over to the bed, and sprawling out on it. *One day Aliyah...One day you will not ruin it by talking.*

Chapter Thirty-One

Josen lay in one of the two beds in the room he and Kaino would be sharing. He was not surprised the other man had not come up yet. Knowing Kaino, he would be occupied for quite some time.

He was used to seeing Kaino like this. It didn't bother him. What did bother him was how those two women treated Aliyah.

He could still picture her face, growing red with anger at the general lack of respect they gave her. He snorted, remembering her threatening them and how she looked like she was going to back it up. He wished he had stepped in and said something, but he had been thinking about Ellie.

Be happy, her words came to him again. He thought of Aliyah and how he had almost kissed her tonight. He had wanted to, or at least most of him had. A small part of him still clung to the idea that Ellie was gone, and it was his fault. He had tried to push that thought away, but Aliyah had seen that hesitation.

I don't want to be a distraction. I want it to be real. Her words had cut into him like knives. Was he using her as a distraction? No. Could it be something real? Could he put aside the last feelings of guilt about Ellie's death and love again? Could he choose to make Aliyah happy and by doing so find happiness himself? He hoped so. He imagined dancing with Aliyah tomorrow and found he hoped he would get the chance.

He debated going back to Aliyah's room to explain. He hadn't meant to pull away from her. He feared he had done something inexcusable, and she would reject him. He hoped that wasn't the case. Sleep evaded him for quite some time as those thoughts swirled around his mind. It was a relief when sleep overtook him, and he let himself drift into the blackness.

***

Josen had slept fitfully. He only vaguely remembered Kaino stumbling in early in the morning. He looked at where his friend lay sleeping, just having made it to bed. Josen shook his head as Kaino let out a snore.

Josen pulled on his boots and a smile played on his lips as he thought of Aliyah's boot comment the night before. He was just about to head out the door when a slip of paper sticking out from under it caught his eye. He grabbed it and took it towards the candle to read. It was addressed to "Master Josen." The script was elegant, but unknown. As he began reading, his breath caught.

Master Josen,

Happy Solstice, I hope this finds you well. I heard a rumor you would be attending the Maiden Dance this evening. It would be a great honor if you would come observe me. I will be the one in blue.

With Love,
Aliyah

He reread the letter at least five times. He was shocked at how something as simple as a note from her made his heart race- Ellie had never sent him notes, but then again, he had never sent her any either. This form of courtship had never occurred to him, and it brought a smile to his face. He would have to find a slip of paper and slide it under her door. If he hurried, he could probably catch her before she left to see some of the festivities.

He wished he had kissed her last night. He imagined what it would have been like, her soft lips on his and the feel of her pressed against him. He found himself studying the note once more. She had signed the note "with love" and he wondered if that was how she truly felt. He wrapped the note in the baby swaddle for safe keeping just in case.

He went downstairs to the main room. It was empty. The windows showed a view of the town bathed in pale early morning light. The sun had not even crested over the mountains to the east and the sky was painted in shades of pink and orange. He found the innkeeper, a man named George. He had a giant mustache and a twinkle in his eye and had been here most of Josen's life.

"Ah, Master Josen, I hope you slept well," George said. He was righting chairs that had been stored on the tables for the evening cleaning.

"I slept quite well, thank you," Josen said, keeping his tone light. "I was wondering if I could trouble you for a piece of paper and a quill, if you don't mind. I just need to write a note to one of my friends."

"Ah, that young miss you arrived with? She was down here last night during our evening clean up asking for the same thing." He gave Josen a smile. "She sure is pretty, that one."

"Umm yes," Josen felt flustered. *Aliyah is pretty, and confident, and funny, and charming...*

He was unaware of George leaving and coming back with the writing supplies. The man cleared his throat to get Josen's attention and he jumped at the sound.

"Here you go, Master Josen," the older man said, placing the items on the table. "When you are finished, just leave them right here. I'll put them back when I'm finished setting up this room." Josen gave him a nod and the man walked off, taking down more chairs as he passed.

Josen didn't know where to begin. He was glad George had supplied him with not one but three different sheets of paper. He had a feeling he was going to need all of them.

***

In the end, he only needed two sheets of paper. The first one contained so many scratched out words it was practically illegible. By the time he had figured out what to write, the sun had peaked over the mountains and the room was starting to get crowded. He folded the paper carefully once dried, making sure to write "Lady Aliyah" on the front of it.

He hoped she was still asleep as he slid the note under her doorway. He couldn't see a light under the door, and he took that as a good sign. He was just leaving when he heard a slight cough behind him. He turned around to find himself staring at Aliyah. His heart stopped. He hadn't considered getting caught. Slipping a paper under her door was one thing, but getting caught in the act was another.

"Good morning, Master Josen," she said with a smile."

"Good morning." Why did he have to sound so nervous? He took a deep breath. "I hope you slept well. I was just coming to see if you were up yet and would like to join me for breakfast."

"I would love that." She gave him a smile before adding, "However, I just came back from the bathing room and need a few minutes to get ready for the day. Will you save me a seat at the table? Preferably one not next to a wall?"

Josen nodded. He turned to leave, fearful at what she might think when she found the letter. He did not want to be around when she read it. "I'll save you a seat," he said as he forced himself to keep a steady pace as he walked nervously down the stairs.

***

Aliyah was not expecting to see Josen outside her door. Embarrassment ran through her, and she half expected him to demand what her letter had been about, the other half of her expected him to just give an outright refusal. She had not expected him to extend an invite for breakfast. She had assumed she would eat with them, but they had eaten most meals together since having met. He had acted nervous, and she hoped her letter hadn't been too forward. *Maybe I should have sent that rather inappropriate letter to Kaino.*

After her "dance lessons" with Anne, she had been too pent up to sleep- despite how tired her body felt. She had tossed and turned for a few hours, thinking about dancing, 'for the enjoyment of being pleasing to the eye" as Anne had called it.

It seemed a silly notion to Aliyah. She had spent a good majority of her life trying to "please" others. But could she enjoy it if it were her own choice? What if she wanted to be pleasing? What if she wanted someone to look at her, see her, and enjoy her. Not because of her powers, but because of who she was?

It was that thought that had her getting out of bed hours after the main room had gone quiet.

She had shuffled down the stairs, trying not to disturb any other guests with her movements. The inn staff were still cleaning the large room and they did not seem put out to get her a piece of parchment, quill, and ink. She had taken the items back to her room where it had taken at least another hour before figuring out what to say.

By the time she had completed her note, she was too exhausted to deliver it. Instead, she had curled up on the bed and slept for a few hours before being awoken to a crying baby next door. With a sigh she had gotten out of bed and had decided that it was as good a time as any to deliver her note.

That had only been an hour prior. After dropping off the note, she decided to use the privy and wash up in the washroom. She really could use a bath. She was thankful she had woken up so early, as after she left the washroom other patrons were beginning to line up for it.

But now she was clean and anxious for breakfast. She slid her door open and almost didn't notice the note that had been slipped under the door. *So that's what he was really up to.* Her palms were sweaty as she reached a shaking hand down for the note. "Lady Aliyah" was written on the front in a large scrolling script.

Fear of rejection coursed through her. *Did he have to send it in a note? And then invite me for breakfast?* There was no reason to postpone reading the note if he was waiting for her.

My Dearest Aliyah,

It is a deep honor to receive an invitation to observe a lady as fine as yourself performing the maiden dance. I look forward to the opportunity. May I also be so bold as to request the dance directly following?

With tender affection,

Josen

She had to reread the note a few times due to her shaking hands. She couldn't believe he had accepted her invitation. She hurried to finish getting ready, combing out her long hair and putting it into a neat braid. She would have to figure out how to do something fancier with it later. She found herself bouncing down the stairs as she went to find Josen.

The dining room was jammed with people trying to eat breakfast. She had to stand on her tiptoes to see around a group of tall, cloaked figures sitting at one of the many tables strewn about the room.

Josen was sitting at the same table as the night before and Aliyah was pleased to see Kaino had not joined him yet. *Don't need another repeat of last night, that's for sure.* She laughed to herself as she remembered the rather nasty note she had written to him before ripping it up. It would have done no good to deliver it. She hoped he would have a massive hangover anyway.

Josen stood and smiled at her nervously as she sat down across from him. It was odd to see his uneasiness and it made her feel better about her own awkwardness.

"Hi," she said. *Should I say something about the note? Will he?* She didn't know.

"I ordered you some breakfast. You like bacon, right?" He sounded nervous.

"Among other things," she said, trying to put him at ease. "So, tell me, what are your plans after this fine meal? I am assuming Kaino will not be joining us?"

"No, I don't think he will join us for a while. He got in extremely late last night and barely made it to his bed before passing out- at least that's the position I found him in this morning." He gave a little laugh.

"Serves him right," Aliyah muttered with a roll of her eyes. That caused Josen to laugh even harder.

"I am so used to traveling with him, I guess I have grown accustomed to his... dalliances."

Aliyah raised an eyebrow. "Dalliances... more like annoyances. But if that's what he is into... guess we know why he never wants to settle down." Their food came out at that time, and they dug into it.

"I was hoping you would like to accompany me to the market fair this morning," Josen said quietly as they ate. "Solstice markets can be quite spectacular, and you never know what items of interest one might find. Not to mention the food or entertainment that is set up with it. It would be a great honor to escort you through it."

A jolt ran through her as she thought about strolling through the market with Josen. She smiled at him before responding, "I would like that very much."

He wasn't exaggerating about the market being spectacular.

After they had finished eating, they went out to where the market sprawled across the village green. It was not as big as the one in Vendin, but it was enjoyable, nonetheless. Little ramshackle stalls were interspersed among colorful tents. Somewhere music was being played. The soft sound of flutes and lyres being strummed intermixed with the sound of children laughing.

Josen offered her his arm and she took it shyly. There was something different about holding hands around a campfire in the cover of darkness compared to promenading through the market on his arm. People would see. She found she rather liked the idea of people seeing.

She gripped his arm tighter the closer they got to the market, and he began to explain things with which she was unfamiliar- necklaces with beads believed to ward off evil spirits, perfumes made of flowers that only grew on the tops of the Vendi mountains, figurines carved into wood depicting stories of legend. The food, however, was the most interesting.

It was intriguing how a mountain range dividing a continent could change culture so dramatically. From spiced meats to fruit ciders, and something Josen referred to as candy floss, it was all a unique experience. He had her try them all, finishing off items she did not like. They had just wandered down a different row of the market when Aliyah saw a delicacy she recognized.

“Starcake!” She towed Josen toward the cake, stopping just short of the stall. She hadn’t thought of the pastry in years.

“You’ve seen Starcake before?” Josen asked her curiously.

“Oh, I’ve never seen it, but it was my father’s favorite food from Myral. My mother tried making it for him on many occasions, but each time turned out to be an utter disaster." She wiped a tear from her eye.

"He never seemed to mind. He always took her attempts as an act of love. Although he told me once, he sometimes wished she wouldn’t try so hard because then she would just beat herself up after it failed.” She gave a sad smile. “My father always told me, if he were to bring me to Myral, the first thing he would have me try is Starcake.”

“Well then, I am sorry it was not the first thing I had you try. Had I known, I would have had Grandma Nettle make some for you.” He held up two fingers, indicating they would like two slices of the cake. He placed the silver for them on the counter of the stall before taking a slice and handing it to Aliyah.

She took a tentative bite of the cake, aware of Josen watching her. “Oh! That is divine!” Aliyah said, as she let out a small moan of delight. “I’ve never eaten anything like it!” She found herself taking more bites. It was flaky and sweet and the pudding in the middle was a stark contrast to the outer crust.

Josen laughed before holding out his uneaten piece to her. “Here, I figured anything this good is worth having two of.”

“You don’t want it?” She asked, taking it from his outstretched hand.

“I’ve had my fair share of Starcake in my life- I'd rather enjoy seeing you experience it for the first time.” He had a twinkle in his eye she had not seen before. It made her smile in response.

They began walking again, and Aliyah nibbled at the slice of Starcake. They passed many more stalls containing homewares, rugs, and scarves. There were also many stalls containing wreaths of flowers, not only for the home, but also for hair. Aliyah had seen many women wearing these, the flowers making them look as if they were queens of some faraway floral land.

Josen stopped at one of the stalls and pointed at a floral crown. It was made of greenery intermixed with deep blue roses and small yellow buds. He paid the man behind the counter for it and then placed it delicately on Aliyah’s head.

“Just as I thought,” he said softly, voice catching. “It matches your eyes.”

Her breathing sped up and she half expected him to kiss her right then and there. However, he gave her one of his smiles reserved just for her before pulling her down an aisle they hadn't been down. They were halfway down the aisle when the village bell began ringing, calling for all the eligible men.

"Come on," she said, eyeing him wryly. "Weren't you going to participate?" She tugged him along toward the space designated for the contests and he joined her with a laugh.

Chapter Thirty-Two

Aliyah had never been to a fair before. They weren't common in Gralanth, and her aunt would never have allowed her to attend if they were. She found everything to be so fascinating- especially the men's sports.

She clutched Josen's arm in the gathered crowd. People were cheering those currently competing and she winced as a man missed a barrel and landed hard, falling to the ground. Next to barrel jumping was an obstacle course and archery. further down there was javelin and ax throwing and a dueling ring.

"What shall it be, my lady?" Josen eyed her with a smile. "What shall I compete in to win your attention and prove to you my strength?"

She couldn't help it, she laughed.

"What is so funny?" Kaino said, coming up behind them. Aliyah jumped at his voice.

"Ah- he's awake!" Josen said, giving his friend a broad grin. Kaino looked shocked at seeing the expression on his friend's face. He looked to Aliyah for help.

"Josen was just asking me what event he should compete in," Aliyah said, still gripping Josen's arm. She knew Kaino didn't miss the way she pulled Josen tighter to her as the crowd started to get thicker around them.

"Trying to win her attention, eh Jos?" Kaino teased. "Then I suggest dueling."

"You know we can't duel ordinary men, Kai- it's not proper."

"Then I, Master Kaino, challenge you, High Protector, to a duel," Kaino said loudly enough for those around them to hear. People stopped what they were doing and turned to stare at them.

Aliyah looked between the two men. "Jos, you don't need to fight to win my attention- you already have it." She put her hand to his chest and whispered it so only he could hear.

"I appreciate knowing," he said back quietly. "The challenge has been issued quite publicly though, and it would not be honorable to ignore it." Then much louder, "I accept your challenge."

The crowd started cheering. Aliyah felt herself being pulled along by Josen toward the dueling ring. The crowd pushed at their backs. She glared at Kaino. "Was this necessary?" She asked him.

"Oh quite!" He said with a laugh. "People love watching the Ringada fight. Think of it as our gift to them- and you!" He winked at her.

"Josen please," she turned to him. He was looking stoically at his friend as if assessing him. "Please don't get hurt- either of you."

They had stopped in front of the dueling ring. He turned to look at her and bowed. "My lady," he said before ducking into the ring.

She watched him go with trepidation. The crowd surged around her until she was pressed up against the ropes marking the ring.

"What shall it be?" Kaino called out to the crowd. "Knives? Staves? Swords?" He listened as the crowd erupted into cheering with each one.

"Swords it is then," he began, untying his tunic and pulling it off. Aliyah started, wondering what he was doing and then realized Josen was doing the same. The women in the crowd began cheering even harder.

So that is what Kaino meant when he claimed this was a gift. Aliyah wanted to throttle him. Instead, she found herself staring at Josen. She hadn't seen much when she had burned his clothes away and she had been too embarrassed and far away to notice much detail.

She was unprepared for him to turn and start walking back toward her, shirt in his hand. A collective gasp went through the crowd as he approached her. "My lady, would you be so kind as to hold onto this for me?" He held out his shirt and she took it mutely, staring at a large tattoo that stretched across the left side of his chest. It was the antlered qilin of the Ringada intertwined in vines and flames.

She forced her eyes away from the tattoo to meet his. He was smiling at her warmly. "We'll talk about it later," he said before running a gentle hand down her face and walking away. An older woman next to her sighed and Aliyah looked away from Josen to the woman next to her. The woman was swooning more than Aliyah.

"If I wasn't a married woman," someone whispered from behind.

When Aliyah turned back to the ring, she noticed Kaino had left his shirt in the dirt. The two men faced each other now.

"First to draw blood," Kaino said, addressing not only Josen but the crowd as well. A pit formed in Aliyah's stomach. This was not what she had in mind when she teased Josen about wanting to compete. She watched, unable to look away, as the two men bowed and drew their Ringada blades.

***

Josen wished his friend were still passed out in their room. He had meant what he said about showing off to win Aliyah's attention, but he had not intended on being goaded into a fight with Kaino.

Not that he was worried about losing, Kaino had only bested him a handful of times before and each time he had been distracted by something else. This time he wouldn't be. He threw himself into the fight, dodging out of the reach of his friend's blade and pushing back with his own.

"So," Kaino whispered to him conspiratorially as Josen blocked his blade. "I think we have everyone's attention- especially Aliyah's. What do you say we give them something spectacular to remember."

"What?" Josen asked as he thrust his blade toward Kaino.

"I'm thinking more on the lines of *training*," Kaino said, as he dodged the blade and whirled around without waiting for a response.

I really hope he regrets this, Josen thought as he lit his blade on fire.

***

Aliyah listened to the crowd cheering but didn't understand their pleasure in watching the fight. The men were evenly matched but she still watched horrified as Josen dodged Kaino's attack before meeting him with one of his own. They paused.

Are they talking? She couldn't imagine what they could be talking about in the middle of a fight.

Then Kaino made an announcement. "And now," he said loudly to the crowd. "How about we make this a little more exciting and add some magic?"

Aliyah felt her heart drop. She had seen Josen use his magic many times before, but not against another person. A grarg yes, but not a friend.

She couldn't breathe. All she could see were the flames twisting down his blade. She leaned forward clutching the rope of the dueling ring as the crowd pressed around her clapping and screaming. She could feel someone pressing into her back before being jostled away. She gripped the rope tighter, letting out a gasp as he threw a fireball toward Kaino.

She squeezed her eyes closed, panic rising within her. "You are going to miss it!" The older woman next to her said as she gave Aliyah a nudge.

"Just tell me when it's over," Aliyah said, tears forming behind her closed eyes. Memories of the study came back to her. The heat of the flame being held against her cheek. His voice as he screamed at her to make it bigger. He'd thrown fireballs at her in anger. Always deliberately missing but getting close enough to singe her skin. His hot hands left burns on her arms as she struggled to extinguish his flames-

The sound of the crowd breaking into a frenzy cut through the memories. Aliyah shuddered as she opened her eyes. Josen had Kaino pinned to the ground with his flaming sword at his friend's neck.

"Yield," Josen said, loud enough to be heard over the roaring crowd.

"I yield," Kaino said, and he smacked Josen's boot three times for good measure. Josen extinguished his flames. Both men were laughing as Josen removed his foot and extended a hand to help him off the ground. They shook hands before they turned and bowed to the crowd.

***

Josen was relieved he had finally been able to pin Kaino to the ground. He hated fighting until the first draw of blood and Kaino knew that. It had been nice to let off some energy and he had to admit he had missed sparring with his friend. However, there was a time and place for everything.

He turned to look for Aliyah and saw her holding onto the rope with white knuckles. She had her eyes cast down and looked as if she was going to be sick.

Shouts of "Congratulations High Protector" and "That was quite a show" called out to him as he went to stand before Aliyah. He nodded his thanks to the crowd as he reached her.

"Aliyah?" He said her name gently, and she brought her head up to look at him. Her eyes were completely void of any gold and it startled him more than anything. "Are you alright?"

She nodded her head but didn't speak. Her breathing was shallow and soon gasps started escaping from her mouth.

In one swift motion, Josen jumped over the rope and threw an arm around her. He glared at the still gathered crowd and they gave him room to lead her away. He pulled her back toward the inn but continued walking past it toward the lake, keeping both arms around her. When they made it to the lake, he stopped at its edge and sat down, bringing her with him. She fell limp against him, and he heard her gasping even harder.

"Aliyah? What's wrong? Please talk with me," he put his hands to her face, trying to see. She began sobbing.

He wondered what caused her to react like this and he realized with a start she had already told him so many weeks ago.

Nothing good in my life has ever come from fire. He felt awful.

"Aliyah?" He said her name so quietly he was afraid she wouldn't hear. "I'm so sorry! I didn't mean to frighten you."

She looked up at him and he noted the gold flecks were returning.

"It wasn't you," she gasped between sobs. "It was him! It's what he did to me!" The tears began falling even harder and he was afraid she would hyperventilate.

She took deep shuddering breaths trying to calm the tears and Josen put a comforting arm around her. She slowly melted against him as she had two nights prior.

"I'm so sorry Aliyah, I didn't understand how badly that would upset you. If I had, I would never have let Kaino suggest we fight with magic." He began rubbing her arm in comfort.

They stared out at the lake. Its waters were calm and smooth. The clouds reflected on the water and Josen had never seen anything more serene. He could have sat there for hours.

"Jos?" Aliyah said, turning her head so her cheek was against his tattoo. The feel of her wet cheek against his skin made him realize he was still shirtless.

"Yes Aliyah?" He looked around for his shirt, seeing she still had it in her lap.

"Thank you. I know I'm a mess and I'm sorry if I ruined your victory." She pressed closer and he could feel her breath on his skin.

She pulled back, realizing she still had his shirt. “Sorry,” she said with a slight hint of color to her cheeks.

“It’s alright, Aliyah,” he said as he took his shirt from her and put it back on.

“Can I ask about the tattoo?” She blurted with another blush. She sounded almost back to normal, and he was glad to answer her question.

“It’s the mark of the High Protector,” he began. “When you are named Heir, you are given the tattoo of the vines and a depiction of your magic to remind you where your loyalties lie. When you become the High Protector, the qilin is added to remind you of the weight of your station.”

“Did it hurt?” Aliyah asked, leaning into him again. She put a hand over the tattoo as if she could feel it beneath the shirt.

“The first one did. I was only fourteen when my father named me Heir. My mother had just died, and he worried he would never get the chance to see me raised to adulthood. He had the ceremony performed years before he should have.” He cringed remembering the feel of the needle against his skin.

“I had the qilin completed the day after finding Ellie,” he paused and felt her look up at him. He didn’t meet her gaze. “You saw me just over a year after her death. I know I wasn’t the most civil and

I wouldn't hold it against you if you thought I was rude and disrespectful."

"I figured something awful must have happened to make you so bitter," Aliyah said, still trying to meet his gaze.

"Before then, I was more than bitter. I was numb with anger and hatred. They put the needle to my skin to complete the qilin and I didn't feel anything. I wished I could have felt something-anything other than the grief and anger I felt at the time." He planted a kiss on her hair and looked at her.

"But then you came along, and everything brightened. Everything changed. I found a purpose outside my search for revenge. I found *you.*" He pulled her closer to him.

"I am glad you found me," she said into his shirt. "I am sorry you had to go through all of that to find me, but I am glad to be here with you."

Chapter Thirty-Three

They sat talking by the lake for the rest of the afternoon. It was peaceful. Few others wandered out this far and they were able to just be the two of them, with no reputation to uphold.

Aliyah had never heard Josen laugh so openly, and it made her feel lighter. He showed her a side of him few others got to see, and she felt honored because of it. She wished the afternoon would last forever. But, sooner than she expected, the afternoon was over, and Josen was escorting her back to her room to get ready.

They had just wandered back into the inn when she heard Anne call out to her.

"Miss! Your dress has been laundered and I was just about to take it up to your room!" She shuffled from behind the bar counter holding the blue satin gown.

"Thank you, Anne," Aliyah said, reaching over to take it from her.

"Would you like help with your hair? Not that you can't do your own hair, Miss," Anne scrambled. "I meant it more that it would be an honor to help a lady such as yourself get ready for the evening."

"Oh, that would be quite lovely. Thank you. Will you please meet me in my room?" Aliyah asked with a nod to the woman. Anne gave her own nod and started up the stairs with the dress.

"What station does she think I have?" Aliyah wondered aloud.

Josen laughed. "She saw you with me and suspects there is more between us than the story we originally told. I guess we didn't keep to that story well, did we?"

"Not in the slightest," Aliyah agreed with a laugh. "Although it was Kaino's story, so I guess they still might suspect he's my brother. Lucky me- I get to be related to him," she teased as Josen escorted her up the stairs.

They came to her doorway and stopped just outside it. Aliyah's breath caught as she remembered standing in the same position the night before. She hoped he would kiss her.

He had kissed her plenty of times on her hair or brow that afternoon, but his lips had never strayed further down her face. She looked up at him expectantly.

He laughed at her expression as he grabbed her hand. He bowed to her, bringing his lips to graze the back of her hand. "My lady." The way he said it made her shiver and she smiled at him.

"May I have the honor of escorting you to the dance this evening?" He looked up from her hand to meet her gaze and her heart skipped a beat.

"Yes," she breathed, and he kissed her hand again before standing up and striding away. She watched him go, pleasantly surprised and suddenly very warm. *Maybe it's a good thing he only kissed my hand...*

She fumbled with the door and was relieved when Anne pulled it open from the inside. Aliyah took deep breaths trying to calm herself as she sat in the chair and let Anne start combing through her hair.

"That is a beautiful flower crown, Miss," Anne said, lifting the crown to inspect it. "It matches your dress and your eyes just perfectly. We need to incorporate it for the dance tonight. She began to weave Aliyah's hair up through the crown and into an intricate style.

Aliyah had grown quite fond of the woman during their dance lessons the night before and Aliyah knew she was hoping to impress the man she had been courting for quite some time.

"I suspect he will ask me any day now to marry him. I just don't know what is holding him back," she complained to Aliyah.

"I hope you don't mind that I asked the Masters to watch me. I only did it to make Filb jealous. We have been courting for months- everyone else that started courting around the same time we did is already married. I'm not getting any younger."

"Aren't you my age?" Aliyah asked. Anne went on as if she hadn't heard her.

"Now that Master Josen," she had said, putting the finishing touches on Aliyah's hair. "He seems like he would be a good catch. You are so lucky your brother introduced you! I wonder if he will be proposing tonight! I see the way he looks at you- it can't be that far off!" She laughed to herself as she helped Aliyah up and into the dress.

"It's not like that," Aliyah told her. *How I wish it could be that simple.* "Josen- I mean Master Josen- is a fine catch but he has and is still grieving. I don't think he will be ready for anything like that for a long time."

"What- the woman ran off with his brother? That happened to a cousin of mine. Messed him up for years. He still will not come to family parties. Says he doesn't want to see her. Don't blame her though- he isn't much of a looker, that one."

"No, no. It's not like that at all. The woman, he was married to her and she...died."

"Oh, bless his heart! I had no idea! Well, just think, miss, he must be getting over her if he is willing to be courting you!"

"Courting me?"

"Sure miss! Courting! I saw you in the market today- mind you, I wasn't spying on you, I just happened to be out wandering the market. He bought you Starcake didn't he?"

"What does Starcake have to do with courting?" *Honestly, do I know nothing?*

"Starcake is only shared with those who people care about. It is often customary for couples to buy Starcake for each other as a sign of endearment. Usually, it marks the start of their courtship! It is often eaten again at weddings and other special occasions the couple experiences. Do they not do this in your village?" Anne gave her a perplexed look.

"No... they do not."

"Hmm. Well, the way he looked at you and the way he dueled for you are two obvious signs that he would very much like to court you, Miss. That really was an amazing fight." She looked off fondly, remembering the spectacle the two men had made earlier.

"He didn't tell me," Aliyah whispered, feeling confused. She had been hoping this is where their conversations and feelings had been heading, but if he was giving her obvious Myralian courting signs, she had no clue.

She was relieved when Anne deemed her hair ready and left her alone to get dressed. She carefully undressed and slid into the gown. She stood in front of the small mirror, admiring Anne's work while thoughts of Starcake and courting customs swirled in her mind.

***

There was a small knock at her door a while later and she didn't hesitate before opening it. Josen stood in the hallway waiting for her. He held out a bouquet of flowers identical to her crown. He looked her up and down, a look of appreciation on his face. "These are for you."

She reached out to take them. His eyes went wide, and he sucked in a breath as he took in the mutilation of scars and burns that crisscrossed both arms.

Aliyah pulled her arms behind her back. Josen was staring at her as if he had just seen her for the first time. Shame for what had happened to her threatened to crush her and she couldn't meet his eyes.

He took a step into the room towards her, and she took a trembling step back. *Stupid, so stupid! If only he had gotten me a dress with sleeves!*

"What did he do to you?" He asked, his voice a low growl. His voice sent shivers up Aliyah's spine, and she didn't fight him as he tugged one of her arms towards him.

"When you said he cut into you, I believed it. But Aliyah! He mutilated you! Why didn't you tell us sooner? It's been weeks and we could have taken you to a healer or..." he trailed off, taking in the tears that had formed in her eyes. "Aliyah, I am so sorry!"

He put the flowers on the small dresser before taking her into his arms.

She clung to him, recollection of exactly what she had lived through returning. This was worse than her memory of the study earlier that day. These were physical and his reaction verified how horrific her experiences had been.

She buried her face in his freshly pressed shirt. "The pain is gone. They are just scars," she mumbled into his chest. She felt Josen's arms tighten around her and he held her like that for a while before speaking.

When he did speak, his voice was calmer, soothing even. "You are so brave Aliyah. Few people could do what you did or live through what you have and still smile after." He lifted a hand to her chin so he could stare into her eyes. "You may be the bravest person I know, and it is an honor to be in your presence."

"It is a relief to have shared this part of me," she whispered. "To have someone see me and not be ashamed. I'm broken Jos. I've been broken over and over until I hardly knew who I was anymore. But being with you, I finally feel I can be myself-scars and all." His arms gripped her tighter at her words and she could feel the thundering of his heart against her face.

Music began playing outside in the distance. Her open window let in the slow soft sound that gradually grew as various instruments joined in. Josen continued holding her, lifting her chin so he could stare into her eyes. "I am honored you feel comfortable enough to share your broken pieces and all with me." Slowly he began to sway with her, releasing her jaw to take one of her hands. He brought his other hand to her waist, and she immediately moved hers to his shoulder.

He pulled her in close before leading her into a slow dance. She followed along, hesitantly at first. Her feet soon found the rhythm and she was thankful her father had taught her to dance so many years ago. The slow song turned into a quicker tempo and Aliyah found herself laughing as Josen whirled her around the tiny bedroom. He didn't throw her into deep dips like Kaino had, but he did pull her into him more intimately. She was breathless by the time the song changed.

This new beat was familiar to her, it was the one Anne had clapped out for her as they practiced the steps for the maiden dance the night before. She paused, feeling nervous before stepping back. He let her go with a wry smile and then a look of amazement as she danced just for him.

She moved through the twists and turns as Anne had taught her and brought her hands up to clap at the appropriate times. By the time the dance had ended she was winded but laughing. Josen was still staring at her, as a slow song- the pairing song as Anne had called it- began.

She stepped forward tentatively and took his hand. “I believe you requested this dance specifically?”

He gave her a soft smile before stepping forward and pulling her into his arms once more.

He held her in almost an embrace, and they found themselves swaying to the music. No fancy footwork or intricate twirls- just his arm around her with their hands clasped together. She rested her head against his chest, not caring if the floral crown was crumpled as he rested his cheek on her hair. Occasionally, his arm would tighten around her, pulling her in closer as he kissed her hair. She had never felt happier.

Of course, Kaino had to ruin it.

Neither of them had realized the bedroom door had been left open. Between one slow song and the next, they heard a coughing sound behind them. They both turned to find Kaino leaning up against the doorframe, arms crossed, a look of mock annoyance on his face.

"I've been looking everywhere for you two! The party is out there" he gestured toward the open window. "Yet here you two are having one of your own. The least you could have done was invite me," he pouted.

Josen let go of Aliyah's hand but kept his arm around her. She wanted to punch Kaino for the interruption. Instead, she shot him a murderous glare that he seemed to take in stride. "I'm sorry Kaino-our disappearance from dinner last night didn't bother you, yet the stars above, we didn't join you for the dance." She rolled her eyes at him.

"I was just making sure you two weren't sitting in your respective rooms sulking. It's a party! Now will you please come out there with me? Or do I need to drag you both out by the ears?" He said it with a mischievous gleam to his eye that showed how thrilling he thought that idea would be.

"We will be out in a second," Josen said, giving Kaino an expression Aliyah couldn't read. It seemed, however, Kaino could. He chuckled to himself before turning on his heel and leaving them.

Without letting go of Aliyah, Josen reached over and shut the door. He sighed, "I guess he would have found us anyway. Wish I would have thought of closing the door sooner." He gave the now closed door a look.

"Do you want to go out there?" Aliyah asked quietly.

"Not particularly. Although Kaino will just keep badgering us if we don't." He gave a rueful shake of his head.

"Well then, I guess we had better go out there before he hauls us out of here by force," she said with a laugh, turning to leave. Josen's arm tightened around her.

"Aliyah, wait," he said. The nervous tone to his voice caught her off guard and she turned to look up at him. His eyes were warm, and he held her in place as she stared at them. When he spoke again, his voice was quiet,

"One more dance, please? He will give us that much time."

She gave him a soft smile before taking his hand.

***

Josen had wanted to wipe the smug expression off his friend's face. *Later,* he thought as he turned to close the door behind him. He wanted to reclaim the moment he had been having with Aliyah before Kaino's interruption.

Dancing with Aliyah was pleasant- more than pleasant even. Holding her in his arms made him feel whole again.

She wasn't a replacement for Ellie, those scars left in her absence would always remain. No, Aliyah was more a bright beacon of light in his own personal darkness. She chased the shadows of grief away and gave him purpose again. She made him feel *love* again.

"One more dance, please?" He found himself asking and he was thrilled beyond measure when she accepted. She snuggled in close to his chest, her eyes closed, as they swayed to the music floating up to them. He dared to plant a soft kiss on her brow instead of her hair and she sighed happily before looking up at him. Did he dare?

Tentatively, he let go of her hand to lift her chin, the pose a mirror of what he had attempted to do the evening before. Her breath caught as she stared up at him with her blue eyes, eyes he found himself getting lost in. "Aliyah," he whispered her name like a caress before bending his head down to meet hers.

He had intended for the kiss to be soft, nearly the whisper of a butterfly's wings. He had not expected the way Aliyah would melt into him and kiss him back. Her lips moved in tandem with his and he found himself moving his hand away from her chin and into her hair. He held her even tighter to him, regretting the layers of silk between them. She clung to him, pulling him closer as well.

The rest of the world seemed to fall away while dancing with her. Kissing her made him feel like the rest of the world could burn and he would be unaware of the ashes that remained. He pulled back and found they were both breathing hard, tangled up in each other's arms. He rested his forehead on hers and held her there as the music played on.

“I’ve wanted to do that for a while,” he said as his breathing became more even. He placed another kiss on her brow before continuing. “The more I got to know you, the more I began to have feelings for you. Aliyah,” he was cut off as she leaned up and began kissing him again. This time the kiss was soft, yet somehow deeper.

“Josen,” she said after a while, breaking the kiss, “you have my whole heart. My heart has been yours all along and I am so grateful it was you who saved me that day. You say I’m brave because I can smile after everything I’ve been through? That’s only because you are worth smiling for. *You* Jos- not anyone else.

“I had never been in love until I met you, but I would gladly go through everything again just so I could be with you.”

He brought both hands up to cradle her face. He held her there and looked into her eyes.

"Is it sad of me to say I am thankful for the grarg attacking you?" He began. "Not because you were hurt but because your scream pulled me out of a deep stupor I had been in for so long. Seeing you there, lying motionless on the ground, it snapped something in me. For once, I began to care about something other than my misery. I cried over you that day, thinking we had been too late to save you. And then your eyes opened, and I've been getting lost in them ever since.

"Aliyah," he said, feeling a rush go through him as he said her name. "I want you to know my heart is broken and bruised and I once thought it scarred beyond repair, but it is yours. All of it. You have patched it up and made it something new, something I never thought I would have again. You did that." He pulled her in close for one more kiss and the world dissolved into nothing.

Chapter Thirty-Four

By the time they made it out to the party, the sun had set, and the moon had risen into its place high in the sky. Giant bonfires had been lit and it was by that light people mingled and danced with one another.

The music was louder than it had been inside the inn. Josen led Aliyah through some quick dance steps different from the ones they danced inside. She felt light and airy after their conversation and the dancing added to that effect.

There was something so relieving about having declared how she felt to him. To discover he felt the same way about her was more than she could have hoped for. She knew what today meant to him and she hoped he would look on the solstice with fondness for more than one reason.

She found herself laughing as he threw her into dips and twirls, and she enjoyed the way his laugh wove in and out with hers. Kaino was dancing next to them with a different woman than any of the those that had approached him the night before. Aliyah could see he had a line of girls waiting to dance with him. A few of the girls had tried to ask Josen to dance but he had firmly told them his "attentions were already taken." Aliyah felt bad for the girls but was pleased she was where his attention lay.

Word must have gotten around; they were able to dance with relatively few interruptions. When slow songs were played, he held her close, reminiscent of how he had held her in her room. When the tempo increased, he led her through the footwork. He seemed to be enjoying this almost as much as she was.

"Would you like some food?" He asked, motioning to where the villagers had brought out food to share on long tables. Aliyah nodded and he twirled her over there without breaking stride. They stopped to admire the dishes and he went to grab a plate for them. There on the table lay a few pieces of Starcake. Thinking of what Anne had told her, she didn't notice when Josen had returned.

"I had quite an interesting conversation with Anne about certain... courtship rituals I was unaware of," she said, giving him a smile. "From what I understand, it is customary to give the person you are intent on courting some Starcake?" She bent down and dished a slice onto the plate.

"With that being said, I am giving you this Starcake to erase any doubts you might have about my feelings and intentions towards you." She raised an expectant eyebrow at him until he slowly picked up the pastry. He paused to smile at her before taking a bite. A bit of the pudding got on his nose, and she giggled at the sight.

"What's so funny?" He asked, mouth full of cake.

"You have pudding on your nose!" She giggled again as she watched him reach up and wipe the pudding with a finger. She was not prepared for him to reach out and wipe the pudding onto her nose.

Now it was his turn to laugh as she attempted to wipe it away. It just continued to smear, and he hurried to grab a napkin, dabbing her nose for her.

She turned back to the food with a laugh. "Let's see, any other food with special meanings I need to be made aware of? Or any other food you want to introduce me to?"

He directed Aliyah to find an unoccupied spot on the ground just outside the ring of firelight. Many other couples sat in this same area eating food and conversing under the stars. She also noted the cloaked figures she had seen at breakfast the morning mingling around this area as well.

She wondered how hot they must be continually covered up.

She looked at Josen who was piling food onto the plate. She smiled to herself as she folded her skirts under her, being careful of the delicate fabric. Josen soon joined her, scooting close so his arm was behind her as he leaned back.

"I hope you don't expect me to eat all of that," Aliyah teased, eyeing the overflowing plate of food. "I will not be able to fit in this dress again if I do."

"That would be a shame," Josen said, picking up something that looked like a tart. He held it out to her, "I tried to find food I thought you might not have tried- nothing with any hidden meanings. We leave hidden meanings to things like Starcake." He put the tart into her mouth, and she took a tentative bite. It was even more delicious than Starcake.

"I figure anything you don't want to eat, I will finish off for you," he said with a grin as she took another bite of the tart. He ate a tart of his own before introducing her to other foods. She found she liked most of the food, but she was glad when Josen finished off the plate.

"Ugh!" She said, lying back on the grass with a hand over her stomach. "I haven't been this full in a while." She turned her head toward where he now lay next to her. "I might need a break from dancing for a minute or two."

He continued looking up at the sky and she snuggled closer to him, raising herself on one arm to stare into his eyes. "What are you thinking?" She asked softly.

It took him a while to answer, and Aliyah was afraid he wouldn't. "I'm thinking," he finally said, "about how happy I am. I haven't felt this much joy in... well, a long time." He intertwined his hand with the one she was not leaning on, moving so their hands rested on his chest, right over his tattoo. He let go of her hand, leaving her fingers splayed. She could feel the thump of each heartbeat beneath her hand.

"I'm thinking," he said again, "how feelings like this can either make or break a man. I vowed to myself to never love again. Yet, here I am, fully falling for an amazing woman I was so fortunate to encounter- despite the circumstances."

He shifted to his side and lifted his hand to her face, tracing the shape of her jaw with his thumb. When he spoke his voice was tender, "I'm also thinking I should have kissed you a lot sooner." He bent his head closer, and the tracing stopped as his mouth met hers.

***

When Aliyah made it back to her room, the first light of dawn was peeking over the mountains. Her feet were sore from dancing, and she fell onto the bed in an exhausted heap of skirts and silk. Despite being tired, the night had been wonderful. She had never expected to feel the way she did for Josen, and it filled her with unexpected joy.

Dancing with him, and just being held by him, had a way of making all the dark days of her past worth it. Had she known this was what awaited her at the end, she would have endured anything to get to the point of being held by him.

Kissing him was even better. She smiled as the smell of him lingered on her and she sighed as she tried to get comfortable on the bed. She would change later.

Her body relaxed into a peaceful slumber, and she dreamed she was standing with Josen in a large field. Music began playing in the distance, a soft melody reminiscent of ones played during the solstice. Josen took her into his arms and began moving them in time with the rhythm.

She lay her head against his shoulder, feeling the rise and fall of his chest. Suddenly he was ripped away from her, dissolving into nothing. She stood there; arms stretched out as if she could reach for him. "Josen?"

There was no reply. Instead, she felt her body being yanked every which way, and she lost her footing in the tall grass, falling to the ground. "Josen!" She cried out panicked as she thrashed and bucked at the unseen hands pulling her through the long grass.

"Ah, she was always a feisty one," a cruel voice said, as if from far away. "Should we kill her?"

"Yes let's," another voice said, this one low and gravelly. "We can kill her and enjoy her magic. It's been too long since we have tasted *Wyvanni.*"

"Hush!" Said a third voice, a female voice. "We do what the master has ordered. Then, when he is done with her, maybe he will share some of the scraps with the rest of us!"

She recognized the last voice. Suddenly the dream faded. Gone were the blue sky and tall grass. Gone were the invisible hands. Instead, she opened her eyes to find herself being carried by a figure in a hooded cloak. There were other figures with it, and she realized she had seen these figures at the inn and all throughout the solstice.

Awake, she kicked and thrashed as Kaino had taught her. It threw the hooded figure off balance and she found herself tumbling to the ground. She landed hard and realized her hands and feet had been tied. She tried to roll away as the figure came toward her again. But the floral crown which was still in her hair got stuck in some low hanging branches of the tree, pinning her in place. She yanked and pulled at it but was not fast enough.

The figure loomed over her and hooked an ashen hand around her wrist. The other hand reached up and unhooked her hair and remnants of her floral crown from the branches. As it did, Aliyah was able to see the face under the hood.

"Linna?" Aliyah gasped. Shocked, she didn't resist as Linna pulled her over her shoulder and started running again.

Anger at what had been done to her friend coursed through her. Fear of what they might do to her hit her next and she started to struggle harder against Linna's grip. With an exasperated sigh, another grarg came up behind Linna and held a dark cloth to Aliyah's nose. Then the world went dark.

Chapter Thirty-Five

It had taken Josen quite a while to fall asleep after leaving Aliyah at her door. Their parting kiss had been tender and full of promise.

Oh Aliyah, he thought with a sigh. *You dangerously brave woman.*

He had meant what he told her. He had never expected to feel so happy again. Yet here he was, falling in love with her. He was glad to have admitted it at last. To find out she felt the same way in return... it was more than he had ever hoped for.

Kaino let loose a rather loud snore from where he lay sprawled out over the mattress. *At least this time he made it to the mattress and isn't lying on the floor.* He rolled his eyes at his sleeping friend as another loud series of snores commenced.

Stretching, Josen pulled aside the tan curtain to see what time of day it was, it was almost midday.

He stood up and put his boots on, intending to go check on Aliyah. He didn't want to disturb her, but if she was up, maybe she would want to go for a stroll?

He walked down the long hall to her room, noticing how quiet the inn was as its patrons slept off their solstice fun. He knocked quietly on her door and was startled when it swung open.

"Aliyah?" He called out softly as he pushed the door fully open. Instead of finding her asleep in her bed, he found twisted bed sheets thrown on the floor. Her pack lay where she had left it and her boots were next to it.

He backed out of the room, his worst fears running through his mind. *Aliyah taken. Aliyah killed. Aliyah gone.* He thought he was going to vomit. He stumbled back to his room, throwing open the door with enough force to rattle the mirror that hung above the small dresser.

"Kaino!" He shook his friend awake, the panic rising in his voice. Kaino responded by grabbing a pillow and covering his head. Josen only shoved his friend harder. "Kaino, wake up! Aliyah is gone!"

Kaino's eyes opened groggily. "What?" He said with a yawn.

"Aliyah! She isn't in her room!

"Are you sure she isn't just in the privy?" Kaino asked, rubbing the sleep from his eyes.

"Will you just come look please?" Josen's voice had an edge to it Kaino hadn't heard in a while. It got Kaino out of bed. He rushed down the hall, not caring to get fully dressed. He skidded to a stop outside her door.

"You're right," Kaino breathed as he entered the room. His eyes roamed the room, looking for clues. "We know the grarg have been after her, but how did they get past our defenses? Why now? We haven't seen any grarg for weeks!"

"I don't know, but do you think you will be able to track her?" Worry clouded his voice, and he didn't notice the flames that were starting to twist up his arms.

"Jos, we will find her," Kaino said, putting a hand on his friend's shoulder before walking back toward the room. "Meet me outside with the horses in five minutes. There is going to be hell to pay."

Josen watched his friend stalk back toward their room before grabbing Aliyah's pack and boots and going down the stairs himself. He entered the dining room to find it completely spotless, none of the serving staff in sight. He was just heading past the last row of tables when he heard a low moan. He turned to find George lying face down on the ground.

He knelt next to the man, feeling for a pulse. The steady beat of the man's heart thumped beneath his fingers. He rolled the man over onto his back. As he did so, the man woke up.

"What-" George began, looking up at Josen groggily. Then recollection set in. "Grarg! They stormed through the door and knocked me upside the head!" He clutched at Josen's shirt. "Did you chase them off, Master Josen?"

"No, but I'm afraid they took my friend," Josen said, helping him off the floor and into a chair. "Do you know how many there were?"

"About four to five- no wait! Probably more. I only saw the ones in front of me, but I was attacked from behind." He ran a hand over the tender spot on his head. "Got me really good, they did."

"We'll find them," Josen promised, before heading out to the stables. He didn't know how he would live with himself if they didn't.

***

It took Kaino longer than he would have liked to find the trail. He could feel Josen's anticipation and anger. It was a whip driving them forward. They spent a good half the day going the wrong direction on a false trail that had been perfectly laid out for them. It led them right back to the inn and Kaino half expected Josen to burst completely into flames as he let loose a string of curses. Kaino hadn't seen his friend this angry since they had found Ellie lying in a pool of her own blood.

Time had seemed to stop for Josen since that moment. He had been different, so encompassed by his grief and anger. At the beginning, Kaino had to coax him to eat and drink, and was aware of how little his friend had slept. He didn't want to see Josen fall into that same pattern of barely existing. *He can't go back there- I can't watch him go back there.* Fate had a cruel sense of humor if that was the case.

He urged Maelstrom to go faster, aware of Raynar traveling riderless behind him. They stopped only now and then to make sure they were on the correct path. For all he could tell, they were. They had just rounded a bend around dusk when he saw it. He would have missed it if not for the bright yellow in contrast with the dark green of the foliage. There, on the ground, tangled with some low-lying branches, lay pieces of a blue and yellow floral crown. He got off his horse, holding the pieces up to Josen.

"Aliyah?" He asked.

Josen nodded, too anxious to speak.

Kaino looked around the area and found a few more pieces trailing down a small side path. This path was easy to miss as it veered off from the one they currently were on. He walked the path for a long way, noting more yellow and blue flowers strewn about.

"Jos- they went this way!" He called, leaping back onto his horse. They followed the trail slowly, looking for more flowers. It led for quite a while before leading off towards the bank of the Arthom River. The flowers stopped before the churning waters.

Of course, they would have a boat waiting, Kaino groaned inwardly. He tried to show more confidence than he felt when he glanced toward his friend.

"Jos," Kaino said softly.

Josen looked up sharply from where he had been staring at the water.

"They had a boat waiting for them. They could be miles ahead of us by now," he stopped and took a breath before continuing. "We can push our horses to the brink of exhaustion all night but-"

"There is no but, Kai. Who knows what they are doing to her? Who knows if she is even- if she is even..."

"We will find her," Kaino said soothingly, not showing his exhaustion as he got back up on his horse. "We know the Arthom is too choppy in early summer to travel against the current. The best we can do is travel downstream and look for any signs that they've have stopped."

***

They followed the river until the moon was high in the sky. Josen, aware of Kaino's exhaustion, begrudgingly agreed to stop for the night.

It grated at him. Memories of racing back to Ringard now intertwined with his horror and frustration at not being able to find Aliyah. He forcefully pushed his emotions aside as he saw just how exhausted Kaino was. Bloodshot eyes were covered by drooping eyelids. He didn't say a word to Josen as he saw to Maelstrom before grabbing his bedroll and finding a spot to lay down.

Within moments he was asleep. His quiet snores intermingled with the sounds of the churning water.

Josen took the first watch. Not bothering with a fire in the chilly air, he found himself staring at the sky. The stars glistened like frozen tears in a sea of black. He felt tears of his own running down his cheek.

Chapter Thirty-Six

Aliyah! A woman's voice called to her. Unfamiliar but commanding. *Wake up Aliyah! You need to wake up.*

Aliyah tried opening her eyes. They were heavy. When she got them open a slit, she thought she could make out the form of a delicate blonde woman a little older than her kneeling next to her.

"Please, Aliyah!" The woman begged. *"Josen is on his way, but you need to wake up."*

Icy water forced itself into Aliyah's nose. Adrenaline coursed through her veins, forcing her body to wake from its drugged slumber. Panicked, she thrashed and was relieved when unseen hands pulled her head up from where they had been forcing it down into the water. She gasped for air but found herself heaving up water instead. The heaves turned into coughs that scratched her throat and she was so preoccupied she didn't notice the person who had approached her until he spoke.

"Well, well, well."

She went still at the sound of Sir Caldryk's voice. She looked up at him from where she knelt in a puddle of water and vomit. He looked the same as he had at the manor except, he was now missing an eye. The gaping hole left in its place looked as if someone had torn it out with their bare hands. Aliyah found herself retching.

"Admiring my new look?" He said with a sneer as he motioned to his face. "It is unfortunate you ran away that day. Madra was not pleased with me when she found out my plans, but you... why, she has delightful plans for you that pale in comparison to what she did to me."

Still trying to regain her breath, Aliyah forced herself to look away from the gaping hole in his face. Instead, her eyes focused on their surroundings. In front of her was a giant lake of clear blue water. On the far side was a waterfall, the sound of it echoed in the stone outcropping where she was being held. On the other side of the clear lake, a wide river flowed. Its calm meandering was a stark contrast against the waterfall's rapids and mist.

"I realize I may have been too hasty in my assumption of what needed to be done," Sir Caldryk had continued, dragging Aliyah's attention back to him. "Why bring magic back to all Gralanth when I could take it for myself? With you, my little *Wyvanni*, I can overthrow Madra and rule the whole of Gralanth- all of Myral even."

He motioned and firm hands gripped Aliyah by the arms and hauled her to her feet. He turned and began to walk further back into the outcrop. "Come along, Aliyah, dear. It is time for you to learn about what your future holds."

***

The outcropping was the entrance of a cave. Sir Caldryk paused a little way into the cave and lit a lantern hanging from the wall. Taking the lantern off its hook, he continued into the cave. Aliyah didn't resist as the rough hands dragged her into the dark gloom.

It was as if the cave would never end. Farther and farther, they walked, dodging stalagmites and stalactites as they went. A luminescent glow radiated from some of the walls, throwing her captors into a strange light. Time became meaningless as they continued to travel through the cave. Aliyah had just begun to wonder if they would ever see the light of day again when the cave opened into a well-lit antechamber.

Large reliefs of figures in ancient garb lined the walls. Some in the throes of battle, others worshiping a woman clad in armor as she stood next to a man who wore similar armor but brandished a curved blade.

Aliyah continued looking around the chamber and her eyes came to a relief of an image she had seen before. Two females and two males in robes grasped hands, the image of the Vendi Mountains behind them. Below the image stood a stone box. Pieces of what had once been the top littered the ground and a giant mallet lay next to the box.

As they approached the stone box, she could see the whirls of ancient writing carved into the sides. On the top the sigil of the Ringada was carved. The horns of the qilin looked to be edged with gold and it glimmered in the light of the lanterns around the room.

"This is what Ringada do to *Wyvanni*, Aliyah," Sir Caldryk said as he gripped the other side of the box. "They are afraid of the magic you possess. It has been that way since the very beginning." He walked away from her then, motioning to the reliefs on the walls.

"As you can see, *Wyvanni* were once coveted, worshiped even. They were seen as an integral part of winning wars. The ancient queen was one herself," he stopped, hands clasped in front of the relief of the woman and man in armor. "She was said to be a fair ruler, kind to her subjects, and peace prospered in the land. Who would want to go to war against the kingdom with a *Wyvanni* and her bonded lover?"

He paused and looked at Aliyah, who was staring at him confused. "Unfortunately for her," he continued, "she decided to experiment with her powers. It had been easy to bond with her lover. How many people can one person bond at once?" He walked over to the next relief; one Aliyah hadn't paid attention to. Unnerving creatures stared out from it. Their clawed hands and hungry eyes had been skillfully carved.

"And so, the grarg were born. Unable to share the power between more than two people, their magic and the essence of the person was taken, drained by the queen and her lover. But the grarg weren't useless. She found they made a more effective army than many of those who served her. Their subservience was incomparable. Their only wish in life was to do their mistress' bidding in hopes she would give back a fraction of what she had stolen from them."

Aliyah glanced a look up at the grarg holding her. She didn't know who he had been originally, but she felt pity for him and for what was taken.

"The Queen was finally brought down by a group of *Wyvanni* who sacrificed themselves to entomb the ancient Queen and take magic from those who followed her... Gralanth and Myral became separated by a new mountain range and where one nation continued to prosper, the other was punished, having their magic taken away." His hands were in fists now as he walked back over to where Aliyah stood.

"But their plan only worked for so long. My father-in-law and I went on a "hunting" trip. We were part of a secret society that wanted to bring the ancient Queen back. Thinking we could wake her and ask for a boon, we foolishly searched for her and found her here." He tapped the stone box.

"My father-in-law spoke to her first and in her anger, she killed him. Not wanting the same fate, I was forced to grovel, and she granted me permission to speak.

"When I told her what I had been doing and what cause I was working for, she was delighted and awakened my magic as the boon. What she didn't tell me was the magic came with a cost. My magic may have been awakened but it belongs solely to her.

"I began to look for an alternative solution. Imagine my surprise when I discovered another *Wyvanni* could negate what had been done to me. The only way I thought I could achieve it was by getting you to sacrifice yourself. However, upon further research, you will not have to kill yourself after all. Instead, by bonding you to me, I shall regain the entirety of my magic and make a grarg army of my own."

Aliyah was speechless. She had no idea what bonding entailed. The thought of it- particularly to him- sounded horrible. Her heart began to pound faster as he pulled a knife from his belt and stalked toward her.

She fought against the hands that held her and felt its nails dig into her skin in response. Holding her in place. She braced herself for the sting of the knife and was shocked when he stopped in front of her, the hilt of the knife held out to her.

"Take it," he commanded.

Aliyah stared unmoving at the blade.

"Take it," he said again, "and give your blood freely so I may bind myself to you. We haven't much time- Madra is probably already aware of what we are up to. She will kill you if given the chance. But with you by my side, we shall be unstoppable."

Chapter Thirty-Seven

"Josen!" Ellie's voice had never sounded so panicked.

His heart skipped a beat and he looked from where he lay toward the sound of her voice. She stood, glowing radiantly, in front of the entrance of a cave. *You must hurry! She doesn't have much time. You need to save her!*

"Ellie?" He croaked out with his hoarse voice. She shimmered in the early morning sun, and he realized the area around her looked different than the area they were currently located. A waterfall spit up mist in the background and he realized with a jolt where Ellie was.

"Hurry! I will stay with her as long as I can, but she needs you now!" Ellie faded into nothing, and Josen bolted upright.

"Kaino, wake up! I know where Aliyah is!"

***

Both men dismounted their horses. The horses wandered off looking for appetizing vegetation. Nothing moved inside the cave.

It had not taken long for Josen to relay to Kaino his conversation with Ellie. It might have been their long history as friends, or maybe it was the desperation in his eyes, but Kaino had believed him. It also had not taken long for them to find the waterfall.

"Look at this!" Kaino's voice was excited as he knelt next to what looked like a puddle of vomit. Josen took a step forward and his breath caught as he saw the blue and yellow flowers strewn next to the puddle.

"You did it, Jos. You actually did it." Kaino said with disbelief. "

Kaino watched as Josen crouched before ducking into the cave. His feet were near silent on the stone ground beneath him. Kaino was just as quiet as he ducked into the cave after him.

The cave was little more than a tunnel that led into a deep dark abyss. Not wanting to alert anyone by creating a flame, they moved with their hands along the wall, pausing when they felt it veer sharply to the left.

Listening for any sounds, Kaino moved ahead of Josen. It was amazing how magic shifted his senses when he was in the dark. He walked a few steps away from Josen when he heard a gasp of pain up ahead. He reached back for Josen, and the other man joined him.

"I heard something- be prepared," Kaino said, keeping his voice low. He moved off down the hallway again and felt Josen moving behind him. Suddenly, the dimmest of light was seen up ahead. The tunnel veered off to the right and the light was coming from around the bend. They moved to the other side of the tunnel.

"Pathetic," a deep cold voice said from within the light. "Weak. That's what you are. But don't worry, I will help you find motivation. You are mine and you will give me what I want- one way or another."

A scream echoed through the tunnel. There was just enough light for Kaino to see Josen react. He stood up, blade out, and began to advance toward the light. Kaino followed behind him.

"I told you once, you can make it stop. You can make all the pain end. You will never have to feel the bite of steel again, Aliyah. All you need to do is one simple thing..." The screaming intensified.

***

Josen acted on instinct as he moved into the chamber. Aliyah's screams echoed around him as she lay chained to the floor. Her skirts lay about her in tatters, her legs and hips exposed through the slices.

Both her arms were bleeding from long thin cuts that had been sliced into her. Pools of blood had formed around her, and he blanched at the sight.

"Aliyah," he said, as he took a step toward her. She didn't respond.

He hadn't noticed a dark figure kneeling next to her, a long thin blade in its hand. The figure turned its head, and he could see it was a man. A long scar ran down his face and one of his eyes was missing. The man laughed, a deep sinister laugh, before reaching out and slashing the blade down Aliyah's arm. She screamed again as it left a long gash in its wake. Josen watched in horror as the man lifted the blade to his mouth and licked the blood off the weapon.

"Intoxicating," the man said with a pleased sigh. There was no emotion to his voice, just numbing coldness. "Her power that is. Wouldn't you agree, Master Josen?"

"I wouldn't know what you are talking about," Josen said, glaring murderously at him. His heart began to beat faster, and he had never wanted to kill anyone as much as this man. "Since it seems you know my name, wouldn't introductions be in order?" Conversations with Aliyah ran through his mind, and he had a feeling he already knew who this monster was before him. It didn't matter who he was though, Josen and Kaino would kill him. Josen gripped his sword tighter, sending flames down the blade. The flames crackled ominously.

"Why, I'm Sir Caldryk, her fiancé. And you," he said, pointing the bloodied blade toward Josen, "are done getting in my way." He snapped his fingers and hooded figures detached themselves from shadows at the edge of the chamber. The figures began advancing toward Josen.

"I believe you know a thing or two about fighting grarg, but I've always wanted to see a Ringada in action. Purely selfish of me, but then again," he looked down toward Aliyah, "I am not a man that likes to share."

***

Aliyah's vision went in and out. The pain from where he had touched her was all she knew- that and the feel of the cold blade biting into her skin. She had refused to take the knife from him. He had shown her how displeased he was with that choice. She had been unprepared for the grarg to grab her and chain her to the dais. She had thrashed and bucked as he ripped her dress and forced himself on her.

She had wished he would kill her and make it stop. She had begged him for it as he had straddled her. Pleaded with him as he hungrily took from her. The manacles on her wrists and ankles chaffed from where she had pulled against them trying to escape. He had liked that. He had liked seeing her fight against him- especially as he told her she belonged to him.

When forcing himself on her didn't work, he brought out the knife. He cut into her, screaming at her to bond to him. He had cut deep enough to draw blood. Again, and again, and again. Her arms, her face. She screamed as she felt the knife dragged from her collar bone to her right breast.

Then the bite of cold steel stopped. Was the monster talking? It seemed that's all he did, talk and pain, talk and pain. She had stopped listening to him...Had it been hours ago? Days ago? Time had ceased to have meaning. All that remained was pain.

She braced for the cold kiss of the blade. It didn't come. Whimpering, she opened her eyes, daring to look at the monster. He was talking, but not to her. He spoke to someone farther down the cave. Someone she couldn't see.

Aliyah could see the blonde woman from earlier. She knelt next to Aliyah, tears pooling in her eyes. She put a soft, comforting hand on Aliyah's arm.

"Shh.... everything will be alright," the woman said. "You are safe."

"Please," Aliyah begged, her voice hoarse from screaming. "Please help me."

There was another voice in the chamber now. A familiar voice that cut through the fog of pain and captured Aliyah's attention.

“I don’t know what you are talking about. But since it seems you know my name; wouldn’t introductions be in order?”

She craned her neck searching for the source of the voice and found Josen, sword drawn and blade aflame. She had never seen him look so threatening as he stared at the monster above her.

He was here. He had come for her. Maybe the pain would finally stop. She whimpered, despite herself, and he dared glance at her. His eyes went wide with horror as he took in the sight of her. She wondered what she must look like after Sir Caldryk was done with her.

“Jos,” she cried. Tears formed in her eyes, and she began crying. “Jos,” she kept repeating his name like it was a lifeline. He took an advancing step towards where she lay and then stopped when the monster began talking again.

“I believe you know a thing or two about fighting grarg, but I’ve always wanted to see a Ringada in action. Purely selfish of me, but then again, I am not a man that likes to share.” Sir Caldryk’s voice was cold, and Aliyah felt him turn his attention back towards her.

Aliyah watched in horror as grarg detached themselves from the walls around them. She knew they were there; she had felt their dispassionate eyes on her as Sir Caldryk took what he wanted from her. She hadn't realized how many there were.

She tried to awkwardly brush her tears aside to look at Josen. His expression softened for a fraction of a second as he looked towards her. It filled her with a hope that had been dampened by the pain. Warmth filled her as she looked into his eyes, and something whispered inside her. Something she hadn't been aware of until the wolves attacked them. Something she hadn't fully understood until now.

Staring at the man she loved, the whispering grew louder, and she felt it then- a phantom thread that connected them together. A thread formed by love and joy. A thread formed by hope.

She focused on it, feeling where she ended, and he began. She could feel his pain and horror at finding her chained and bleeding. Horror that mirrored her own shame at him finding her like this. They were just flickers, impressions of feelings, but the more she focused on it, the more substantial it became. The pain faded into the background as she forced herself to focus on him.

She watched as the first of the hooded figures reached for him. Josen sprang into action. He was a blur of motion as he dodged and slashed at the creature. He took its head off with little effort before the next one attacked. Aliyah could feel Josen's focus as he fought creature after creature. She could almost sense his movements before his body responded.

Grarg began falling, their lifeless corpses lying in smoldering heaps on the ground. The scent of smoke and burning flesh was overpowering. More grarg fell to the ground and Aliyah was vaguely aware of Kaino entering the melee. As she turned her focus towards him, she was shocked she could feel him as well. Different from how she could feel Josen, but she could feel whispers of a thread. A thread built by shared laughs over inappropriate jokes. It felt wholly like Kaino.

She focused this newfound awareness around the room. She could sense where the grarg were, but instead of whispers she was met with numbing blackness and impressions of insatiable thirst. It threatened to consume her, and she pulled her awareness away and back toward Josen.

Josen was fire. She could feel the magic whirling within him. His passion was a billow urging and shaping the flames. The flames begged to be released. She watched as he dispatched the last grarg and approached where she lay.

Sir Caldryk backed away, casting his knife aside as he drew a small sword at his waist. He stood to meet Josen. “I was hoping it would come to this,” Sir Caldryk sneered. “When I heard you were a fire user, I was intrigued. My dear fiancé left me to run off with another with a passion just as formidable.” He looked down at Aliyah. She glared at him.

“I told Madra about you,” he continued, holding his sword out defensively toward Josen. “She was upset when she discovered what we had been up to.” He looked down at Aliyah as if blaming him for the loss of his eye. “She made me a deal. Bring you to her and let her finish you off or she would kill me. Alas... You did not take me up on my offer and now I will be forced to take you and your friends to her."

“We are not going anywhere with you," Josen threatened, taking another step towards where she lay. Kaino joined him and the two began advancing toward the dais.

“Ah yes, he who would take what is mine. She really is quite enjoyable. She has a fight to her that just makes it so much more satisfying. But pity, you will never know.” With that, he lunged towards Josen.

Josen was ready. He met the blow with a fiery one of his own. It made the monster off balanced, and he barely moved fast enough to avoid Josen’s next blow. Both were lethal dancers, but where Sir Caldryk had received training with the sword,

Josen *was* his sword. Parry, thrust, parry, thrust. The sound of their swords clashing echoed in the chamber.

Cold hands touched Aliyah's wrists and she turned to look at the woman. She was nowhere to be seen. Kaino knelt in her place. His usual laughter was replaced with horror at her condition.

"Aliyah, I'm going to have to bind your wounds before you move. What did he do to you?"

She didn't answer. Instead, she lay quietly as pieces of her already tattered dress were pulled off. A new kind of pain began as Kaino began to wrap her arms. Tears welled in her eyes and she let out another whimper.

"Shh... it will be alright. Josen will take care of him." He said it with such surety that Aliyah wanted to believe him. She looked at him through a new onslaught of tears.

"He-" there were no words to describe what the monster had done to her. She pulled weakly against the manacles. She felt Kaino shift his attention to unpicking the locks. She closed her eyes and listened to the sound of the fighting as it echoed around the chamber.

Chapter Thirty-Eight

Josen dodged a swipe of Caldryk's sword before rushing him, trying to get past his defenses. It didn't work. Caldryk blocked him again. He tried a new tactic. He let Caldryk come to him and began to retreat towards the dark tunnel he had entered from.

"You remind me of him," Caldryk sneered as he began to advance toward him. "The way you act- the way you fight." He spat the last word.

"I honestly have no idea who you are referring to," Josen said, blocking another hit. He made it another step towards the tunnel.

"The Executioner," Caldryk said with evident hatred. "He does her bidding like some faithful lapdog. It's pitiful. She's got him bound to her so tightly, you think what she did to me is bad," he gave a laugh. "Pity, you might never see him again. The once wise leader of the Ringada, cowed by a mere woman." He paused, slashing halfheartedly, letting his words sink in.

"I wonder," he said in a mocking tone, "what Aliyah would have made you. Would you have become her faithful lapdog- her hound to do her bidding? You and your father could have swapped notes and compared stories." He slashed down harder with his sword.

Caldryk's words troubled Josen as he tried to dodge. Josen dared to spare Aliyah a glance. Caldryk, upon seeing him distracted, began attacking him with new vigor. Josen blocked too late and swore as his sword was knocked out of his hand.

***

Aliyah heard the clatter of a sword hitting the ground. She turned to look at the monster. His sword pointed toward Josen. "And now," he sneered, "I will have the pleasure of killing you in front of the ones you love."

Something cold rolled through Aliyah. She reached out with her magic, finding where Josen stood in the room. Strangely, he wasn't panicked. She could feel his emotions about the situation and see flickers of thoughts. He would attack Caldryk only with magic if necessary. She watched as if through his eyes as a flaming whip began to form in his hand. She felt panic as she witnessed

Sir Caldryk tossing his sword away and a whip of his own formed as well.

She shifted her attention to Caldryk. His magic called to her, linked to her by her blood. She could feel him. His dark desires and his mind twisted with greed. He would never be satisfied. He would always want more. He tried to make the flames of his whip brighter and Aliyah pulled back on the magic. It responded.

Instead of bright flames, his flames winked out, the whip disappearing from his hand. Panic rose in him as Josen cracked his whip at Caldryk. He narrowly dodged and tried to create the whip again.

Oh no you don't! Aliyah put all her concentration into pulling his magic back.

He tried harder, sending a look her way. Josen's whip made contact and wound around Caldryk's wrist. Aliyah could feel his pain. She let out a whimper.

"It's alright," Kaino said from beside her. Unaware of what she was doing. "I almost have your hand free- there!" She felt her own wrist become free of the cold metal as he leaned over to work on the other hand.

Kaino's distraction had allowed Caldryk to form his own whip again. Aliyah refocused, berating herself for allowing him control. She tried to seize it from him. He held onto it tighter, flickers of thought of her binding him in heinous ways flooded his mind. The fear of her taking over drove him to attack with more fury.

Aliyah was shocked at that fear. He was her living nightmare and yet he feared her? The one he abused and put through hell? Wasn't this what he had wanted? What he'd screamed at her to do?

An idea began to form in her mind. She reached out gently. Where her previous attempts to take over had been rough pulls and shoves, this was the caress of a lover.

Shocked at the softness of Aliyah's mental touch, he dropped his guard, allowing her to seize control. Instead of winking out his flame, she spoke from where she lay on the ground.

"Stop!" She called to the two men. Her voice was small but firm as it echoed effectively around the chamber.

"Stop!" She forced a wall of flame from Caldryk to come between the two of them. She felt Caldryk's panic as the fire burst out of him and he realized her control.

Kaino released her other hand and helped her to a sitting position. She kept her grasp firm on Caldryk's magic. Both men stared at her, Josen with relief and Caldryk with fear. She pulled on his magic again, making him shudder.

"It doesn't feel good, does it?" She said with another squeeze, venom dripping in her voice.

"To have someone take control and do things to you against your will?" Another squeeze, this one brought him to his knees. They were eye-level and Aliyah could see the panic in his features.

"You said all along you wanted me to be your *Wyvanni*, that I am yours no matter what" she spat. "You should have thought long and hard about what bonding would entail because you messed with the wrong *Wyvanni*." She released his magic, and his screaming began.

***

Josen watched horrified through the wall of flames as Caldryk began to smoke from the inside out. Aliyah sat on the ground, held up by Kaino. A mix of hatred and concentration twisted her features. She didn't look toward him. Instead, she kept her focus on the screaming Caldryk.

Josen looked at the man. A hole formed in Sir Caldryk's stomach and flames began to peek out. He bucked and screamed as his fire escaped him, burning away flesh in the process. Josen gagged.

"Every pain you caused me," Aliyah said, and Josen turned to look at her. "Everything you took from me. Do you feel it? Do you feel the emotion I lend to your magic?"

I don't know how he couldn't feel it, Josen thought.

"You wanted me. Wanted me enough to take me against my will. Now you will never take anything again."

With that, fire burst through Caldryk's mouth, now opened in a silent scream. Fire also began to pour through his eye sockets and soon he was nothing but a flaming corpse. Then, with a whoosh, the flames suddenly died out and all that remained were ashes.

Josen turned to where Aliyah sat, slumped against Kaino. Her lips had a faint bluish tint, and she shivered. He began walking toward them but stopped when she looked at him. She flinched when she met his eye.

"Aliyah," he said, voice quiet. "Aliyah, it's me. It's Josen." He took a tentative step toward her and her eyes refocused. "It's alright, you are safe." Another step.

He felt her then, a brush on his consciousness. The brushing became more urgent, a shove instead of a caress. He stopped, standing in place, and felt her touch his magic. He let her inspect him, sending her soothing thoughts.

I'm not going to hurt you. You are safe. He will never touch you again. He repeated these to her and with them also came feelings of guilt. *I'm sorry I wasn't fast enough. I'm sorry I couldn't kill him for you. I'm sorry I wasn't there to prevent them from taking you.*

She studied these thoughts more, taking her time. He could feel her rifling through them. Sweat beaded on his forehead as she dug deeper.

Feelings for her intermixed with feelings of grief for Ellie. Memories strung together like beads on a necklace. She looked at each one before moving to the next. Memories he didn't want to think about. His wedding day to Ellie. Ellie laughing over dinner at their small wooden table. Ellie holding a hand on her stomach, telling him she was pregnant. Ellie as she lay in his arms, a smile on her lips as he played with her hair. Then the panic.

The panic of not being in time to rescue Ellie. Finding Ellie dead. Holding her limp form in his arms as he said goodbye to her. A funeral pyre with smoke rising high into the sky. Then nothing but moments in time where life seemed to hold no meaning. She went through these faster. Then she stopped.

This memory was of Aliyah. The moment he first saw her. She inspected this one and he could feel her shock at how the sight of her pulled him out of whatever darkness he had been in.

The next memory was of holding her as she cried, lifting her into the bedroll after she fell asleep. The memories kept coming.

Traveling with her. Sparing her looks when he thought she wasn't looking.

Feeling a desire for her he hadn't expected to ever feel again. That desire stumped her. He could feel her questions. Was it because of what she was or who she was that he wanted her? So he showed her.

She let him take control and he flipped through memories.

Conversations with her he cherished. Wanting to make her happy because she deserved happiness. He showed her how he felt when he gave her Starcake and when she gave him some in return. He showed her how overwhelmed with joy he felt when she danced the maiden dance for him. He showed her how he felt when she said she loved him.

"I love you Aliyah," he said aloud. "I'm sorry I wasn't enough to save you." There, he said it. He felt her mental tug on his magic, as if to pull him toward her. He took small careful steps until he stood before her. He knelt, reaching out a hand for her and she surprised him by flinging herself into his arms and crying against his shirt. The mental tug disappeared.

"I'm so s-sorry!" She wailed into his chest. He held her tighter. "I h-had to kn-know if you l-loved m-me or just my m-magic." Her words came out choppy through the tears.

"It's alright, my love," he said, planting a kiss in her hair. He waited for Kaino to remove the shackles on her ankles before lifting her into his arms. She was exceptionally light. “I’m sorry we didn’t get here fast enough,” the tears began to form in his eyes, and he planted another kiss on her forehead.

“It’s not your fault,” she whispered into his chest. “None of it. But you came for me. You really came for me. He- he told me you wouldn’t. That you were just trying to use me. That you didn’t love me and if, by chance, you did, you wouldn’t want me when he was done with me. He told me that while he- he.” She stopped, breathing hard.

He shifted her in his arms so he could see into her eyes. She avoided his gaze.

“Aliyah,” he whispered while Kaino grabbed his sword and a lantern where Sir Caldryk had placed it on a wall. “I love you, no matter what. I will always love you. Even after what he...” he gulped, imagining what had happened to her. “Know that no matter what he did to you- no matter what he took from you- that doesn’t change the way I feel about you. You are still you, and I love you.”

“Even if he forced himself on me?” Her voice was barely a whisper. Her tears began falling harder and he hugged her tighter to his chest.

“Even then,” he said, emotion seeping into his voice.

They began walking in silence down the dark tunnel. Kaino moved in front of them holding the light. He was quiet, giving them privacy. Aliyah's breathing became more regular. Josen had thought she had fallen asleep when she spoke again.

"Jos?"

"Yes, my love?" He looked down at her as he walked.

"Please don't leave me alone. When we get back to Ylen, I-I don't want to be alone." She pressed her face into his chest, and he could feel her shuddering in his arms.

"You won't be." He planted another kiss on her hair. She relaxed at that, and he felt her body go still as her breathing slowed.

The night was dark as they emerged from the cave. They went a little way down the trail to where they left the horses. Josen took care not to jostle Aliyah as he carried her. She had fallen asleep as they had traveled through the tunnel. Now that they were outside, he could see the pallor of her skin in the moonlight. She had lost a lot of blood.

Kaino whistled for the horses and all three of them appeared on the trail. Kaino ran to where Aliyah's pack was attached to Raynar's saddle. He pulled out her blue cloak and draped it over where she lay in Josen's arms. She stirred.

"Aliyah," Josen said quietly. She looked at him through groggy eyes. "The horses are here. I'm going to put you on Raynar and tie you to him with some rope. We need to get you to a healer."

She nodded. With help from Kaino, Josen was able to get her on the giant horse. She leaned toward the horse's head as if dizzy and they attached her to the saddle. When they were sure she wouldn't fall, they mounted their own horses. They took off at a steady pace, Kaino in the front and Josen in the rear. Josen was thankful for Raynar's loyalty and training as the stubborn horse followed them back towards Ylen.

The trail widened and Josen brought his horse up next to Raynar. Aliyah was asleep in the saddle.

"Jos," Kaino called to him softly with concern. "Is she alright?"

"Physically or emotionally?" Josen asked, without looking away from Aliyah. Her face was peaceful but every now and then, she would wince at the horse's movements.

"Did he do what I think he did to her?" Kaino's voice had an angry edge to it.

"Yes," Josen whispered before continuing angrily. "He did. If he were not dead already, I would kill him with my bare hands. Use that knife and slice into him for every single one of her scars." His breathing was ragged.

"I would help you," Kaino said, just as upset. "There would never be enough torture for a man like that. However, watching Aliyah do that to a person..." he shuddered. "I've never seen anything like it. I was afraid she was going to do it to you! What did she do to you?"

"She inspected memories," he said slowly. "I was afraid she was going to hurt me as well, but then she started going through my memories. Memories of her. Memories of Ellie. She wanted to know my intentions. If what I told her had been true."

"And what was that?" Kaino asked curiously.

Josen looked over at Aliyah again before taking a deep breath and responding, "That I love her."

Epilogue

Her fingers clicked against the stone throne she sat on. He eyed her from where he stood at the side of the stone monstrosity.

She didn't notice. Her gaze was far away, seeing through the eyes of another. He turned his attention inward and was able to see what she was seeing through the bond they shared. The bond he despised. He tried to bury those feelings. They would only bring pain.

Instead, he watched as his son entered a poorly lit chamber. Josen's attention was on something just outside the line of sight of the creature's eyes he looked through. Josen took a step toward something, and the eyes of the creature followed with its gaze.

There on the floor, next to the monster Caldryk, lay a female figure. She was chained to the ground, and he could see the abuse Caldryk had inflicted upon her.

The creature focused on her face. Horror washed through him. It was the same girl from the manor. She was supposed to be on her way to Ringard. How did he catch up to her?

He turned his attention toward his mistress as she sat atop her throne. Her back was straight and golden hair was wound tight into an intricate style. In the center of it all was a black crown. It seemed to pull all the light toward it. A contented smile played on her face as she watched the events unfold. He swallowed before turning his attention back to the fight. He hoped his son would kill Caldryk and then in turn kill him. He was tired of playing her games.

Madra let out a shrill laugh that echoed around the stone chamber. "I see why you kept him from me. Your son is quite the fighter."

The Executioner jumped, looking through the bond at what she saw. They had switched eyes and were looking through the last remaining grarg. The rest lay on the floor with smoke rising from them.

"Yes, truly he is skilled and passionate- just as you were all those centuries ago." She gave him a long, penetrating look. "He will make a fine addition to our legion. Who knows, he might be as invaluable as you. You would like that, wouldn't you? To be bound to your son?"

"It is an honor to be bound to and serve one such as yourself, my lady. However, I know my son and he will not come willingly."

"Oh? And you are sure of that?" Her tone was mocking. "I'm sure, with enough *persuasion*, we can get him to do anything we want. Particularly if it involves that *Wyvanni.*"

A chill ran down the Executioner's back, but he forced himself to give her a bow. With his face to the floor he responded, "Whatever you command, my lady."

The End of Book One

Acknowledgements

I would be remiss if I did not take this opportunity to thank those who have helped make this novel a reality. First and foremost, I would like to thank my husband, Jacob. From listening to me talk about story plots and character development, to supporting me in this dream, this book would not be here without you! I love you, Babe!

Also thank you to my parents for being the best parents a girl could wish for- and the greatest Nana and Pa for our little guy. I am who I am today because of the love and support you have always given me. Your encouragement to go after my dreams and make them a reality means the world!

Thank you to my BFF, and fellow "Electro-cutie" Jess Martin. You have been one of my strongest supporters since the beginning and you deserve all frappes from Beans! Seriously- the fact you let me springboard ideas off you and still do... I could go on forever about all the reasons I am thankful God put you in my life. He knew I needed a Jess- even before I did!

I want to give a huge shout out to my beta readers: Jess Martin, Katie Craig, Rachel Griffin, Ashley Gibby, Elizabeth Gurney, and Rachel Olson. Your insights and suggestions really helped make the story better.

Also, thank you to Debbie Oakeson for doing my final edit! You rock Aunt Debbie!

I started writing this story in October of 2020. Life had been hard the past few years, and we were going through fertility treatments. What started off as a way to keep my mind occupied, turned into writing a full novel. This story is special. I know all authors think that, but this one was a way to process things in my life- as well as things in the lives of those closest to me.

Everyone has experienced grief, heartache, pain, loss, trauma... I wanted to write a book that resonated with the reader as much as it resonated with me. So, thank you, dear reader. Thank you for letting me take you on a journey into the lands of Gralanth and Myral.

May you enjoy the journey to come.

About the Author

K.L. Hester was born and raised just outside of Salt Lake City, Utah. Surrounded by the beautiful Utah mountains, her imagination was allowed to run wild. When she isn't reading or writing, she can be found spending time playing board games with her family or RPGs with her husband and friends. She lives in Utah with her husband, son, dog, and two cats. *Wounds of Ash* is her debut novel.

Keep up with her on Instagram at @KLHester_author

Ingram Content Group UK Ltd.
Milton Keynes UK
UKHW010818260623
424053UK00004B/326

9 781088 141632